D0898023

Sunshine
and
Shadows

Sunshine and Shadows

A NOVEL

Ila Yount

Rutledge Hill Press
Nashville, Tennessee

Published in Nashville, Tennessee, by Rutledge Hill Press, Inc., 513 Third Avenue South, Nashville, Tennessee 37210

Library of Congress Cataloging-in-Publication Data

Yount, Ila, 1928-
  Sunshine and shadows : a novel / Ila Yount.
    p. cm.
  ISBN 1-55853-201-3
  I. Title.
PS3575.O88S86   1992
813'.54—dc20

92-32432
CIP

Manufactured in the United States of America
1 2 3 4 5 6 7 — 97 96 95 94 93 92

To my children:
Cecil, Cindy, and David

Sunshine
and
Shadows

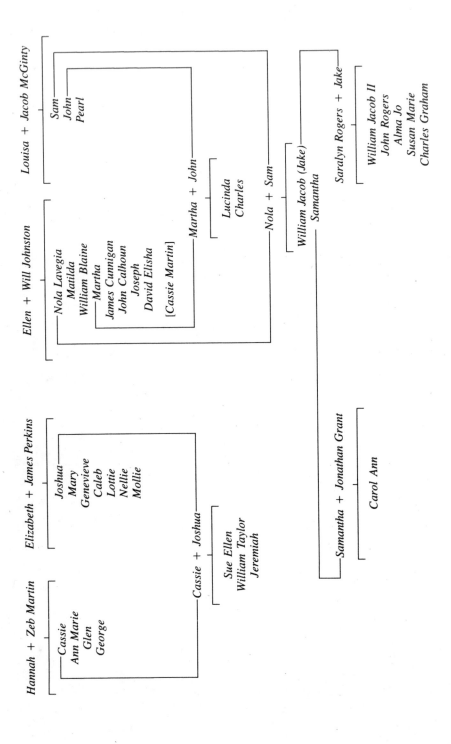

Prologue

Cindy turned around slowly in the middle of the room, overcome by a sense of familiarity even though she had never been there before. Walking over to the staircase, she laid her hand on the bannister and shivered, as if the people—her kin—who had placed their hands in this same place long ago were here with her.

She went to the hearth at the great stone fireplace and stood on it, feeling through her whole body the presence of women who had labored there feeding and warming their families. The opening was large enough for an adult to stand in it. To the right of the fireplace, a door led to the dog trot that connected the house to the kitchen. The door to the left led to the bedroom of her great-great-grandparents, Will and Ellen Johnston. She glanced at the staircase, which was illuminated by the window at the top. Another door, half hidden by the stairs, opened into the dining room.

"It's just like they described it," she murmured to herself.

"You'd better be careful, Cindy," her husband warned her. "That floor may not be as strong as it looks. You might end up falling through it."

"Oh, Daniel," she laughed. "The way my great-great-grandfather built this house, it will never fall down."

"Just the same, you'd better be careful. I don't know why I let you talk me into spending the night here. We could have driven down tomorrow just as easily."

"No, if we waited until tomorrow, we wouldn't have time to do any exploring," Cindy replied. "I've wanted to come here for so long, and since we're bringing flowers for the graves on Decoration Day, I intend to see everything while we're here. We can still look around this old place tonight, and tomorrow morning we'll find the log cabin and the cemetery."

Daniel shrugged. "Well, then, come on and help me carry in the sleeping bags. I want to get settled in as soon as we can. I don't want to go stumbling around out there after dark."

"All right, but as soon as everything's in, I want to go exploring," she answered.

After spending a half-hour carrying in food, lanterns, and sleeping bags, they had everything unloaded and settled. They left the flowers they had brought with them outside in buckets of water, then went exploring.

The yards and fields surrounding the house were overgrown with weeds and broom sage. They located the path leading to the porch by the trellis at the end of the yard. Cindy recalled her mother's descriptions of the roses that had climbed the trellis, forming a bower of fragrance in the summertime.

"I want to walk around to the back of the house and see if I can find Ellen's springhouse," Cindy said. "Everyone said it was her pride and joy. Look, there's the stream. Let's follow it. I'm sure we'll find it."

They waded through the weeds surrounding the stream and followed it until they came to a partially collapsed log structure straddling the water.

"This must be it!" Cindy exclaimed. "Look how the stream is lined with rocks from here up."

"Careful, Cindy, that whole floor is gone. Better watch your step," Daniel warned as she entered the little building.

"Don't you know anything about springhouses, Daniel?" Cindy laughed. "They don't have floors. Just dirt. It makes them cooler. Oh look! Look how carefully she lined the stream along here. I bet that's where she kept her milk and butter. Feel how cool it is, even with half of the roof gone."

Cindy knelt down and ran her hands across the moss-covered rocks at the edge of the stream, thinking of the many hours it had taken Ellen to put them in place.

"This is where she found Cassie," she said softly. "Imagine what it must have been like for that poor child, wandering alone over the mountainside. She must have been desperate by the time she came across Ellen's springhouse."

"Why was she out there in the first place?" Daniel asked.

"Her stepfather had turned her out," Cindy answered sadly. "He had been molesting her, and when she got pregnant, he threw her out, claiming the baby wasn't his."

"How could her mother have let that happen?" Daniel exclaimed. "She must have known what was going on."

"I think she was so beat down herself, she didn't dare stand up to him," Cindy answered before changing the subject. "Let's look around some more, Daniel. I think that's the barn over there. Looks like it's almost gone too."

By the time they had finished exploring the old house and grounds, the light had faded. Daniel lit the kerosene lanterns, placing them around the room, where they cast tall shadows against the dark walls of the house. Cindy shuddered as she looked up at the dusty cobwebs hanging from the high ceilings.

"Looks kind of spooky," she laughed nervously. "Maybe this wasn't such a good idea after all."

"Well, it's too late to back out now," Daniel told her. "I don't want to carry all this stuff back out in the dark. So let's spread the tablecloth and eat. I'm starved."

They sat around the edge of the cloth as they ate the simple meal and remained lost in their thoughts.

"How long has Nola been dead?" Daniel finally broke the silence.

"Almost five years," she answered. "Why do you ask?"

"Oh, I don't know. I was just thinking of the last time I saw her. It was her hundredth birthday, and I don't think she liked me too well."

"She liked you as well as she did any man," Cindy laughed. "She was kind of soured on men because of the way her husband did her. She had a hard time forgiving him. I think after her best friend, Cassie, moved away and her children married, she was pretty lonely for a while, until she moved in with my mom. I always thought she just sort of lived on the tail end of other people's lives. She never seemed to have a place of her own after she lost her boarding house."

"Whose graves are we going to visit tomorrow?" Daniel asked. "Is she buried up there, too?"

"No, she's buried beside her children," Cindy answered. "These are the graves of her parents and her sister. They've been there a long time, and as long as I can remember, someone always goes up there and puts flowers on them on Decoration Sunday. Grandma went herself until she got too weak to make the trip. Mother says she thinks she was almost ninety the last time she went."

Daniel shook his head and laughed. "She must have been some kind of tough cookie. Imagine walking that far at that age."

"Well, there used to be a fairly good road up there. At least it was good enough for a horse and buggy to maneuver. Anyhow, compared to some of the other things she did during her lifetime, that was nothing," Cindy said. "She came up in a hard time. I wonder if I could have done half as well as she did. Oh, well, I guess we'd better get to sleep. It's been a long day and I'm tired."

They rolled out their sleeping bags and settled down in them. The last thing Cindy remembered was the movement of a rotted curtain hanging over the window. She thought sleepily to herself that it looked like someone had walked by and disturbed it. Maybe she's still looking for her family—or maybe just someone to love her the way she loved Sam, Cindy thought. Poor Grandma, she never did find anyone. Or maybe she did. Maybe she just couldn't ever love anyone else like she loved him.

A tear slid down her cheek and was absorbed by the ancient floor that she slept on. As sleep claimed her, Cindy thought she heard a voice crying, "Good-bye, Cassie, good-bye. Don't forget us."

CASSIE

Cassie turned and looked at the cabin as the mules slowly pulled the wagon out of the clearing and began the climb up the mountain. Her eyes were so filled with tears that the cabin was only a blur. Angrily, she brushed the tears away, refusing to be denied this last look at their home.

The bright carpet of red and yellow leaves surrounding the cabin gave it an almost mystical appearance, as if it were floating in a sea of color. Never had the poplars and oaks displayed their autumn colors as blatantly as this year. A sugar maple standing at the edge of the yard added a punctuation mark to the scene with its deep red leaves dripping color onto the ground.

As they rounded the bend that took them out of sight of the cabin, sobs shook Cassie's shoulders. Joshua leaned over and covered her small hand with his large work-callused one.

"Please don't cry, Cassie," he said sadly. "You know I can't stand for you to cry. It just tears my heart out to think I've made you so sad."

"Don't pay me no mind, Joshua," Cassie told him as she bravely tried to stem her tears. "I'll be all right directly, I reckon. It's just the sight of our home lookin' so lonesome with everything gone from it. No curtains on the winders, and no smoke a'risin' from the chimney. I never thought it'd look so sad, like it knows we're a'leavin' it."

"We'll be back some day. You just wait and see," Joshua told her. "You do understand why I have to go, don't you? You do know that I'd rather stay right here in the cove with you if I could, don't you?"

"Yes," she whispered. "I know. I ain't a'blamin' you, Joshua. It ain't yore fault yore pa died. I know you got to go help yore ma. Don't fret now. I'll be all right in a minute."

As the mules pulled Cassie and Joshua's load of belongings up the mountain trail, the morning fog began to engulf them. Although it had

1

lifted in the cove, the higher they went the thicker it became until the mules were wading chest high in the gray swirling mist. Joshua was hard put to follow the crude trail and twice took a wrong turn that took them into dense mountain laurel thickets. Finally, he gave the mules their head and let them follow their own instincts.

Cassie pulled her shawl more tightly around her shoulders, thinking that the gray mist had penetrated her whole being. She was as miserable inside as the weather was outside. The baby she was carrying gave a kick in protest of her hunched position, and she was quickly brought out of her reverie. She straightened up, automatically cupping her swollen belly in her arms. Absently, she massaged her stomach.

"Are you all right, honey?" Joshua asked worriedly. "Is anything wrong?"

"No, nothin's wrong." She smiled weakly at him. "It's just the baby's way of tellin' me to straighten up and quit a'feelin' sorry for myself, I reckon. It's tired of me a'settin' all slumped over."

"As soon as we get to the top of the mountain, I'll stop and let you stretch awhile," he told her. "Right now, I'm afraid the brake might not hold if we stopped. It's so steep here."

The sun that had been struggling to break through was beginning to have some effect on the fog, and soon it was burned away except for a few stubborn swirls that clung to the trees. The sun's rays seemed even brighter as they shone through the yellow leaves of the poplars. Soon Cassie was caught up in the wonder of the colors around them, and she was surprised when Joshua pulled the mules to a stop, announcing that the top had been reached.

Gratefully, Cassie climbed down out of the wagon to stretch her tired back. She was in her seventh month of pregnancy, and the discomfort of the rough ride made her feel as if every bone in her body had been jarred loose.

Joshua put his arms around her, and quietly they looked back down the mountainside toward the home they had just left.

"Cassie, I know how you loved our cabin, but I promise you, we'll be happy where we're going," he said quietly. "I know it'll be different, but what we brought with us is what will count. As long as we love each other, it won't matter what kind of house we live in."

"What's yore ma's house like, Joshua?" she asked him. "You never have told me much about it, 'cept it was a farmhouse. Is there room enough for us? I don't want to feel like I'm a'puttin' anybody out."

"Don't worry," he laughed. "You won't be putting anyone out. As well as I can remember, there's seventeen rooms in our house. That's counting the dining room and the library too."

"Seventeen rooms?" Cassie exclaimed. "How many young'uns has yore ma got?"

"Well, there were eight of us in all," Joshua said. "There's my two older sisters, Mary and Genevieve, who're married and live in Nashville. Then I'm next, and then comes Lottie, Caleb, Jonathan, Nettie, and Molly."

"What do you mean, a libery?" Cassie asked him. "I never heard of nobody havin' a libery in their house."

"Well, it was really Papa's office," Joshua explained, "but Papa loved to read, and he kept all of his books there so Mother called it the library. I think she thought library sounded better than office," he chuckled.

"Joshua, you never told me yore folks was rich!" Cassie exclaimed. The distress she felt was plainly written on her face.

"I don't suppose I ever thought of us as being rich," Joshua said slowly. "Although I suppose compared to some we are. Papa always insisted that we work alongside of the field hands, though, and I suppose we just thought of ourselves as the same as them in many ways. Frankly, I always sort of envied them because they went to their cabins at night and didn't have to clean up and sit at a big table. They always seemed to have more fun than we did, and I was always anxious to get through with supper and go play with them as soon as I could."

"How can I ever fit in such a place as that?" Cassie cried. "I won't know the proper way to talk nor eat nor nothin' else. You'll be ashamed of me, Joshua."

Joshua turned her face up to his and cupped her chin in his hand. He looked sternly into her eyes.

"Cassie Perkins, don't you ever let me hear you say anything like that to me again. There's not a fancy dressed lady in the whole of Tennessee that could hold a candle to you. You'll learn what you need to know. Look at how much you've already learned from Nola."

At the mention of her friend's name, Cassie's eyes filled with tears.

"Oh, Joshua, do you ever think we'll see her again?" she wailed.

"Of course, we will," he assured her. "You just wait till we get settled, and you can write to Nola to come for a long visit. We'll be happy, Cassie, you'll see." He gave his wife a quick hug. "Now, come on and let's get back in the wagon. I aim to be nearly to Tennessee by nightfall."

Wearily, Cassie climbed back into the wagon, some of the anticipation about her new home dulled by this new worry. She wondered if Joshua's family would be as accepting of this little mountain girl as Joshua was.

Resolutely, she set her eyes toward the trail ahead of them as they began their steep descent of the mountain. Few words were spoken between the two young people as Joshua turned all of his attention to the mountain trail.

As the sun was setting, they were beginning the climb of yet another mountain, and Joshua found a suitable campsite near a stream. Cassie was grateful for the bountiful basket Nola Johnston and her mother, Ellen, had brought them before they left that morning.

"I'm afraid if I had to fix it, you'd do without any supper tonight, Joshua," she said wearily. "I don't know if I'll even have the strength to eat, I'm so tired."

After the mules were fed and tethered for the night, Joshua spread their bedding out under the wagon. The last thing Cassie remembered before she drifted off to sleep was the plaintive "Whoo" of an owl.

"I guess I know who," she murmured, "but I'm beginnin' to wonder how?"

TWO

Days of hard travel followed each other until they all became a blur of bone-shaking endurance for Cassie. They traveled as long as they could during the day, then struggled to prepare a simple meal over their campfire before falling into their covers for a night of exhausted sleep. At first, Cassie tried to wash the dirt and grime from their travels off each night, but the last two days of the journey she was too tired to make the effort.

They came in sight of Joshua's home after three weeks of travel, both so weary they could summon little enthusiasm for celebration. Cassie was grimy from the dust of the trail and her hair, uncombed since that morning, was straggling down her back and falling out from under the edges of her poke bonnet. The dress she was wearing had originally been blue, but was now a dirty grey, and her pregnancy made her feel like her body had disappeared and she was all belly.

Before they turned up the drive to the house, Joshua pulled the mules to a halt and looked in dismay at Cassie.

"What's wrong?" she asked him. "You look like you've swallered yore tobaccer. Yore plumb green around the gills."

"Oh, Cassie, I forgot," he gulped.

"Forgot what?" she asked. "Whatever it is, it's too late to go back for it now."

"No, it's not anything like that," he said. "It's that I forgot to tell you that Mother doesn't know about you."

"What do you mean, she don't know about me?" Cassie asked in bewilderment. "What is there to know, 'cept I'm Cassie and I'm yore wife."

"That's what I mean," he said lamely. "She doesn't know we're married. You remember that I told you how opposed my mother was to me coming to the mountains, don't you? She never understood why I didn't want to stay at home and help Papa on the farm, and she thought that the mountains were uncivilized and wild. That first summer that I went home, she pitched a fit when I started back and she forbade me to leave. Well, when I left anyway, she told me she didn't want to hear from me again until I'd come to my senses and taken my rightful place at home. The first thing I've heard from home was my Uncle Grover's letter telling me about Papa. He said my mother needed me but was too proud to write me and ask me to come home. She's never had much of a head for business and things are in a pretty bad mess. That's why I felt like I should go home and help them." He took a deep breath.

"I'm sorry I've waited so long to tell you, honey, but I guess Papa's death just kind of pushed it out of my mind. You're not to worry, though. Everyone's going to love you as soon as they meet you. It's just that sometimes it takes my mother awhile to accept things that weren't her doings, and at first she might not be too happy about me being married."

Cassie looked in dismay at him. Then she looked down at her swollen body and dirty dress.

"My stars," she uttered weakly. "What'll they think of me? I look like somethin' the cat drug in."

"Don't worry," he said quickly. "It'll be all right. Besides, you don't look any worse than I do."

Worriedly, he reached up and tried to push her hair back off her face and into her bonnet. She slapped his hand away angrily.

"It's too late to try to pertty me up now," she said sharply. "They'll just have to take me like I am. Oh, Joshua Perkins, I could just strangle you."

Sheepishly, Joshua took up the reins and started slowly up the road to the house. Cassie looked through a blur of tears at the large, rambling, white house they were approaching. In her eyes, it seemed to go on forever. It was a two-story house with a wide porch encircling the ground floor and a smaller portico jutting out from the middle of the upper floor. Large oaks surrounded the house, and Cassie thought that she had never seen anything so imposing. Behind the house were small outbuildings that she later would discover housed the field hands. Flat fields, some plowed and some covered with the stubble of the previous year's harvest, surrounded the great house. In the distance she saw a huge barn almost as big as the house itself.

I bet the critters live better than we did back home, she thought to herself.

As Joshua and Cassie approached the house, people spilled out of the front door and rushed to meet them. Cassie thought there must have been two dozen people or more. Actually, there were only ten people, but they came in such a rush that the whole porch seemed full.

A young boy, who appeared to be about fifteen, ran out and eagerly took the reins of the mules from Joshua as he jumped down and began hugging and thumping people on the back. Cassie shrank back against the seat of the wagon, wishing she could crawl into the back and disappear. She was suddenly aware of how dirty and disheveled she looked.

A woman swept out of the door and down the steps. Everyone moved back out of her way as she flung her arms open to Joshua and embraced him. She was short and plumpish, and he had to bend down to hug her. Her hair was swept up on top of her head in ringlets and was faded blonde in color. Cassie surmised that this must be Joshua's mother.

"Oh, my son, my son," she exclaimed. "At last you are home where you belong! I thought I would never see you again after you went to those terrible mountains. But here you are at last, back with your family.

"And who is this?" she asked as she spied Cassie. "Why, you've brought a servant girl with you. Well, never mind, come on in, you must be exhausted. Caleb, see to the mules and show the girl to one of the cabins."

She took Joshua by the hand and began drawing him toward the steps. Cassie sat where she was, frozen in embarrassment and dismay.

"Mother," Joshua said, pulling his hand from hers and turning her around firmly. "This is not a servant girl. I have some grand news for you. This is Cassie, my wife. I'm sorry to spring this on you with no warning, but we were married almost two years ago. I would have written you, but if you remember, we didn't part on the best of terms the last time I was home. Here, Cassie, come on down and meet my family."

Joshua reached his hand up to Cassie. She stared at him in fright for several seconds before timidly placing her hand in his.

Elizabeth Perkins stopped dead in her tracks at her son's announcement. She turned just as Cassie stood up. Elizabeth stared, taking in Cassie's swollen figure and dirty clothes. She threw her hand up to her mouth, gave a cry of dismay, and swooned in a dead faint. As Cassie watched her, she thought, She looks just like a big old hooty owl a-settlin' down on the ground.

Joshua lifted Cassie down and set her firmly on the ground, then turned to his mother and lifted her up. He carried her into the house. Almost all the family crowded through the door behind them.

Cassie stood on the huge stone at the foot of the steps, looking up at the house where Joshua and his family had disappeared. The boy Caleb was still holding the reins of the mules, gazing at her in silence.

"What must I do?" she wondered. "Where on earth have I come to?"

A girl, who looked to be about twelve years old, suddenly appeared at the door.

"Joshua says for you to come on in," she said to Cassie. "I reckon Mother will be all right in a minute or two."

Awkwardly, Cassie climbed the steps, holding her skirts up to keep from tripping on them. The girl stared at her and gave a tentative smile.

"Are you really married to Joshua?" she asked.

"Well, if I ain't, I shore ought to be," Cassie answered her as she placed her hand on her stomach.

The girl glanced at her and blushed.

Cassie stared in awe at the handsome room they had entered. She forgot the people momentarily as she tried to take in the rich furnishings and ornate opulence of the room. Her eyes finally rested on Joshua's mother, who was lying on the settee upholstered in a beautiful floral tapestry.

The family had gathered around her, with several of them patting her hands. She was lying still with a cold cloth across her forehead.

When Joshua saw Cassie, he sprang up and rushed to her side. "Sweetheart, I'm sorry," he said. "I knew it would be a shock to her, but I didn't think it would knock her off her feet. Forgive me for leaving you standing there, but I had to help her. Are you all right?"

At the sound of Joshua's voice, his mother sat up and stared at Cassie. With one look she took in every speck of dirt and evidence of grime that the trip had inflicted. As her scrutiny traveled down Cassie's body, she took in the pregnancy and, moaning, sank back on the couch and covered her eyes again.

Joshua ignored her and began introducing Cassie to the people in the room.

"Cassie, these are my sisters, Mary, Genevieve, Lottie, Nettie, and Molly. You met Caleb outside, and this is my little brother, Jonathan. This is my Aunt Jenny and my Uncle Grover. This is my wife, Cassie, folks. I hope you'll make her welcome," he finished.

One by one they nodded to Cassie as Joshua introduced them, staring curiously at her. Cassie could only stand and look back at them in silence. She clenched her hands as hard as she could, determined to hold back the tears that she felt welling up in her.

Finally, Joshua's Aunt Jenny broke the silence.

"Come with me, child," she said kindly. "You must be exhausted. Let me show you where your room is. Grover, you help Joshua fetch her things. I know she wants to get out of these dirty clothes and freshen up after her long trip."

Gratefully, Cassie followed her up the long staircase, relieved to be out from under the scrutiny of Joshua's family. She stumbled as she neared the top and would have fallen except for Jenny's arm around her.

The room Jenny took her to was large enough to contain their whole cabin. It was furnished in dark mahogany furniture with a huge bed dominating the room. The bed was covered with an ivory-colored heavy woven spread.

"Here's a bowl and pitcher," Jenny told her. "I know you must be longing to wash up a little. Here, let me help you."

Without waiting for permission, Jenny began untying Cassie's bonnet strings. Cassie's fingers felt numb as she fumbled at the buttons on her dress, and Jenny reached up and deftly unbuttoned them.

"Oh, my dear, what beautiful hair you have," she said as the bonnet fell to the floor. "Look at the curls. What I wouldn't give for hair this color and this curly. How far along are you?"

"I'm near eight months along," Cassie murmured, trying to hide her bulging stomach as her dress fell around her knees.

"Now, don't you be shy with me," Jenny admonished her. "My goodness, I've had six of my own, and now I've got four grandchildren. I reckon I've seen my share of expectant mothers. Well, well, so Joshua found himself a bride in the mountains, did he?"

"Yes'm, I reckon he did," Cassie said. "He never told me that his Ma didn't know till we got here. I reckon it's a big shock to her."

"Oh, don't worry about Elizabeth," Jenny laughed. "She'll get over it. Most everything's a shock to her anyhow. She faints at the drop of a hat. She'll be up and rippin' around in no time, you'll see. Now, I'm going to leave you to your privacy while you wash and change. When you're ready, just come on down and we'll have a little something on the table. You must be starved to death."

Jenny swept out the door and closed it firmly behind her. Cassie turned around and stared at the high-ceilinged room and the furnishings in wonderment. Then, locating the washstand, she poured water into the bowl and picked up the bar of scented soap, smelling it and shaking her head in amazement. Once she and Nola had added some cinnamon to the soap when they made it, but this smelled like nothing Cassie had ever experienced before.

"Why, it smells like a whole flower garden," she murmured to herself. "Do you think I should rub it on me? Maybe it's just to smell."

She looked around, but saw nothing else to use, so she gingerly lathered her face and arms with the soap. When she had finished, she quickly wiped and dried the soap with the wash cloth, then replaced it in the dish where she had found it. She rinsed off, and, rather than dirty the towel hanging on the washstand, she pulled her petticoat up and dried her face and arms on it.

"Well, Joshua, this is a fine mess you've got me in," she said. "How on earth can I show my face down there again? These people are a'gonna hate me. I can tell they think I ain't no better'n a mangy old hound dog. Oh, Nola, I wisht you was here so's you could tell me what to do."

Flinging herself on the bed, she beat the pillows and cried in frustration.

THREE

A knock at the door caused Cassie to sit up and dry her eyes. Hastily, she stood and smoothed her slip down, turning and looking for somewhere to hide.

"Cassie, it's me, hon," Joshua called. "May I come in?"

"Oh, Joshua, of course," she cried in relief.

Joshua opened the door and peeked in. He was holding one end of a trunk, which he set down halfway through the doorway.

"I'll take it, Uncle Grover," he said over his shoulder. Cassie heard Joshua's uncle walk away as her husband dragged the trunk through the door.

"I'm sorry it took so long—" he stopped, taking in Cassie's tear-stained face. He shut the door, then crossed the room and took her in his arms. What little composure Cassie had mustered melted when she felt his arms around her, and she broke into sobs again.

"Oh, Cassie, can you ever forgive me for what I've put you through?" he begged. "I'm a low-down inconsiderate jackass. I couldn't blame you if you never spoke to me again."

As Cassie heard the misery and self-loathing in his voice, she began to feel a little better about the situation. She pulled back a little, dried her tears on her petticoat, then peered up at him. He looked so miserable that she felt her heart going out to him.

"I don't reckon it'd be possible for me to go very long without speakin' to you, Joshua," she sniffed. "Don't take this to mean that I've forgive you for what you done though. I'm still powerful mad at you."

"I don't blame you," he said hastily. "But if you can forgive me enough to put that pretty green dress of yours on and come downstairs, everyone wants to make up to you for that bad reception they gave you. They're just as sorry as I am for the way things turned out. Here, let me help you

11

get dressed. I remember we put your dresses in this trunk, didn't we? I know when you brush your hair and put on that dress, you'll be beautiful."

"Humph, you needn't think a few sweet words is a'gonna make up for everything, Joshua," Cassie told him sharply. "How-some-ever, I reckon my manners is just as good as theirs, so I'll get myself dressed and go down. 'Sides, your Aunt Jenny said they had somethin' fixed for us to eat, and I'm near about starved."

They found the dress and Cassie pulled it on, feeling that she looked much more presentable in it than in the dress she had just removed. Nola's mother, Ellen, had made it for her and had allowed for her growing figure, so that the pleats and folds somewhat camouflaged her condition. The jade color was definitely becoming to her, and when she had brushed out the tangles in her hair and put some cold water on her eyes, she began to feel more human.

"Ah, sweetheart, you look beautiful," Joshua said softly. "I don't think I've ever seen you look any prettier. Except maybe that first time I saw you at the schoolhouse in the cove. You wouldn't even look my way, no matter how hard I stared either."

"I reckon I seen you just as plain as you seen me," Cassie giggled. "I just didn't want you to know I was interested."

"You hid it well for a long time," Joshua said drily. "I thought you'd never let me near you, no matter how much I longed to be. But here we are now, two old married people. Come on, honey, let's go downstairs now."

Reluctantly, Cassie left the room with Joshua, wishing that she didn't have to but knowing she must. She resolutely squared her shoulders and followed him down the stairs. She was relieved when she saw that the family was already seated in the dining room. Cassie's face fell as she looked at the elaborate settings of dinnerware and silverware. How would she ever manage, she wondered.

A brief silence fell over the room as the two young people entered. Their surprise was evident as they gazed in slack-jawed amazement at Cassie. Her hair was a flaming halo around her face, framing her creamy complexion and green eyes with soft ringlets that fell halfway down her back. She seemed like a different person from the dirty, stumbling girl who had gone up the stairs.

"Oh, my!" Joshua's Uncle Grover exclaimed in admiration. "Joshua, how did you ever persuade this vision of loveliness to marry you? Come here, my dear, and sit beside me."

He sprang up and held the chair next to him for Cassie. She smiled demurely and sat down, folding her hands in her lap and peering at the people around her. What she saw in their faces was a mixture of awe and admiration. She suddenly felt much better.

I'll jest remember what Nola told me and use the forks and such in order as they come, she thought. Thank goodness we talked about manners, and she learned me how to act in perlite company.

Joshua sat beside her, giving her hand a reassuring squeeze.

"Joshua, come and take your place at the head of the table," a petulant voice demanded. "Now that your dear Papa is gone, you are the head of this family."

"Not tonight, Mother," Joshua said mildly. "I think I want to be near my bride right now. Perhaps tomorrow night, but for now, I'm more content here."

Cassie looked up and intercepted a venomous glare from her mother-in-law.

Well, so this is how it's a-gonna be, Cassie thought. I reckon I'd best be on my guard.

A gentle nudge from Joshua roused her from her thoughts as he began urging food on her. She turned away and began filling her plate, suddenly feeling ravenous. Any discomfort she might have felt was forgotten as she ate and at the same time tried to answer the questions that were hurled at her.

"Is it really very wild in the mountains where you lived, Cassie, and is it true that Indians still live there?" Lottie asked her.

"Well, I don't rightly know what you mean by wild," Cassie replied. "But we've got some Cherokee Indians livin' across the mountain a'ways. They don't never bother us none though."

"How deep does the snow get in the winter?" Jonathan asked. "I heard it covers the treetops up."

Cassie and Joshua both laughed at this exaggeration.

"I've seen it drift over the cabin winders," Cassie said. "But I ain't never seen it cover the trees."

"Joshua says sometimes it's too cold to have school," Molly said. "How can you learn if you don't go to school every day?"

"I reckon when you've got a teacher as good as your brother, you just naturally learn more." Cassie smiled at Joshua.

"That's enough of these questions," Jenny interrupted. "My goodness, let the poor girl eat. She's hardly had time to take a bite. You'll have plenty of time to ask her questions later."

Cassie smiled gratefully at Jenny, then bent to her plate and began to eat. Conversation rose and fell around her, and she watched as the family vied with each other for attention. She pondered at the difference between

Joshua's family and the Johnston family where she had lived. There they had treated each other with a courtesy that was obviously lacking here. Longingly, she remembered the gentle kindness of Nola's parents, Will and Ellen. She wondered what it was going to be like becoming a part of this family.

When the meal was finally over, Cassie found herself so exhausted that she didn't know where she would find the strength to climb the stairs.

"Joshua," she whispered, "do you think I could be excused from helpin' with the dishes tonight? I'm just plumb wore out."

"Of course, you can be," he grinned at her. "Come on and I'll help you up to bed."

"Goodnight, everyone," he told the family. "Cassie and I are just totally exhausted, and, if you will forgive us, we would like to lie down in a real bed for the first time in weeks. Tomorrow we'll answer all of your questions and catch up on all of the news, but for now, I think we need to rest ourselves."

A chorus of disappointed protests greeted his announcement, but he pushed them aside and firmly led Cassie toward the stairs, supporting her with his arm around her.

"It shore was nice of yore ma to put on a spread like that just for us," Cassie told Joshua as she searched through the trunk for their night clothes. "How did they know what day we was a-comin' anyhow?"

"They didn't know," he laughed. "And that wasn't anything special. Just their usual evening meal. Well, maybe a little extra because my sisters are here from Nashville."

"Their usual meal, you say?" Cassie asked. "My goodness, what do they do for special days? I never seen so much food."

"I guess it is different for you," Joshua said. "But you'll get used to everything soon."

"I reckon," Cassie yawned. "Just as long as I don't have to do all the cookin'."

Cassie barely remembered pulling her gown over her head before she sank down in the soft mattress and surrendered herself to sleep. She slept soundly but dreamed of being in a strange land surrounded by strangers, and all of them were holding out empty plates demanding that she fill them. Just when she began to stir restlessly, Joshua rolled over and put his arms around her. She sighed in her sleep and snuggled safely against him.

FOUR

Cassie woke the next morning and lay still for a moment, confused and wondering where she was. When she remembered, she sat upright in the bed and looked around frantically for Joshua. There was no sign of him, but as she started to get out of bed, her hand touched a note pinned to his pillow. It read:

> Darling Cassie,
>   You were sleeping so peacefully, I couldn't bear to wake you. I'll see you at noon meal.
>
> Joshua

Her heart sank, and she wondered frantically what she would do without him there to guide her.

Listen to yoreself, she thought. You sound like some young'un afeared to be parted from its ma. You got to learn to stand on yore own two feet sometime, and I reckon this is jest as good a time as any. I'll jest git myself dressed and go downstairs and help with the chores.

First, she made the bed and tidied up their room, putting their clothes in the huge dressers. She picked the least wrinkled of her dresses, and, after washing her face and hands, she brushed her hair and prepared to go downstairs. Before she left, she took out a clean apron and put it over her dress.

What in the world will they ever thank of me, she worried. It's way past sunup. I ain't never laid in bed this late in my life. I reckon they'll thank Joshua got hisself a lazy woman for shore.

She opened the door and crept cautiously to the stairway, peering around curiously. No one else was in sight, and she decided everyone must already be out working in the fields.

Cassie entered the dining room and looked around. The table was set for breakfast, but no one was there. On the sideboard were containers with food in them, kept warm by the burning candles under each dish. As Cassie looked in astonishment at the various contraptions keeping the food warm, a Negro woman entered the room. Cassie jumped back in embarrassment at being discovered peeking in the dishes.

"Mornin', miss," the woman said. "Is you ready for some breakfast?"

"Why, yes, I suppose I am," Cassie answered. "Has everybody else already et? I'm sorry if I've put you out any."

"Why, law, no, they don't never get up this early," the woman laughed. "Nobody but Mr. Joshua has eat. It's early yet. Sun ain't been up but just an hour or so. Mr. Joshua, he said he was itchin' to git out and look things over. That's why he's up so soon. You jest set now and tell me what you want, and I'll serve you."

"Why, I reckon I ain't too tired to fix my own," Cassie laughed. "Is these the plates we're supposed to use? Mrs. Perkins shouldn't have got her good stuff out just for us."

"Why, this ain't the good stuff," the woman laughed again. "This is jest the everday china."

"Oh," Cassie said quietly. "Looks pertty fine to me. But I ain't used to a lot of fancy dishes where I come from. We jest had two sets, and neither one of 'em looked as good as these. What's yore name? Mine's Cassie."

"I'm Belle, ma'am," the woman replied. "And I'm right pleased to see what a fine lookin' wife Mr. Joshua got for hisself. I been with the family a long time."

"Well, I'm mighty pleased to meet you, Belle," Cassie said, "and soon's I get through eatin' I'll come and help with the dishes. I sort of laid down on my job last night I was so tarred. Seems like the trip took more out of me than I ever thought it would. I reckon this baby I'm a'carryin' takes some of my strength. I feel fine this mornin' though, and I'm ready to help with the chores if you'll but tell me what to do."

"Huh?" Belle said in amazement. "What you mean help with the chores? Ain't nothin' here for a fine lady like yoreself to do. Miz Perkins don't trouble herself with housework, and I know she don't 'spect you to neither."

Cassie paused with the fork halfway to her mouth and stared at Belle.

"What do you mean nothin' for me to do?" she asked. "Of course, they's somethin' for me to do. For one thing I've got a whole basket full of clothes we dirtied on our trip that needs a'washin' and ironin'. I can help with the cookin', too. There must be a powerful lot of cookin' to do to keep all these mouths fed. I'm a good cook, if I do say so myself."

Belle shook her head in disbelief. She backed hastily out of the dining room and fled into the kitchen, muttering as she went, "Miz Perkins ain't gonna like no such a'doin's as this."

In the dining room Cassie reached for another light, flaky biscuit and filled it with butter and preserves from the dish before her. She finished her meal, picked up her plate and silverware, and looked for the kitchen.

She went through a small sitting room, then, following the sounds of dishes, went through a long covered porch into the kitchen where she found Belle bending over a pan of dirty dishes, still muttering to herself. She deposited her plate and silver in the dishpan and reached for a drying cloth and began drying the dishes Belle had rinsed and set out to drain.

"What you doin'?" Belle asked in alarm. "Don't you know Miz Perkins'll have my hide, she catch you here a'helpin' me?"

"Why on earth should she?" Cassie asked. "It don't 'pear to me you got anybody else to help you. Was you goin' to do all these dishes by yoreself?"

"I allus does," Belle answered defensively. "They used to be three more girls to help in the kitchen till Mr. Perkins died and set 'em all free. Since then they ain't nobody to do the work but me. I'd a'gone too, but they ain't nowhere for me to go nor nothin' for me to do. Miz Perkins give me a place to live and food for my belly, so I reckoned I's jest as well off to stay where I am. 'Sides, I done got too old to be a'travelin' 'round. I jest does what I can, and the rest goes without bein' done."

"Don't Mrs. Perkins or the girls help any?" Cassie asked.

"No'm," Belle replied. "They's ladies, and ladies don't do housework."

"If they don't do no housework, then what on earth do they do?" Cassie asked in amazement.

"You know," Belle said. "They does lady things. They goes to parties and sews them little picture things and fans theyselves a lot."

"My stars, I'd go crazy if I didn't do nothin' but fan myself and go to parties," Cassie muttered. "Here, show me where these dishes and things go so I can put them up."

"Now, Miss Cassie, Miz Perkins'll have my hide for shore," Belle exclaimed in alarm. "Please jest leave them dishes and go on about yo' business."

"This is my business," Cassie replied firmly. "I'm Joshua's wife, and I heard his mother say last night that he's the man of the house now, so I guess that makes me the woman of the house. Now, when I get these things put up, we'll dust the furniture in the settin' room if you'll find me a clean rag. I noticed last night that it needed a good cleanin'."

Belle rolled her eyes in resignation and went looking for a dust rag, shaking her head and mumbling dire predictions of terrible consequences as she shuffled off.

When Elizabeth Perkins finally rose at ten that morning, she found Cassie busily dusting furniture with the help of Lottie, the eldest daughter.

"Good morning, Mother Perkins," Cassie said cheerfully. "It's a right pert mornin', ain't it? I noticed the furniture was in need of a little dustin', and I thought I'd take care of it while I was a'waitin' on you to get up and tell me what you wanted me to do."

"You—you what?" Elizabeth Perkins asked. "What on earth are you doing? Where's Belle? If the furniture needed cleaning, then why didn't you tell Belle to do it? Why on earth would you be cleaning furniture— and what's Lottie doing?"

"Cassie showed me how to rub the oil on the furniture and make it shine, Mama," Lottie said proudly. "Don't it look nice now?"

"Oh, my—oh, my!" Elizabeth exclaimed. "Well, I never! I never in my life thought I'd see the day when my son brought home a common servant for a wife. What on earth am I to do? What will people think? Lottie, you put down that dirty rag right now and go and wash your hands."

"I'm sorry if you don't approve, Miz Perkins," Cassie said mildly, "but it seems to me it's too much to expect Belle to cook for this big family and keep this big house, too. I'm used to pullin' my own weight, and I reckon that's what I aim to do. I'm not no servant though. Not yours nor nobody else's. I do what I do because I want to, not because I'm somebody's servant. I reckon the quicker you and me understand this, the better off we'll all be."

Lottie held her breath, expecting her mother to explode any minute. She shrank back behind a chair and eyed the nearest door so she could get away when the explosion came.

Elizabeth Perkins stared at Cassie with contempt and exasperation, then turned on her heel and sailed into the dining room, where they heard her screaming for Belle to bring her some fresh eggs.

Quietly, Cassie resumed rubbing the furniture. Lottie looked at her with big round eyes for a moment, then picked up her cloth and started helping her.

When Joshua came in at lunch time, it was to find his mother in bed with a sick headache and Cassie cheerfully helping a wide-eyed Belle carry food to the table. He grinned and began helping his plate.

When Cassie sat down with him he asked her, "Everything going all right for you this morning?"

"Why, of course," she answered cheerfully. "Why wouldn't it be? I reckon it'll take me a day or two to find where everything belongs, but with Belle a'helpin' me, I'll get settled in a'fore long."

She ate on, oblivious of the glances being exchanged among the rest of the family.

FIVE

Joshua's sisters Mary and Genevieve decided it would be wise if they left for home that very afternoon. As soon as the noon meal was over, they packed up and left for the train station. They did not disturb their mother with farewells but left her notes, promising to return soon.

I reckon they know how put-out at me she is, Cassie mused. And they don't want to get caught in the crossfire. I hope I ain't done somethin' that'll set her against me for good.

Belle had drawn the line at letting Cassie do her own washing and was in the back yard bent over the wash tub, busily scrubbing clothes and muttering under her breath. After Cassie finished up the noon dishes, she decided she was feeling a "mite tired" and went up to her room to lie down. As she lay on the bed, her eyes wandered around the room, taking in the furniture and marveling at the richness of the pieces. When she spied a desk in the corner, she rose and went to it, curious about the cleverness with which it was constructed.

As Cassie looked the desk over, she spied paper and pen sitting in readiness on the desk top. On impulse, she took up the pen and began a letter to Nola.

> Dear Nola,
> Well, you'd never beleeve yore eyes if you could see me now. I'm a settin in a big fine house the likes of which I never seen before. Joshua never told me his folks was rich and its come as some kind of shock for me. Course I think I was some kind of shock for them too—specially his ma. She never knowed nothing about me on account of Joshua hadn't told his folks he was married. They've been nice to me for the most part though. His Aunt Jenny and Uncle Grover lives near by and I think we'll be

friends right off. And his sister Lottie is nice too. She's about twelve year old and is a sweet little thing. His older sisters is kind of snooty, though, you know like them Davis girls was at home. Lucky though they live in another town and I don't reckon I'll be bothered much by them. I'm not sure about his ma. I reckon when we get to understand one another things will be alright. They's a old colored woman named Belle who has been doing most of the work by herself. I guess when she gets used to having some help she'll be right glad I'm here. She sure is scared of Joshua's ma though.

You seem so far away Nola. What I wouldn't give for a look at you right now. I can't hardly stand the thought of you and yore ma not being here when my time comes. I don't know how much help Joshua's ma will be. She don't seem to know how to do much of anything. Maybe Belle will know how to help.

Please write to me soon and tell me all the news in the cove. Give everybody a howdy for me and tell your ma I miss her too.

Yours truly,
Cassie Perkins

Cassie wiped a tear from her eye as she signed the letter and addressed it. A wave of homesickness swept over her, and she threw herself down on the bed and cried herself to sleep. That was where Joshua found her when he came in from the field that afternoon.

Cassie opened her eyes, forgetting for a moment where she was. She smiled sunnily at Joshua as he took her in his arms. Then her smile faded as she remembered that they were no longer in their little cabin in the mountains.

"Oh, Joshua," she said tearfully. "Do you think I'll ever learn to live in this big house? I don't want you to be ashamed of me. I feel like such a ignorant bumpkin, and now I think I've done gone and made yore ma mad at me right off."

"Listen, Cassie," Joshua said firmly. "I could never be ashamed of you, and you should never be ashamed of yourself. You are a beautiful, bright, wonderful woman, and I am proud to call you my wife. As for my mother, don't worry about her. She'll come around soon, and if she doesn't, then it's just her loss."

"I don't understand why it's wrong for me to want to help with the housework," Cassie said. "I wouldn't feel right not to earn my keep. Belle says that all ladies is supposed to do is set and make little needlework and fan theirselves. Joshua, I tell you right now, I'd go out of my mind if that was all I could do."

Joshua threw back his head and laughed. "I can't imagine you just sitting around fanning yourself either, Cassie," he said when he could catch his breath. "You go right on and do whatever you want to. This is your home now. Mother may put up a fuss for a while, but she'll come around and probably be grateful for the help, although I'm sure she'll never admit it.

"You have to understand how it's always been for her, Cassie. She was always used to a house full of servants to do the work. When Papa died, he left a paper giving all the slaves their freedom, never dreaming he'd go before she did, and she just doesn't know how to manage any other way. You will just have to help her to learn to do some things for herself."

"I'll try, Joshua," Cassie said earnestly. "That is, if she'll let me. I don't want to set her against me, but it just ain't in me to become somethin' I ain't."

"Don't you change one single bit," Joshua ordered her sternly. "I love you just the way you are, my little mountain wildcat.

"You know you're going to have plenty to do when this baby gets here. How much longer do you figure it's going to be?"

"Well, from what Nola's pa said, it should be about four more weeks," Cassie replied. "That's somethin' else we got to talk about. Who're we gonna get to help me when the time comes? I don't reckon yore ma will be much help."

"No, I don't think she will either," Joshua smiled. "There's a doctor in town, and we will send for him when the times comes. I have to go in to town in a day or two on some business, and I'll speak to him then."

"A doctor!" Cassie exclaimed. "Well, I don't see no need for that. Ain't there no granny women around that could help?"

"I don't know of any," Joshua answered, "but you're not to worry yourself about that. I'll take care of the arrangements. Now, I hear Belle ringing the supper bell and I haven't even washed my face yet. Let's get ready and go down."

"Oh, my goodness!" Cassie exclaimed, jumping up. "Here I've been a'layin' in bed all afternoon and pore Belle down there fixin' supper all by herself. What must she think of me?"

"I expect she thinks you're some kind of angel sent from above," Joshua grinned. "Don't worry, she's used to doing things by herself, so don't jump in and make her feel useless, or she might take it in her mind to leave with the rest of them. Lord knows I wish one or two had stayed on. The few hands Uncle Grover was able to hire are as sorry a lot as I've ever seen. Tomorrow I'm going to get Caleb and Jonathan out and put them to work. Maybe you could help me motivate them like you did Lottie."

"I don't know what that big word means, but if it means what I think it does, just tell them if they want to eat, they'd best help make the vittles," Cassie retorted.

Elizabeth Perkins was seated at the foot of the table when Joshua and Cassie came into the dining room. She ignored Cassie but smiled lovingly at Joshua.

"Now, Joshua, you must sit at the head of the table," she urged him. "You are the head of this family now and you must assume your proper place."

"That being the case," Joshua replied thoughtfully, "then Cassie's proper place should be at the foot of the table where you are."

Elizabeth's face paled, then flushed dark red. She glared malignantly at Cassie, but made no move to leave her place at the table.

Cassie put her hand on Joshua's arm and gave it a gentle squeeze.

"I wouldn't think of askin' yore ma to move," she said softly. "I'll just sit beside you, Joshua. That way I can help Belle carry in the vittles. It's closer to the kitchen."

"Very well, Cassie," Joshua replied. "You sit where you are most comfortable. I don't care much about who sits at the head or the foot of the table. It seems silly to me."

The meal was eaten in cold silence. The only sounds were the dishes being passed and muted conversation between Cassie and Joshua. Belle looked fearfully at Elizabeth as she shuffled in and out of the dining room with the food.

When all had finished their meal and rose to leave the table, Cassie held Lottie back when they moved toward the living room.

"Lottie," she said quietly, "me and Belle could use your help for just a few minutes. Help me clear the table so Belle don't have to walk her legs off. Mrs. Johnston used to say, 'many hands make light work,' and I reckon that's shorely true when you're a'clearin' up after a meal."

Lottie glanced fearfully at her mother, but Joshua urged her, "Go on, Lottie, do what Cassie says." With one last glance at her mother, Lottie started picking up plates and carrying them to the kitchen.

"Please, Cassie, can I help, too?" Molly begged. "It looks like fun."

Cassie smiled to her. "Why shore, I reckon you can if'n you're a mind to."

Elizabeth turned her back and swept up the stairs to her room, bypassing the evening gathering in the living room. Joshua thoughtfully watched her retreating back, then turned toward his younger brothers, who were trying to slip out of the house.

"We'll want to talk for a minute, boys," he said quietly. "Come into the sitting room with me."

Wide-eyed, they followed him, perching nervously on the edge of their chairs and wondering which of their pranks had caught up with them. Cassie, pausing on one of her trips to the kitchen, stood in the door, giving Joshua her support.

"This is a big farm," Joshua began slowly. "And if we are going to make it work, we'll all have to pitch in and help. I know you've all been slacking off since Papa died, but from now on everyone will have jobs to do, and I will expect you to do them."

"I ain't no field hand," Caleb said defiantly. "Mama says it's the Negroes' place to do the field work. We're the owners, and it ain't right that we should lower ourselves to do menial work."

"Ain't? Did you say 'ain't'?" Joshua asked coldly. "You may not consider yourself a field hand, but you are surely talking like one. As for whose place it is to work, I might remind you of the good food you put in your belly tonight. If you wish to continue enjoying the taste of it, you will contribute your share of labor to the growing and harvesting of it. But, of course, it's your choice. If you feel like it's beneath you to dirty your hands in honest labor, then I suggest you look elsewhere for your food."

"Mama won't allow it," Caleb said defiantly. "You can't tell me what to do."

"I am back here because the place was falling apart and you are one step away from the poorhouse," Joshua said evenly. "I was perfectly happy where I was and would be happy to return there and take up my profession again, but I cannot turn my back on my family. On the other hand, I do not plan to carry the full burden by myself. Everyone will pull their own weight as long as they are living under this roof. Do I make myself clear?"

"Yes," Caleb muttered. "Does that mean we can't have any fun anymore? Can't we go fishing or swimming anymore?"

"Of course, you can," Joshua said mildly. "I'm no tyrant. There will be plenty of time for fun, too. I just want you to realize that no one gets a free ride around here. Everyone has to pull their own weight. Besides, Caleb, as soon as you're old enough, I plan to go back to teaching and turn the farm over to you."

"Me?" Caleb yelped in horror. "Not me. I don't want to be any farmer. I can tell you that right now, Joshua. I hate farming. I'm going to be a banker or something I can make a lot of money at and get rich so I don't have to work at all."

"Well, until then, you'll just be a farmer like me," Joshua said drily. "Now, go on about your business, but be sure you're in bed at a decent hour because I plan on getting you up early tomorrow."

As the boys were leaving, Lottie and Molly returned from the kitchen chattering excitedly about their new jobs. Impulsively, they hugged Cassie.

"Cassie said if we helped her and Belle, she'd teach us how to make a quilt for our doll beds," Lottie said to Joshua. "I like Cassie, Joshua. I'm glad you picked her out for your wife."

"So am I, Lottie." Joshua smiled at Cassie. "I have a feeling that Cassie is just the breath of fresh air this old house needs."

Upstairs a door slammed loudly.

SIX

T he days began to settle into a regular routine at the farm. Cassie soon had the house in order and cleaned to her liking. She was worried how she was going to tactfully get Elizabeth out of her room to clean it, but Elizabeth solved the problem herself when she announced at supper one night that she was going to visit a neighbor the next day.

"Oh, are you a'goin' to a quiltin'?" Cassie inquired eagerly.

"A what?" Elizabeth asked, momentarily forgetting to ignore Cassie. "I don't know what you're talking about."

"You don't know what a quiltin' is?" Cassie asked incredulously. "Why, I never knowed anybody that didn't know what a quiltin' was before. They're just about the funnest things there is. We used to have quiltin's regular when we was back home."

"Well, I am not going to any quilting. I am going to visit my dear friend, Isabella Timmons," Elizabeth said coldly. "I will not be home until late afternoon."

While they were washing dishes that evening, Cassie told Belle, "We'll get started on Mrs. Perkins's room as soon as she leaves tomorrow and have it all clean and put back together for her when she gets home. That'll be the lot of it then, and I don't mind tellin' you I'll be glad of it. The way I'm a'feelin', this baby is goin' to be comin' soon, and it pleasures me that we've got the house all cleaned up before it gets here. I know there'll be some little time that I won't be much help to you, Belle. But I think the girls're learnin' fast, and they's lots they can do to help till I get back on my feet."

"Miss Cassie, I keep tellin' you it ain't fitten for you to be helpin' me with the cleanin'. Miz Perkins sho don't dirty her hands with no house-work. Ladies ain't supposed to do such things," Belle told her.

"I know what you keep sayin', Belle," Cassie smiled. "And I've told you a hundred times or more, I'm not no lady if that's the way I'm supposed to act. You work too hard, and I don't think it's gonna hurt any of us to help you out."

Belle shook her head in resignation. "You sho is somethin', Miss Cassie. I reckon you's jest about the finest lady I done ever seen. You jest don't know it yet."

Supper dishes washed and the kitchen tidied up, Cassie took off her apron and went into the study. As soon as the evening meal was finished, Joshua had gone there to work on the books.

"Joshua," she began, but stopped when she saw that he was slumped over the desk, sound asleep.

"Oh, my goodness," she sighed. "You're just plumb tuckered out, ain't you? Well, come on, it's off to bed for you."

She roused Joshua and picked up the lamp. Together they made their way upstairs. Joshua pulled off his boots and fell tiredly across the bed.

"Now, Joshua, don't you fall asleep before you put your nightshirt on," she admonished him. "You're just a'workin' too hard. You got to get you some more help. I don't see how you expect to work all this land with no more help than you got. It's more'n one man can do. Can't you find nobody else that wants to work?"

"I've practically combed the bushes," he said tiredly. "Besides, I'm barely scraping up enough to pay what I've got. Sorry as they are, they're better than nothing. Uncle Grover says I'm lucky to have them. All of the good workers have gone north, thinking they'll get rich up there."

"Hmmm," mused Cassie, "looks like they's somethin' we could do. If I wasn't in such a motherly way, I could help you, but the way things are, I sure wouldn't be much use to you."

"You do too much now." He smiled at her. "I know how hard you've been working getting this place cleaned up. You should be taking it easy now. I don't want you doing anything that might hurt the baby."

"Don't you worry about me," she told him. "I'm strong as a horse. You know me and Nola and Martha helped in the fields at home. Soon's I get back on my feet, I'll be out there with you."

"That really will cause Ma to blow her top," he grinned at her. "I can just hear her now!"

Cassie could hardly wait to get Elizabeth out of the house the next morning so they could get at her room. She and Belle spent the better part of the day scouring and cleaning the room. When they finished, Cassie stood back and looked with satisfaction at their work.

"Well, now that's what I call a right good job," she said with satisfaction. "I bet Miz Perkins will be tickled pink. I wish we could have aired the bedclothes another day though. Never mind, we'll give 'em a good one next spring."

"If'n you's a'spectin' any kind of thanks from Miz Perkins, you might as well fergit it," Belle snorted. "I ain't never heard her say 'thank you' for nothin' yet."

"Oh, well, I don't care if she don't," Cassie laughed. "It's just give me a fine feelin' to know my house is all clean and ready for this young'un. I reckon I can rest easy now till my time comes."

If Elizabeth noticed the change in her room, she didn't acknowledge it to anyone. When she came in, she muttered something about having a sick headache and Belle bringing her a light supper to her room. Then she disappeared for the evening.

When Belle returned from picking up Elizabeth's empty dishes, she told Joshua, "Miz Perkins say for you to come up to her room, Mr. Joshua. She say she want to talk to you right away."

Puzzled, Joshua made his way up the stairs to his mother's room. Cassie was startled to hear the sound of shouting, then a door slamming.

"What on earth?" she asked Joshua when he came downstairs.

"He shook his head at her and stalked into the study. Cassie followed him in, and he gestured at her to close the door behind her. She had never seen such a look of rage on his face before.

"My dear mother," he said icily, "has decided that she wants to have a party. No matter that there's barely enough money to put food on the table. She wants to have a grand party 'now that Belle has finally stirred her lazy hide enough to put the house in order,' she says. I told her there was no money, but that didn't discourage her. She says she will 'manage' the money. I don't know where she thinks she'll 'manage' it from, and I told her so. I also told her that it wasn't Belle who had 'put the house in order,' but that it was you who had scrubbed your hands raw cleaning it. That she ignored. Anyhow, we've had a grand row about it, and she's in her room pouting. Says she refuses to come down."

"Oh, Joshua, you poor thing," Cassie said softly. "Now don't fret so, she'll get over it. I reckon she's just not used to havin' to worry about money and practical things. I bet when she thinks about it for a while, she'll come around."

"Humph," he snorted. "She never thinks about anything but herself. Never has. Papa worked himself into the grave trying to satisfy her. She gave no consideration to the fact that you're about to have a baby and wouldn't feel like having a party. When I pointed that out to her, she said, 'Of course it wouldn't be proper for her to appear in public right now, but I'm sure she could just stay in her room during the party.'

"I have put my foot down on this though, and I don't mean to change my mind. I will hear no more about it."

The next morning Elizabeth stayed in her room, ringing a bell every few minutes for Belle. By noon, Belle, tired from running up and down the stairs, muttered under her breath every time she heard the sound of the bell.

Cassie had watched the morning's events quietly and had taken over the preparation for the noon meal. When the dishes were washed and put away, she took Belle firmly by the arm and led her to the kitchen door.

"Now, Belle, you've about run yourself to death this mornin' up and down them stairs. I think you need a rest. You go to your cabin and don't come back till it's time to fix supper," she told her.

"Oh, no'm, I wouldn't dare do that," Belle protested. "Miz Perkins, she'd have my hide if I did."

"Don't you worry about Miz Perkins, I'll take care of her," Cassie said firmly. "You just go and rest for a few hours. I'll manage just fine."

"You ain't got no business runnin' up them steps in yo' condition," Belle protested.

"Oh, I don't think one trip will hurt me," Cassie said, "and I don't intend to make but one."

"Lawd help us," Belle said, rolling her eyes. "I hopes you know what you're gettin' into, Miss Cassie. She ain't a easy woman to please."

"I think I know what I'm doin'." Cassie smiled at her. "Now, you just go on home."

Belle had been gone for only a few minutes when Cassie heard the bell ring. She waited for several minutes until it rang a second time. After a few more minutes, it rang louder and more impatiently. Cassie smiled and slowly started up the stairs. It rang again before she reached Elizabeth's room.

She pushed open the door and went in quietly. Elizabeth Perkins was sitting at her desk in the window alcove. She did not bother to look up but went on with her writing.

"Belle, where have you been?" she began impatiently. "I rang for you at least three times. Come over here and find my rosebud peignoir for me. I can't find anything since that woman messed my room up."

"This ain't Belle," Cassie said quietly. "Belle was worn out from runnin' up and down the stairs all mornin', and I sent her home to rest for a while. You know, Belle is not very young, and it's hard on her runnin' up and down the stairs ever few minutes. Yore rosebud robe is right there in the front of yore closet. I'm surprised you couldn't see it. I can see it from here."

Elizabeth looked up in surprise at Cassie, then her face hardened.

"What do you mean, you sent Belle home?" she asked. "How dare you interfere with my slaves?"

"Well, it seemed like the Christian thing to do," Cassie said. "I think it was the smart thing to do, too, since the poor woman was about wore out. She sure won't be much use to you if she's too sick to work. Besides, I don't think there's any such thing as slaves no more. I think Belle just works for you. You don't own her. She's belongs to herself, not you."

"Please leave my room," Elizabeth said coldly.

"Gladly," Cassie said softly. "And by the way, you'll just have to do your own fetchin'. The girls went out in the yard to play, and the boys are in the field helpin' Joshua. I'm sure you wouldn't want me runnin' up and down the stairs in my condition."

She turned to leave, then said softly, "Oh, by the way, supper'll be ready at six o'clock. If you're a mind to eat, I reckon you'd better come on down to the dinin' room. Since you don't appear to be sick, I don't reckon anybody's got the time to fetch it up to you."

Cassie closed the door quietly behind her, then grinned as she heard the sound of glass shattering against the door. She hesitated as she heard sobs from behind the door, then shook her head. Like Joshua, she had to stand firm.

Supper was on the table promptly at six and everyone was just about to sit down when Elizabeth swept into the room. She took her place at the foot of the table.

"Well, Mother, I'm glad to see you're feeling better," Joshua said, surprised.

"Thank you, Joshua," she said. "I feel quite recovered now."

Cassie hid a smile behind her napkin.

SEVEN

Just as the first rays of the sun began to appear the next morning, Cassie woke to the beginning of labor pains. Joshua was sitting on the side of the bed, pulling on his boots, when he heard her utter a surprised, "Oh, my!"

"What is it, Cassie?" he asked. "Are you all right?"

"Why, yes, I reckon I am," she said softly. "I reckon I'm about to git ready to have our baby, Joshua."

"What!" he exclaimed as he sprang up. "You mean today, right now?"

"I reckon so," she said. "Now seems 'bout as good a time as any. By my reckonin', it's about time, give or take a week or so."

"Where are you going?" he cried in alarm as she began climbing out of bed.

"Well, I thought maybe I'd better git things ready," she said slowly. "I'm shore it'll be a time yet, and I reckoned I'd better git things together."

"You stay right where you are," he said firmly. "I'll get you whatever you need. This time someone's going to do for you for a change. I'll go get Belle, then I'm going to send one of the men to town for the doctor."

"If it ain't too much trouble, I reckon I'd sort of like it if yore Aunt Jenny could come," Cassie said timidly. "She said if I'd send for her, she'd come."

"Of course, darling, anything you want," he reassured her. "Damn, where did I put my other boot?"

"It's a'settin' right there next to where the other one was, and you better not say that word again, Joshua Perkins," Cassie said sharply. "It ain't fitten to use such words in front of our baby."

"I'm sorry," he said contritely. "But I don't think the baby heard me. I guess I'm excited. Oh, we've waited so long, I guess I didn't think the time would come, but it's here, isn't it? Soon we'll hold our own sweet baby in our arms."

He turned and put his arms around Cassie and drew her to him and held her for several minutes before he gently laid her back against the pillows and rose to go about his duties.

"Belle!" he shouted as he opened the door. "Come up here! Hurry!"

The old woman stuck her head around the edge of the dining room door and peered up the stairs at Joshua where he was standing at the head of the stairs.

"What on earth is wrong?" she hissed in a loud whisper. "You better hush, Mr. Joshua. You'll wake Miz Perkins up a'shoutin' like that."

"I don't care if I wake the whole world up, Belle!" he shouted. "My wife's getting ready to have our baby. Come on up here and stay with her while I take care of things."

"Lawd help us!" exclaimed Belle. "I told her yesterday that her time was close, and she just went on a'scrubbin' and doin' anyhow."

She hurried up the stairs as fast as she could and into Cassie and Joshua's bedroom. She began fussing with the bedclothes and pillows behind Cassie, muttering at her and fussing because she had ignored her warnings.

"Don't take on so, Belle," Cassie said mildly. "I'm all right, and, besides, I think it'll be awhile yet before this baby gits borned. I ain't had but one good pain so far. They wasn't no need for Joshua to get hisself all tore up. I tried to git him to wait awhile, but you know how men are."

"I reckon I shorely do," chuckled Belle. "They's about as much use as a fox in a henhouse at a time like this. If you're all right, I'll go down and put some water on. I reckon we're gonna need some 'fore long."

"I'm just fine, Belle, and don't you be frettin' over me," Cassie said. "I thank you for bein' here though. I reckon I'm a'missin' my folks a'right much now."

"Now, now, Miss Cassie, don't you fret yo'sef. You know I'm gonna look after you. How could I do anything else, good as you done been to me?"

"Thank you, Belle," Cassie said tearfully. "If you don't mind before you go, would you look in that bottom drawer of the dresser and get me the blankets and things that I wrapped up in that pillow case. They's things Miz Johnston fixed for the baby 'fore we left the cove. She said they's everything we'd need at first."

"I sholy will," Belle answered, going to the dresser and laying out the things Cassie requested. "My, my, would you jest look at that. Them's the softest, finest lookin' blankets and cloths I ever seen. Look at that pertty stitchin' around this little gown. What you call that work, Miss Cassie?"

"That's smockin'," Cassie said proudly. "Miz Johnston did the finest smockin' of anybody in the cove. She made that gown just special for my baby. Oh, Belle, it sure makes me homesick for the sight of them." She took a deep breath. "I ain't a'gonna fret though, 'cause soon I'm gonna have my own baby, and I reckon that'll make me and Joshua a real family for sure."

"I'm goin' to go put that water on now," Belle said. "You jest rest easy now and I'll be right back."

As Belle left the room, a sleepy-eyed Lottie looked in.

"Cassie, what's wrong?" she asked. "I heard Belle talkin', and she went flyin' down the stairs."

"Nothin's wrong, Lottie," Cassie smiled. "It's just that I think the baby's comin' sometime soon. Joshua's gone to send somebody after the doctor, and Belle went to get things ready for him. Sit down here and keep me company for a minute."

"Oh, Cassie, the baby, really?" Lottie exclaimed. "It'll be so much fun to have a real live baby to play with. I can hardly wait. Are you all right? Does it hurt a lot?"

"Not yet," Cassie answered, "but I expect it will before it's over. Nothin' I can't bear though. No worse than it was before anyhow."

"Before?" asked Lottie. "You mean you had a baby before?"

"Oh, no, I meant no worse than it was when Miz Johnston had her baby before," Cassie said hastily.

She bit her lip in consternation and glanced quickly at Lottie. Lottie nodded her head in acceptance, and Cassie breathed a sigh of relief.

"I'm so befuddled I don't rightly know what I'm a'sayin'," she told Lottie. "Maybe you could go and ask Belle if she'd come up here a minute."

Lottie flew out of the room, eager to have a job to do. She had not been allowed to watch the births of her siblings, and the whole process was making her nervous. Just as she got to the foot of the stairs, Joshua passed her on the way up.

"I was going to get Belle for Cassie," she said breathlessly.

"Never mind. I'm here now. I'll do whatever needs to be done for Cassie," he said. "You go to the kitchen and help Belle get things ready for the doctor. I sent Jeb after him, but it'll take awhile for him to get here."

Cassie was relieved to see Joshua when he entered the bedroom. He went to her and took her in his arms.

"You are not to worry about a thing now, Cassie," he told her tenderly. "Everything is taken care of, and the doctor will be here in plenty of time.

Just lie back and rest while you can. I'm going to stay right here with you the whole time."

Cassie's labor progressed swiftly as the morning wore on. Joshua stayed by her side most of the time, wiping the perspiration from her face and rubbing her back between pains. Belle drifted in and out of the room, giving advice and offering to spell Joshua. At Cassie's insistence, he finally left the room long enough to eat a lunch that Belle had prepared for him.

As soon as he was out of the room, Cassie motioned Belle to come to her side.

"Belle, would you mind a'findin' me a butcher knife to put under the bed?" she whispered. "I know Joshua don't hold with such things, but I knowed a granny woman who swore it helped cut the pain when a woman was in labor."

"I got one right here under my apron," Belle grinned. "Men thinks they's always got to be a good reason for everything. Some things is just so, and they don't always have to be a reason. You just lay back now and rest while you can. I'll take care of it."

Cassie smiled in gratitude, then let out a deep moan as another labor pain began to course through her body. The doctor arrived before it had run its course. He examined her briefly and then began opening his bag.

"Belle, go and bring me a kettle of that hot water you've been boilin'," he said. "I don't think it'll be very long before this baby is born. Joshua, you go on out now. A husband is about the most useless thing in the world at a time like this. Belle can help me. She's probably delivered about as many as I have anyhow."

"Got your knife under the bed?" he asked Cassie, grinning as she nodded timidly at him. "Well, who knows, maybe it helps. The older I get, the more I find out how little I know."

Cassie decided she liked this funny, gruff man. Sighing in relief, she gave herself over to him. Great waves of pain engulfed her as she reached the final stages of childbirth, and she could only cling to his voice as he urged her, "Push now, push. That's fine, you're doin' just fine."

When it was finally over, she lay back exhausted. She saw Belle take the tiny body to the basin. In her exhaustion, she asked, "Is it dead too?"

"Dead? Why no. Whatever made you think your baby was dead?" the doctor asked, "You have a beautiful little daughter. I want you to know I've never seen such a beautiful head of red hair on a baby before. She certainly does take after her mother."

"Truly?" Cassie asked. "Truly, she's all right?"

"Yes, truly, she is," the doctor answered gently as he laid the baby in her arms. "You've lost a child before, haven't you, Mrs. Perkins?"

Cassie closed her eyes and nodded. A tear slipped down her cheek. "Belle, please call Joshua to come in now."

"Right here he is," Belle said. "We couldn't keep him out no longer."

"Oh, Joshua, just look at her," Cassie cried, the tears welling out of her eyes. "Ain't she just the most perfect baby you ever seen in your life?"

"Ah, Cassie, that she is," Joshua said wonderingly. "But what else could she be with such a beautiful mother? Have you decided what you're going to name her yet?"

"I've been thinkin' on it, Joshua, and if you don't have no objections, I think I want to call her Sue Ellen. The Sue was my mama's name, and I guess you know the Ellen is for Miz Johnston 'cause she was like a real mother to me. Do you think your ma will be hurt that we don't name it after her?"

"This is our child and we shall name her what we want to," Joshua said firmly. "I have no idea how my mother will feel about it, but quite frankly, it doesn't matter as long as you are happy. I think it's a fine name for a beautiful little girl. Cassie, I am so happy."

"Me, too, Joshua." She smiled at him. "I reckon this makes us a real true family now, don't it?"

EIGHT

T

he birth of Cassie and Joshua's baby brought much excitement
and joy to the household. With the exception of Elizabeth, everyone in the
family had been by to see the new baby by the end of the day. Elizabeth
sent word by Belle that she felt "indisposed" and would visit when she felt
more herself.

"Hmph," Belle snorted after Joshua had left the room. "You ax me, she
just jealous 'cause she not gettin' all the attention."

"Well, let's not be too hard on her," Cassie said mildly. "It's been a lot
for her to get used to. Joshua springin' me on her and a new baby almost
all at once. 'Sides, once she sees this sweet thing, she'll never be able to
resist her."

"She sho' a fine lookin' baby," Belle beamed. "That red hair, jest like
yours."

Cassie was napping the next morning when she became aware that
someone was in the room with her. She raised up on her elbow and peered
out at the baby's cradle next to the bed. She saw Elizabeth staring at Sue
Ellen.

"Want to hold her?" she asked quietly.

Elizabeth jumped back, startled at the sound of Cassie's voice.

"Why, no, I guess not just yet awhile," she said hastily. "New babies
always make me a little nervous. I could never bring myself to lift one of
mine until they got a little size on them. I always had Belle hand them to
me. She looks healthy enough though, and I don't think I ever saw a baby
with that much hair. Mine were all bald except for a little fuzz on their
heads. Maybe it's because of that red color that she looks like she's got so
much hair."

"I think she's beautiful," Cassie said defensively.

"Oh, yes, I'm sure she is. I certainly never meant to imply that she

36

wasn't," Elizabeth said quickly. "Have you named her yet? I do hope Joshua selected a proper family name for her."

"Well, we consider it quite proper anyhow," Cassie said. "We've named her Sue Ellen. Sue was my ma's name and Ellen is for Miz Johnston who was mighty good to me and Joshua both."

"Sue Ellen, is it?" Elizabeth said. "Well, I suppose that's quite a suitable name for her. Well, I must go now. I have some needlework waiting for me."

She started out of the room, then turned as she reached the door. Looking back at Cassie, she looked her straight in the eyes for the first time since the night Cassie and Joshua had arrived.

"I am glad that the birth was easy, and that you and the baby are doing so well," she said haltingly. "You will have to forgive me for not coming sooner, but I've always been frightened by illness and pain. I remember how painful the births of my own babies were. I am not a strong woman like you or your Mrs. Johnston. I have always been delicate, and my husband shielded me from any unpleasantness. Perhaps too much so."

Turning abruptly, as if she had said more than she intended to, she left the room in a rush. Cassie lay in her bed, slack-jawed at the encounter. When she told Joshua about it later, he only nodded grimly. She suspected that he had been responsible for the visit.

Maybe I need to be a little more tolerant of her, Cassie thought. It may not be all her fault that she's the way she is. Anyhow, I'm a'gonna try to get along better with her if I can. Maybe Sue Ellen is gonna bring both families together.

Cassie was a restless patient and argued with the doctor that there was no need for the week of bed rest he prescribed for her.

"Why, I'll be weak as a kitten if I lay in this here bed for a week," she protested. "My ma was up and workin' in the garden the day after her young'uns was born. I never heard tell of any such."

"You will take care of yourself, young woman," the doctor admonished her. "Your mother probably died a young woman if she did as you say she did. We don't want that to happen to you."

Grumbling and complaining, Cassie endured five days in and out of the bed before she began slipping downstairs to check on things. While she was confined, she took advantage of the time to write her good news to Nola.

Dear Nola,
    Well, I sure got some good news to rite you. We got us a mighty pertty girl baby. We named her Sue Ellen after my ma and

yores. I hope she won't mind none. I reckon I had a rite easy
time, and Joshua fetched a doctor when my time come. Her hair's
as red as mine is, and I think it'll be curly too. Joshua says she
looks like me, and I reckon that way she does.

We are right well settled in now, and I can't wait to be up and
doing again. Tell your ma the dresses and other things she fixed
for me sure come in handy. I think about her ever time I put one of
the dresses on her. It would have been perfec if you and her had
been here when Sue Ellen come. I get so sick for the sight of you
sometimes, I could cry.

I reckon you and Sam is married by now and got a family of
yore own started. Write me all your news soon as you can.

When you write me again, would you ask your ma to send
me a copy of her star quilt pattern—the one she made for Martha
agin her marrying. I crave to start peecin when I can't get out this
winter.

Joshua is busy as ever with the farm and not much help of
any account. I think he misses teaching rite bad, but he's been
helping his sisters and brothers with their lessons some.

Write me soon.

Your friend,
Cassie Perkins

"There, that's done," Cassie said with satisfaction. "I got to get Joshua
to put it in the mail for me when he goes in to town again. I hope Nola
writes me soon. I wonder what she'll think about me havin' a beautiful
red-headed baby?"

A noise at the door made Cassie look up from her letter, and she smiled
as she saw Lottie and Nellie sneaking into the room.

"Shhh," Lottie admonished Nellie, "you better not wake her up. She'll
start cryin' and wake Mama up. Don't you touch her neither. Nobody can
touch her but Joshua and Cassie and sometimes Belle."

"Why can't I touch her, Lottie?" Nellie asked. "I just want to see what
she feels like. She looks so soft."

"Why, who said you couldn't touch her?" Cassie asked the girls. "If
you want to touch her and hold her it's all right with me. Here, Nellie,
come and sit in the rocker and I'll let you hold her in your lap."

"Belle said we wasn't to touch her," Lottie said defensively. "She said
we was too dirty, and we might drop her, too."

Cassie smiled. "Well, I think it would be all right for you to hold her if
I was right here a'watchin' you, don't you?"

Nellie sat in the rocker and held her arms up expectantly, looking at
Cassie with adoring eyes. Carefully, Cassie lifted Sue Ellen out of her
cradle and placed her in Nellie's arms. Lottie looked on enviously.

"Oh, she's so soft and smells so good," Nellie said.

"It's my turn next," Lottie said impatiently. "You've held her long enough, Nellie. Let me have her now."

"Just a minute, Lottie," Cassie said gently. "Give her just a minute more, then you can hold her."

Reluctantly, Nellie gave up her place to Lottie and Cassie placed the baby in Lottie's arms. Lottie looked down at the baby with wonder in her eyes.

"When I grow up and get married I want me a little red-haired baby just like Sue Ellen," she told Cassie.

"Well, then, I guess you better find you a red-haired man to marry you." Cassie grinned. "Now, I guess we better put her back in her cradle before she wakes up. We wouldn't want to disturb your ma's sleep, would we?"

"Why'd you say I'd have to find me a red-haired man to get me a red-haired baby, Cassie?" Lottie asked her.

"Well, I don't see no red hair growin' on you," said Cassie. "And one of you's got to have red hair if you want to have a baby with red hair. Now, you two run on downstairs and get your breakfast so you can help Belle some. You been doin' what I told you to, ain't you? You promised me you'd take my place helpin' Belle till I got able to do it again."

"Yes, Cassie, we been helpin' her good," Lottie assured her. "I been carryin' the dishes in to her, and Nellie's been helpin' too, and I dusted the settin' room just like you showed me."

"Good girls," Cassie said. "I'm right proud of you and when I get up and around again, I'm a'gonna make a special round of them sugar tea cakes you like so good just for the two of you. Run on now, and get your breakfast."

"Bye, Cassie. Bye, Sue Ellen," they chorused as they left the room. "We'll be glad when you can come downstairs again, Cassie," Lottie said. "It's more fun when you're down there."

Cassie watched them go, looking pensively at Lottie as she went out the door.

I reckon Anne Marie must be about Lottie's age now. I wonder what's become of her and our little brothers? I hope Ma ain't lettin' her go through what I had to, she thought sadly.

NINE

Cassie flinched as she tried to pull the comb through her tangled curls. She finally threw it down in exasperation and reached for her brush.

"I wish my hair was as straight as a horse's tail. Nola's hair was so long and straight. She never had no trouble a-keepin' the tangles out of her hair," Cassie fumed.

"Well, as well as I can remember, I recollect she was envious of your curls," Joshua chuckled. "I remember her saying she'd give anything to have hair like yours. Weren't you talking about her dyeing her hair red one time?"

"Yes, but we wasn't serious," Cassie laughed. "Her mama would have had a fit if we'd done such a thing. 'Sides, Nola's hair was a whole lot prettier than mine. I hate my hair. It's so common lookin'."

Joshua threw his head back and laughed heartily.

"Hush, you'll wake the baby," Cassie admonished him, "and then I won't get to go downstairs."

"Sorry," he grinned. "The thought of you calling your hair common just got to me. It's probably about the most uncommon thing about you. I love your hair. Don't you know it was the first thing that attracted me to you?"

"Well, if that be the case then, I reckon there must be some redeemin' graces from havin' red hair," she smiled. "There, that's finally finished. How does it look?"

"Beautiful," Joshua murmured, running his fingers through her hair, then dropping his hands to her waist and pulling her to him.

"Oh, no," she laughed. "Not now, my love. This is the first day that old fuss-budget of a doctor has let me out of this room, and I can't wait to get downstairs and see what's goin' on. 'Sides, you'll be late gettin' the hands to work."

"All right, but I'll see you later. Don't think you've been fooling me though. I know you've been sneaking downstairs before today. Belle told me."

"Why, I don't know what you're a'talkin' about," she said demurely. "You know I wouldn't do nothin' like that."

"I do know you, and that's why I know you *would* do something 'like that.'" He laughed as he went out the door. "You take it slow today, and don't try to scour the whole house the first day."

Cassie smoothed her apron down over her dress and gave one last look at Sue Ellen. She tiptoed out of the room, leaving the door open so she could hear the baby if she cried.

As Cassie started down the stairs, she thought of all the changes in her life in the last few years. My life only started when I found the Johnstons that mornin', she thought. I'd never have met Joshua if I hadn't. Our lives sure got tangled up with each other just because I stumbled into Miz Johnston's springhouse. And now, here we are. We've got a fine little baby girl, and I've got a whole new family. Oh, I am so lucky!

Belle was busy preparing breakfast when Cassie came into the kitchen. She looked up, startled as Cassie bustled through the door.

"Law me, Miss Cassie, what you doin' down here this early? Don't you know you still 'sposed to take it slow?" Belle admonished her. "You got to be careful while you nursin' that baby, else you'll get the weed in yo' breasts. Then I 'spect you'll be sorry."

"Oh, fiddle, Belle," Cassie laughed. "I ain't gonna get no weed nor nothin' else. I'm fine now, and I want everybody to quit treatin' me like I'm sick."

"Uh huh," Belle said skeptically. "Well, first thing you do is go set in the dinin' room and let me bring you some breakfast. You got to eat plenty if you wants to have enough milk for that baby."

"If I get any more milk, I'm gonna bust right out of my dress," Cassie retorted. "I'm gonna fix me a plate right here in the kitchen where we can talk and I can find out what's been goin' on. That big old dinin' room is too lonesome to set in by yourself."

"Whatever you say," Belle said, shaking her head. Everthin' been goin' on just fine. I don't know what you said to them girls, but they been a powerful help since you been confined. I don't watch out, they soon won't be nothin' left for me to do."

"I doubt that'll ever happen," Cassie laughed. "This house is so big, it'll take all of us diggin' just to keep even with the cleanin'."

The two talked companionably while Cassie ate her breakfast. When she attempted to help Belle wash the dishes though, Belle shooed her firmly out of the kitchen, declaring she needed no help. Cassie wandered through the living room, noting that Lottie had indeed kept her promise to dust and keep the room tidy.

"I reckon I'd better check on Sue Ellen," she murmured and started upstairs.

As she entered the room, she was startled to see Elizabeth seated in her rocker, holding Sue Ellen. Cassie stopped and listened to her mother-in-law crooning to the baby. She was smiling, and Cassie thought to herself that it was the first time she had seen her without her guard up. She stood there quietly, seeing for the first time some of the same sweetness of character that had first attracted her to Joshua.

When she looked up and saw Cassie standing in the doorway, she said defensively, "I heard her crying and no one came to see about her, so I thought somebody ought to see what was wrong."

"Why, I thank you, Miz Perkins," Cassie said gently. "I was in the kitchen talkin' to Belle and didn't hear her. You seem to have done a fine job of soothin' her though, she's just about asleep again. Maybe I should put her back in her cradle."

"Of course," Elizabeth said hastily. "But if you don't mind my saying so, I think you should lay her on her stomach. If she lies on her back all the time, it'll make the back of her head flat."

"I thank you for that information," Cassie said. "I'll try and remember it."

Elizabeth placed Sue Ellen in Cassie's arms, and Cassie laid her in her cradle, careful to place her on her stomach. She pulled the blanket up over the baby, patting her on the back when she stirred restlessly. Both women stood looking down at the baby for a long moment.

"Well, I must go back to my room," Elizabeth said. "I was brushing my hair when I heard her. I know I look a fright. It's so tangled."

Elizabeth picked up her brush from the bed where she had laid it and started out.

"I'd be pleased to brush it for you," Cassie offered. "I used to brush my friend Nola's hair for her. Sometimes it's easier for somebody else to free the tangles."

"Well, if you really want to," Elizabeth said as she reluctantly handed Cassie her brush. "I'm awful tender-headed though."

"So was Nola," Cassie smiled. "I'll be real easy, I promise."

Elizabeth sat down at the vanity, and Cassie began carefully brushing the tangles out of Elizabeth's hair. She could see the cradle, which had been placed close by the bed, reflected in the mirror. The baby still stirred occasionally, and Cassie glanced at her intermittently as she gently brushed Elizabeth's hair.

"Eli used to brush my hair for me," Elizabeth said dreamily. "He was always so gentle. I tried having Belle brush it, but she's too impatient. Just pulls the brush through like she's attacking an enemy. You have a soft touch."

Cassie smiled at the unconscious compliment that Elizabeth had paid her, then gently twisted Elizabeth's hair into the swirl that she wore on top of her head and anchored it with the bone hairpins that were lying on the bed.

"There now," Cassie said. "I think that's about how you wear it. You can change it if it's wrong when you get back to your room."

"Why, thank you, Cassie," Elizabeth murmured. "It feels just right. Where did you learn to do that? From your friend Nola?"

"I reckon," Cassie smiled. "We used to practice on each other, me and her and Martha, her sister."

"You must tell me sometime how you came to live with the Johnston family," Elizabeth said. "Were you related to them?"

"No'm, not exactly," Cassie said. "It's a long story and maybe someday I'll tell you. Well, I see Sue Ellen is a'suckin' on her fist now. I reckon that means it's time for me to feed her again. I thank you for tendin' her."

"You're welcome, I'm sure," Elizabeth murmured as she left the room. "She seems like a right sweet little thing."

Cassie smiled as Elizabeth closed the door, thinking to herself, Well, maybe they's hope for me and you yet, but I don't think I'm ready to tell you about me and the Johnstons right now. I'm afraid you ain't ready for that story yet, either.

TEN

"Well, here's something you've been looking for," Joshua called excitedly to Cassie.

Cassie's eyes lit up as she saw the envelope that Joshua was waving. She hurried out to meet him, hands extended.

"What will you give me for it?" he asked teasingly as he put it behind his back.

"Oh, Joshua, don't you tease me now," she implored him. "You know how anxious I am to hear from Nola. Now give it to me!"

Laughing, he handed the letter over and followed his wife into the living room where she carefully opened it and sat down to read it.

"Read it out loud," he said. "I'm as anxious for news from them as you are."

"Hold your horses," she said. "I'll read it as soon as I get things sorted out. Oh, good, Miz Johnston sent me some quilt patterns." She set the patterns aside, glanced over the letter, then started to read aloud:

Dear Cassie,

First of all, everyone sends their love and want you and Joshua to know how much you are missed. Mama is so proud that you named your baby for her, she nearly popped a button. I can't wait to see her. I know she is beautiful, and I am so glad she has red hair.

I am sorry I haven't written sooner, but everything has been happening so fast here, I just haven't had a minute. I will try to catch up all the news for you. Sam and I were married, and we are expecting our own little one. Martha married John, and they are very happy because they are going to have a baby also. Mama says we are making her a grandma too fast, she's not ready for all of this yet! Of course, you know, she loves it.

44

This will shock you I know, but old Willie is married too. He married Nancy Cole from across the ridge. Poor girl!

The twins have gone off to boarding school in Asheville, and that only leaves David and Joseph at home with Mama and Papa. Mama says it's too quiet without all of us noisemakers there, but, of course, we're all close enough to come home quick if we're needed.

Your new home sounds mighty fine to me. I guess your old mountain cabin would seem awful cramped to you and Joshua now. The community misses Joshua, too, because after I gave up teaching, they haven't had a regular schoolmaster since. I know taking care of that big farm keeps him busy though, and maybe he doesn't miss teaching.

Do you think we'll ever see each other again? I wish I thought that someday our children would play together like we did when we were girls. Write me again real soon, and I'll try to do better about answering. Mama says don't forget to plant the flower seeds she gave you.

Your friend,
Nola McGinty

Cassie brushed a tear from her eye as she folded up the letter and put it back in the envelope. She turned to Joshua and threw herself in his arms.

"Oh, Joshua," she cried. "I do miss them so much, and just the mention of the cabin makes me homesick for the mountains and our little home. Do you think we'll ever see it again?"

"Shh, shh," he comforted her as he patted her back. "I miss the mountains, too, Cassie, and I promised you when we left that we'd go back someday. I mean to keep that promise to you. I don't know when it'll be, but we will go back someday."

They held each other for a while, each remembering the happiness of those first months of their marriage. Finally, Cassie straightened up and wiped her eyes. She smoothed out the quilt patterns Ellen had sent her and began reading the notes Ellen had included about each of them. The one that caught her interest the most was labeled Sunshine and Shadow. Ellen had gone to pains to draw a miniature of the quilt square and shaded the pattern in the appropriate areas. She wrote the following note with the pattern:

Cassie,

This is a new pattern I just found and I like the way it makes up and the way it's named. Seems like Sunshine and Shadow is sort of the way our lives are, filled with lots of sunshine, but sometimes there are shadows too.

Ellen Johnston

There were patterns for five other quilts, but Cassie was taken with the Sunshine and Shadow pattern.

"I can't wait to get started piecin' this one," she told Joshua. "There's somethin' about it that just makes me want to set right down and get busy."

Joshua smiled. "Then I'm glad Ellen sent them. While you gather up your quilt pieces, I have to get back out to the field and see if things are being tended to. Caleb is doing a better job, and for the first time I didn't worry about things when I left him in charge this morning. If he'd just get the notion of getting rich out of his head, I think he'd make a good farmer. He seems to have a natural feel for the land—one I fear I shall never have. I'll see you at supper time."

"Bye," Cassie said vaguely, already turning the sketch Ellen had sent in different directions so she could get a feel for the pattern. "Hmmm, I bet I could make a pretty little quilt for Sue Ellen if I can find enough colors to make it work."

Elizabeth came through, and when Cassie saw her, she smiled quickly, an idea forming in her head.

"Miz Perkins, didn't you tell me that you had a lady who made your dresses for you and the girls?" she asked.

"Why, yes, I do," Elizabeth answered.

"I'm just wonderin' if you've got some scraps of cloth left over from the sewin'," Cassie said.

"I'm sure I don't know," Elizabeth said. "You will have to ask Belle about it. I don't keep up with that sort of thing. What on earth do you want with scraps? If you need a dress, we can send for some new cloth the next time Joshua goes into town."

"Oh, no, I got plenty of dresses to do me," Cassie said hastily. "I'm of a mind to start me a quilt for Sue Ellen, and I need some special colors for it."

Elizabeth picked up Nola's letter and examined the quilt patterns Ellen had sent. "Is this what had you so absorbed?"

Cassie nodded. "Don't you think it'll be pretty?"

Elizabeth shrugged and dropped the patterns back on the settee. She turned and drifted out of the room.

Cassie sighed. "Maybe someday," she murmured.

Cassie sought out Belle in the kitchen, who took her to the room where the seamstress worked when she came to sew for the family. It was a large, sunny room, and Cassie fell in love with it the moment she entered. A cushioned rocker had been placed by the window where the seamstress could take advantage of the light. A long table in the middle of the room would be ideal for cutting out patterns, Cassie thought to herself. There was even a small stove in the room for heating the irons. After more exploring, Cassie and Belle found boxes of neatly folded pieces of material. Cassie was ecstatic with the found treasure.

"Oh, Belle, can't you just imagine how many fine quilts all this cloth will make? Why on earth ain't somebody done somethin' with it before now? Miz Johnston wouldn't never have let this much cloth go to waste. I can't wait to get started. Do you think it'll be all right for me to pick out some and use it? Should I ask Miz Perkins first?"

"Humph," Bell snorted. "She don't even know it's here. For all she cares, it could just lay here and rot. She sho' ain't gonna do nothin' with it. You just hep' yo'sef to as much of it as you wants. They ain't nobody gonna care."

Quickly Cassie began selecting light and dark pieces of cloth and laying them together until she got the contrasts she wanted. Then she took the hot irons from the back of the stove and began pressing the pieces and cutting out her patterns. Except for the times she had to stop and nurse Sue Ellen, she worked all afternoon cutting out the quilt pieces. When she finished, she stacked them in neat bunches, the way she would stitch them together. Only then did she stop.

When Joshua asked her how she had passed her afternoon, she only smiled and said, "Just wait for a while and you'll see."

Cassie could hardly wait each morning to finish with her cleaning chores and get started on her quilt top. She fixed Sue Ellen a cozy little basket in the sewing room and kept her there beside her while she pieced the quilt. She chose light and dark shades of the same color to make her designs. When she had enough for a baby's quilt, she decided to make it a little larger, reasoning it could cover Sue Ellen's bed when she was older. Before she finished piecing it, it had become a full-sized quilt.

Cassie and Belle stood back and admired the finished quilt. Cassie had chosen to build her quilt from individual pattern blocks in the style of a full Sunshine and Shadow quilt. The contrasting light and dark shades ranged from a pale pink cotton print she had found to a deep wine that looked almost black in contrast. She counted thirteen rows of thirteen squares each for each of the blocks. In all, she had sewn together 169 two-inch patches to make her quilt top.

Belle helped her find cotton to fill it and a piece of sheeting to make the lining. It took her almost three months to make the quilt top and baste it to the filling and lining.

She stood back and looked at it when it was all put together, proud of the work she had done, but a little sad that it was almost finished.

"How am I gonna quilt it now?" she asked Belle. "Do you know if they's any quiltin' frames here?"

"No'm, not that I knows about, but I knows a ole man over to Mr. Grover's place that could make you some. He's right handy about sech. If you tell him what you wants, he can make it for you."

"Oh, good, could we send for him today?" Cassie asked eagerly. "I'm so anxious to get started."

"I reckon we can," Belle laughed. "You most impatient somebody I done ever seen. Seem like you want everthing yesterday."

Belle was as good as her word, and within a week Cassie had her quilting frames made and set up in the sewing room. She enlisted Belle's help getting the quilt in the frame, and then began the long task of quilting it.

Elizabeth had acted curious about Cassie's project, occasionally peeking into the sewing room but never asking questions. Then one morning Cassie came bustling in with Sue Ellen, ready to work on the quilt for awhile, to find Elizabeth standing transfixed before the quilt. She stopped short.

"This is beautiful," Elizabeth said. "How ever did you figure out to make your colors blend so well? The way the light colors fade out into the deeper shades, then blend out into the lights again, is very striking. Does this pattern have a name?"

"Oh, yes," Cassie answered, pleased at Elizabeth's spontaneous compliment. "It's called Sunshine and Shadow. Miz Johnston said it's like real life is, filled with sunshine, but sometimes there's shadows to contend with, too. I'm glad you like it. I started out to make Sue Ellen a crib quilt, but it just seemed to keep on growin' till it got full sized. Now I'm a'quiltin' it."

Elizabeth watched as Cassie sat by the frames and picked up her needle where she had left it the day before and began quilting in short, precise stitches.

"You certainly seem to know what you're doing," she observed. "Did Mrs. Johnston teach you to do that?"

"Yes'm, she did. She taught all three of us girls to quilt. We started out makin' dolls' quilts and then when we'd practiced enough, she let us set in on a'quiltin'. I hope you don't mind, but I've been showin' Lottie and Nellie how to stitch. They're workin' on their own doll quilts."

"No, I don't mind," Elizabeth said slowly. "In fact, I would like to try my hand at it if I could. It doesn't look as though it would be any more difficult than petit point. May I?"

"Why, sure," Cassie said, surprised at the request. "Just pull you up a chair here beside me at the next block, and I'll show you how to begin."

Cassie instructed Elizabeth on the proper way to thread her needle and knot it so that she could pull the knot into the filling of the quilt and hide the knot. Then she started the needle in and out to show her the proper stitch length.

Impatiently, Elizabeth took the needle from Cassie and, to Cassie's astonishment, began imitating the up-and-down motion that Cassie used to quilt. Her stitches were as fine and even as Cassie's own.

"Why, that's right fine, Miz Perkins." She beamed at her mother-in-law. "I think you was just a born quilter. I never seen anybody do it any better."

Elizabeth flushed and bent her head. Cassie resumed her seat, and the two quilted companionably for almost two hours, chatting about Sue Ellen and the younger girls. Cassie told Elizabeth about the other quilt patterns Ellen had sent her, promising to show them to her when they were done.

When Joshua came home that evening, he was surprised and somewhat taken aback at finding the two women pouring over the quilt patterns, which were scattered out across the dining table.

Well, will wonders never cease, he thought.

The two women smiled at each other, then went back to discussing the patterns. Shaking his head, Joshua went to wash up for supper.

ELEVEN

The quilt established a bond between Elizabeth and Cassie that gradually helped them overcome many of their problems. Each learned to accept the other for who and what she was and become more tolerant of her shortcomings. After Sunshine and Shadow was completed, Elizabeth asked Cassie to help her make a quilt. They chose a star pattern called the Lemon (Lemoyne) Star. Elizabeth wanted to do an elaborate version of the pattern, but Cassie persuaded her to stick with the simple version of the eight-pointed star.

"When we get this one pieced, though, I think it's time we had a quiltin' bee," Cassie told Elizabeth. "It takes too long for just me and you to make it."

"I don't know if any of my friends know how to quilt," Elizabeth said. "If they do, they haven't mentioned it."

"Well, if they don't, we'll just have to teach them," Cassie declared. "Look how quick you learned. Anybody that can do that little bitty stitchin' like you do can quilt. I bet you'll be surprised to find out how many can do this. Let's ask Aunt Jenny first. I bet she can quilt."

This was the beginning of a community quilting project that developed into Cassie's introduction into the town's social life. Those who had never quilted before were eager to learn, and there were many others who were already skilled in the art.

Jenny arranged for the man who made Cassie's frame to make additional ones, and soon almost all the women in their circle had a quilting frame.

Mary Tremaine, matriarch of one of the leading families in the community, gently chastised Elizabeth for not introducing Cassie to the community sooner.

"I declare, Elizabeth," she said after the first quilting bee, "I can't understand why on earth you've been keeping this delightful daughter-in-law of yours hidden from us all these months. She is one of the most refreshing young women I've met in I can't tell you whenever. Why haven't you had a party for her yet to introduce her to us?"

Elizabeth flushed red, and Cassie, seeing her embarrassment, spoke up quickly.

"Why, Mrs. Tremaine, how on earth could she, what with me just havin' a new baby and all? You must know how busy we've all been, tryin' to get settled and take care of a new baby, too. Miz Perkins has just been up to her eyeballs in work. I wonder that she's had time to do what she has."

Elizabeth looked gratefully at Cassie, then turned to her friend.

"Well, as Cassie says, we've been mighty busy, but, of course, that's no excuse for my bad manners. I promise you that just as soon as we can catch our breath, we will have a party for her. And I assure you, it will be well worth waiting for."

"Do you suppose your friend would share some more of her patterns with us?" Jenny asked. "We could swap some of ours with her if she'd be interested. That way, we could all learn some new patterns. That is, if we have any she hasn't already seen."

"I'll shorely write to her and ask," Cassie said eagerly. "Knowin' Mrs. Johnston the way I do, I'm certain she'd be happy to share with us."

Cassie could hardly wait to write Ellen. Her correspondence so far had been with Nola, and she looked forward to writing to Ellen. As soon as the quilting bee broke up, she went to her room and sat down at her desk.

> Dear Mrs. Johnston,
>
> I know you'll be some took back with me writin you instead of Nola, but when I tell you what it's about, you'll understand. First off, I want to thank you for all the quilt patterns you been sendin me. You can't know how much it's helped me. It's been somethin that has made me and Mrs. Perkins have somethin in common—besides Sue Ellen, of course. She's got so interested in the quilts that we've got us a circle goin and are meetin right often. What I'm askin you is, could you send us some more patterns and could we send you some of ours that you might not have? Mrs. Tremaine give me one named Orange Peel to send you. I didn't recall ever seein one like it. I hope it's new to you. Me and all of mine are well, and I hope you and yours are the same. Tell Nola I'll write her real soon. I'd look on it as a favor if you'd do this one more thing for me. You've done so much

already that I know I ain't got no right askin more of you, but I've done it anyhow.

Your friend,
Cassie Perkins

This was the beginning of a steady correspondence between Ellen and these new friends. She shared her many quilt patterns with them, as well as the history of the different quilts, insofar as she knew it. They, in turn, shared their patterns with her. They waited eagerly for new patterns and information from this mountain ally, especially Elizabeth, who began corresponding with Ellen. She was enchanted with the letters Ellen wrote her and developed a new respect for Cassie as she became acquainted with her mountain family through Ellen's letters. After Cassie's defense of her with Mary Tremaine, no one had a stauncher friend than Elizabeth was to Cassie. Her only complaint was that Joshua still vetoed her idea of an elaborate party because of their finances.

The next year was a busy, happy time for Cassie. She and Joshua delighted in every new accomplishment by Sue Ellen. Elizabeth was equally enthralled with the child, feeling more relaxed with this first grandchild than she had ever felt with her own children. When Cassie became pregnant with her second child, she eagerly wrote Nola the news and was delighted to find her letter had been mailed on the same day that Nola mailed one to her. Nola's news was also about new babies. She also was expecting her second child and had special news about Martha and John.

Dear Cassie,

Well, I have some very exciting news for you. First off, I am expecting another baby. I am so happy! Jake is getting to be such a big boy, almost two years old, and I do so long to hold a baby in my arms again. Sam says after this he hopes we won't have any more, but we'll see. Martha and John had twins! Can you imagine? They are the dearest little things. She named them Charles and Lucy. They are both fine big healthy babies and doing well. I'm sorry I can't say the same for Martha. She just doesn't seem to get over the babies' birth. She's so weak she stays in bed most of the time. It's a good thing she and John live with his folks. Mrs. McGinty takes care of the babies with some help from his sister Pearl. I go and do what I can, but I have my hands full at home.

Sam doesn't cotton too well to farming. He'd like to make music all the time, but that don't put food on the table. I have to help with the chores as much as I can. Mama goes and does what she can for Martha, but you know how it is in another woman's house.

Mama wanted me to send along this pattern of Wild Geese A-Flying. She thought you and your ladies would like it. She thinks its wonderful that you've got you a quilting group going. Says it makes her think you still keep to mountain ways.

I'm hoping I'll get me a little girl this time. Maybe she'll get her papa's red hair, and then we'll both have little redheads! Write me soon with all your news. Tell Joshua hello for me, and tell him I hear the state is taking over the schools, so maybe we'll get us a regular schoolmaster at last.

Love,
Your friend, Nola

"Isn't it wonderful that we're both expecting babies at the same time?" Cassie asked Joshua. "I hope Nola gets her little girl, and I'm hopin' for a boy for us this time."

"That would be nice," Joshua said smiling. "But all I hope for is a healthy baby and one that's as pretty as its mama."

"Or as handsome as its papa," Cassie retorted. "Leastwise, I hope it's as smart as its papa anyhow. I been tryin' to read that book you gave me, and I just can't make no sense of most of it. I reckon my mind just don't cotton to poetry. Some of them words, I ain't never heard of before. It's a burden not havin' no schoolin'. I sure don't aim for our babies to grow up without none."

"Don't worry about the book, Cassie," Joshua soothed her. "As you say, some people just don't 'cotton' to poetry. Besides, Shakespeare is not easy reading for anybody. I just thought you might enjoy some of his plays. Most of the language is pretty archaic."

"See there, I don't even know what *that* word means," Cassie lamented. "You're just so much smarter than I am, Joshua."

"I may be smarter in book sense, but I don't think I could have had the good common sense that you've shown in getting around my mother. I never would have believed that anyone could have made such a change in a person as you have with her. I even caught her helping Belle put up the dishes the other day. Before you came, she never would have dreamed of doing such a thing. Then that same day she was weeding your flowers. I hope she didn't pull any of them up. She sure doesn't know anything about flowers, except that they are for decoration in the house."

"Oh, you don't give your ma enough credit," Cassie laughed. "I think she enjoys having something to keep her busy. She just needed someone to encourage her a little. I think your pa must have made her feel pretty helpless. It ain't always good for a man to do too much for his woman."

"I'll try to remember that," Joshua chuckled, "although I don't think there's much chance of that ever happening with you. I never saw such an independent piece as you are."

"When you've had to grub and dig for everything you had, it teaches you to depend on yourself." Cassie smiled sadly. "You know, I been thinkin' lately about my sister and brothers. I hate it when I think about us growing up strangers to one another. I worry, too, about what kind of life they're a'havin'. I hope Pa don't do to Anne Marie what he done to me."

Joshua put his arms around Cassie and held her close against his chest.

"Surely not to his own daughter," he said slowly, his voice harsh with anger. "You were his stepdaughter, but I hate any man that would be that depraved. Why, for God's sake?"

"They ain't no way you could understand what he was like," Cassie sighed. "Maybe some day though, I can go back and find them. I reckon it was cowardly of me to leave 'em behind, but they was so little the mountain would of killed them. If I hadn't found the Johnstons when I did, I reckon it would of killed me."

"Don't talk about it anymore," Joshua begged her. "Just think about what we have now. Sue Ellen is so beautiful, and now we're going to have another child. We're blessed, Cassie."

"I'm blessed in so many ways that I never thought was possible," she said thoughtfully. "It just makes me want to do something for *them*. I wonder if they remember me at all. I reckon I'm just as much a stranger to them. I know Ma was probably never allowed to mention me again. She's probably been afraid to talk about me to them. Maybe some day I'll know."

Joshua hugged her fiercely, tears in his eyes.

Seven months later, their first son was born, and they named him William Taylor Perkins. William was for Will Johnston, Cassie's foster parent, and Taylor was Elizabeth's maiden name. Elizabeth was touched at the gesture from Cassie, and the two became closer than ever with the birth of this second child.

Cassie's happiness was marred only by a troubling letter she received from Nola.

Dear Cassie,
    I got my wish for a daughter, just as you got yours for a son. Samantha was born just one month before your William Taylor and has the most beautiful red curly hair, just like her papa's.
    Papa was so thrilled that you named your son after him. He said to tell you, "You do him great honor."
    Oh, Cassie, I am so unhappy and confused. Sam is so restless

and discontented. He just doesn't take to farming or to married life either for that matter. He has taken up with his old friends and is gone more than he's at home. It's hard for me to tend the two children and keep the farm going, too. If it wasn't for Papa and the boys, I don't know how I'd manage. Mama says it just takes some men longer than others to settle down and I must be patient with him, but I don't know how much longer I can tolerate his behavior.

Well, enough of my troubles. I am so happy for you that everything is well between you and your mother-in-law. How could anyone help loving you? Martha sends her love and congratulations. Her health is still poor, and we worry about her. Write me again soon.

Love from your friend,
Nola

Cassie worried about her friend, and she hurried to write her back, trying to cheer her up and offer encouragement for her faltering marriage. She and Joshua talked until late that night.

"I'm a'feared for Nola," Cassie told Joshua. "It seems to me that Sam's had time a'plenty to settle down if he was a'goin' to. I feel so helpless. If only there was some way I could help Nola now."

"I'm afraid that there's nothing you or anyone else can do to help them, Cassie," Joshua told her. "This is something they'll have to work out for themselves. All you can do is just write as often as you can and let her know we love her."

"You're right, of course," Cassie sighed. "Her folks was agin her marryin' Sam. I reckon they knew best after all. She loved him so, though, and nothin' anybody said could stop her."

Almost a year passed, with the two friends writing each other frequently, when Cassie received a letter from Nola that saddened her more than anything since the day she had left home. It was brief.

Dear Cassie,

My heart is so heavy as I write you this letter. Dear, sweet Papa has left us. A tree claimed his life last August, and nothing will ever be the same again. Mama is devastated and has lost all will to live. She just sits in her old rocking chair staring out the window, as if she thinks he might reappear at any time.

I had not had time to write you that I was expecting another baby, and I suppose it was just as well. It was taken from me after an accident in the buggy. Sam was so unhappy at the prospect of another baby that he had been gone from home for several weeks when it happened. After I recovered somewhat, he left us for good, I suppose. At any rate, we have neither seen nor heard from him in some time. I am back at home with Mama, trying to see to things here.

John bought the farm from me, so I am at least rid of that burden. I neither know nor care what I will do. Each day is just like the other, and I am so unhappy.

                                                                    Nola

Cassie bowed her head and wept for her friend. She remembered the lighthearted young girl she had loved and admired so. Cassie could not believe that fate had dealt such an unhappy life to Nola. She wept, too, for Will, the gentle man who had befriended her and nursed her back to life. She thought back to the times that she had gone to Will for advice and remembered his gentle kindness to her.

"Oh, Nola, if I could only be there to help you out now," she cried out. Joshua could only hold her and share her grief. They talked about Cassie visiting Nola, but both knew it would be foolish for her to try it. Cassie was almost two months pregnant with their third child and had been sick most of the time. For the first time, she had to depend on Belle and Elizabeth to care for her children and the house.

"I'm as weak as a new-born kitten," she lamented to Joshua. "I had mornin' sickness with Sue Ellen and William Taylor, but this time I got mornin', noon, and night sickness. I vow, I've lost twenty pounds. If I could find me some wintergreen root to make me some tea, I bet that'd stop it. That's what Nola's papa always give us when our stomach was upset."

Tears welled up in Cassie's eyes again as she thought of Will's death. Joshua held her until she felt comforted.

"First thing in the mornin', I'll write to Nola," she sighed. "It's little enough to do, but I reckon it'll have to do for now."

While the children were still asleep the next morning, Cassie rose and went to her desk. When she finished her letter to Nola, she felt better. Putting her feelings and thoughts down on paper was like having a brief visit with Nola. She sat and reread the words she had written to her friend.

Dear Nola,

The news of your papa's death has left me heartsore. It just don't seem possible that he's gone. Everything I loved and cherished about the mountains was all a part of his gentleness and wisdom. He was the kind of pa I wish I'd of had, and I thank God that for a short time he was as dear to me as if I had a been his child. After I come to live with you all, I used to pretend that he was my papa, too. I never knew my real pa. Mama said he died right after I was borned, and then she married Zeb Martin when I wasn't much more than three or four years old. You know what kind of a man he was, and he was never no papa to me.

I remember how mad your papa was when he found out my step-pa had got me pregnant and then turned me out. I heard him tell your ma if he could get hold of him, he'd thrash him within an inch of his life. I always felt safe after that. I knew nothing bad was ever going to happen to me again as long as I was living under his roof. He taught me to think well of myself and to not let what had happened to me beat me down. Most important though, your papa taught me that I could trust people again. I don't think I'd of had the courage to open myself up to Joshua if your papa hadn't taught me to trust again. It grieves me no end that I can't come to you now. I been so sick these past two months that I'd be more burden than help to you. I know you're worried about your ma, but I also know how strong in spirit she is. I know as well as I know anything that she'll overcome this in time. If there is a Heaven, and your pa taught me to believe there is, I know that he is there now. When your ma has time to heal and to think, she'll know it too.

I can close my eyes and see the cove between the mountains where we was so happy. I can see your house the way it looked to me that first morning I saw it. Nothing else will ever look so grand to me as that house a'setting in between them two mountain ridges with that wide porch around it. I remember thinking that the rocking chairs setting on the porch looked like they was just waiting there for me to settle in and rock all my troubles away. This house I'm living in is bigger and the trappings are costlier, but it'll never feel as much like home as your pa's place does.

I tried to thank your pa for all he done for me before I left, but he wouldn't have none of it. When I tried to tell him how they'd blessed my life, he said I'd blessed them just as much as all his other children had. You don't know how happy that made me feel, Nola, for him to put me alongside of his children. Nothing he could have said to me would have meant as much as that did.

I'm sure sorry about you and Sam. If I was there, I'd get ahold of him and shake some sense into him. It must hurt even more coming at this time when you need him to be there for you. Don't shut the door on him yet, though, and don't let no false pride keep you from settling things if he comes back again. I know how proud you are, but please, Nola, just remember that pride won't warm your feet at night.

Please give your ma and everybody else my love and tell

them how sad I am about your pa. As soon as this baby comes and I get back to normal, I'm coming for a long visit. Tell them, just remember how much I love all of you.

Love,
Cassie

ELLEN

Nola read Cassie's letter while she was sitting on the porch in Will's favorite rocking chair, the tears running unchecked down her face while she read. When she finished the letter, she sat for some time gazing longingly across the mountain Cassie and Joshua had crossed when they left the cove for Tennessee.

Ah, Cassie, she thought. If only you were here now. I need to talk to someone who could understand how I feel. If only Martha was well, then I could talk to her. I can't burden her with all my troubles. She's got enough of her own. And there's poor Mama, sitting there in her chair, rocking and waiting for something that isn't going to happen.

The words of the psalm came unbidden into her mind. "I will lift up mine eyes unto the hills, from whence cometh my help." She bowed her head and uttered the words, then added her own plea, "But when, Lord, when?" Her reverie was interrupted by Samantha who burst through the door.

"Mama, you better come see what Jake's done," she cried. "He's done spilled jam all over the floor."

Nola scrubbed furiously at the stain on the floor, her tears mingling with the sudsy water.

"I'll skin that Jake alive," she muttered as she mopped. "Spilling that jam all over Papa's floor. He was so proud of this floor. Why won't it come up? Nothing is right anymore. Why can't things be the way they used to be?" She straightened, rubbed the small of her back, and looked up at the ceiling. "Oh, Papa, I miss you so. You're gone and Sam's gone. Why did everything turn out so wrong? Why couldn't things have turned out the way they were supposed to?" With an angry sigh, she went back to scrubbing the floor.

Suddenly, Nola heard voices outside the open front door, including a squeal from her five-year-old son.

"Papa, Papa, you're back!" Jake shouted.

Nola stood slowly, and a shiver ran up her spine. "No," she whispered. Then she heard Sam's voice.

"Whoa, there, slow down, boy." He laughed. "Good grief, what you been eatin', rocks? You shore have grown. Looks like you've added an inch or two. You're shore a sight for sore eyes. Where's yore sister?"

"Somewhere around, I reckon," Jake replied as he ran to the front door, peering in at his mother. "Mama, Mama! Come quick! Papa's home!"

Still shaking her head slightly, Nola walked out onto the front porch. She stared at Sam in shocked disbelief.

"What—what do you want?" she asked.

Sam reached up and nervously ran his hand through his hair as he gazed into Nola's shocked eyes. He stood for a long moment, twisting his hat in his hand. Then, taking a deep breath, he said, "I come to pay my respects to your ma, Nola. It pained me to hear about your pa. He was a good man, and he always treated me fairly. Bettern' I had any reason to expect, I know. I would appreciate it if I could speak to your ma."

Wordlessly, Nola stepped back and gestured for him to enter. He walked into the great room, remembering the time he had come to ask Will for Nola's hand. He remembered how nervous he had been and how Will had looked so steadily at him that Sam felt that he surely could see clear into his soul. He thought of how he had betrayed the trust Will had extended to him and flushed in shame.

"Mama," Nola said in a strained voice. "Sam's here. He wants to speak to you."

Sam looked at Ellen seated in her old rocker by the window. She had a dark shawl draped across her shoulders, and her hair shone starkly white where the sunlight played on it. Sam needed all of his self-control to hide the shock he felt as he looked at this once vital woman sitting so quietly and unmoving.

"Mother Johnston," he said gently, "I'm mighty sorry about Will. He was as good and fair a man as I've ever known. This world will be poorer now that he's gone. I hope you know how much I'm grievin' for you and your family. You might not want to hear any words from me, but I had to come and tell you how sorry I am."

"Thank you, Sam," Ellen said softly. "You were kind to come. I'm sure Will knew how you felt about him. I know it wasn't easy for you to come, and I appreciate it."

She touched his cheek briefly, then turned her face back to the window and resumed her watchful rocking.

Tears sprang to Sam's eyes, and he quickly brushed them away. He knelt there for a moment, then, seeing that she no longer knew he was there, he rose to his feet. He stood for a moment looking down on the still figure, then turned away.

"How long has she been like this?" he asked Nola.

She shook her head at him and motioned him out to the kitchen. He followed her and sank down into a chair at the big oak table.

"I don't remember her hair being this white, she's aged twenty years. What's happened to her?" he asked Nola.

"She's been like this ever since Papa died," Nola said tiredly. "It's just like the fight has gone out of her. She won't do anything but sit in front of that window all day long. I think she keeps holding on to the hope that Papa will come down the path and everything will be all right again. It's all we can do to get her to eat a little something. If it wasn't for Samantha, I think she'd starve to death. I've tried to make it a game for Samantha. I tell her to take a bite, then to ask Grandma to take a bite. It's the only way we can get her to eat anything. I don't know what we'll do if she doesn't begin to accept Papa's death and get on with living. Every day she seems to slip away a little further. I don't know how I could stand it if we lost both of them."

Nola's voice quivered on the last sentence, and she was on the verge of tears. Talking about her mother hurt badly, and it brought back her own grief over Will.

Instinctively, Sam reached out and grasped her hand. For a moment she clung to him, taking comfort in his warm, familiar presence. Then memories of his abandoning her and her children came flooding back and she snatched her hand out of his and stuck it in her apron pocket.

She rose quickly and said nervously, "I guess you want to see Samantha, don't you? She's down for her nap, but it's time she was waking up. I'll go get her."

Before Sam could rise, she left the room. Why did she let him do this to her? Every time she saw Sam, Nola ached to be with him, to feel his arms around her. But she could not find the comfort she wanted with a man who had behaved so badly, who had shamed her and the children.

She looked down at her sleeping daughter. How much she looked like Sam! Nola roused Samantha, brushing her red hair away from a face still flushed with sleep.

"Your father's here," Nola whispered as she picked up her daughter. Samantha snuggled against her as they headed back to the kitchen.

Sam's eyes lit up as he looked at his daughter. Her red curls almost matched his, and the clear blue eyes turned up to his own. He caught his breath.

"Come here, you pretty baby," he said. "Come to your papa. God, she's beautiful, Nola. And she's got so big. She was just a baby when I seen her last, and now she's Papa's big girl. How did you get so big, you pretty thing? Put your arms around my neck and give me a hug."

A noise at the door caused Sam to turn and look. He saw Jake looking wide-eyed at the scene in the kitchen.

"Who's that peepin' in the door over there?" Sam teased. "Come on in here, Jake, and let me see if I can still hold both of my babies on my lap like I used to do."

The invitation was all that Jake needed. He crawled up on Sam's lap and nestled his head on his father's shoulder. Samantha looked at Sam for a minute, then, whimpering, reached for her mother. Nola took the child back and held her tightly to her breast.

"There, there," she soothed her. "It's your papa, Samantha, there's nothing to be afraid of. Don't you see Brother sitting on his lap? It's all right."

Samantha still clung tightly to Nola and buried her face in her bosom. Nola felt a twinge of pain for Sam, then pushed it away. He didn't deserve it.

"Guess it'll take her awhile to get used to me again," Sam said. "She'll soon come around though, won't you, Missy?"

Nola felt her stomach tighten with dread. "What do you mean, get used to you?" she asked. "You can see she doesn't remember you. Do you plan to stay around here? I thought you were fed up with farming and the dull life around this cove."

"Nola, honey," Sam said gently. "I was hopin' that you might want me to stay around. I hoped that you had changed your mind about us. Now that your pa's gone, I thought maybe you'd see that you need me. Haven't you missed me even a little? God, I've missed you somethin' fierce. I've missed my children, too. It ain't right for them to grow up not knowin' their pa. It breaks my heart that Samantha don't remember me."

Nola was shaking her head and moving as far away from Sam as she could. How could he do this to her? No matter how much she loved him, how could he *expect* her to forgive him? She stood with her back to him. He rose and reached out and laid his hand on her shoulder. She was trembling and shrugged his hand away.

"Nola, ain't you never goin' to forgive me? Can't we put all this hurt behind us now once and for all and try to pick up the pieces? I know I've been a lousy husband, but I want to come home now and try to be the kind of man I should be. I want you to be my wife again, and I want to have my family together. I'll do whatever you want me to, if you'll just take me back. I'm beggin' you."

Nola turned and looked at him. For a moment she was tempted to throw herself in his arms and try to erase all of the months of misery she had endured because of his infidelity. She was torn between the powerful attraction she still felt for him and the rigid pride that would not let her yield to him. She thought of the vows they had made to each other that day when they had wed—"until death do us part"—and she clenched her hands together as she clutched their child to her body. She thought of the long nights she had spent in her lonely bed, and the days she had toiled in the field trying to make a living for herself and their children. And she remembered the ill-concealed looks of pity she had seen in the eyes of her neighbors, and the whispered conversations that ceased when she came into a room. The icy hand of injured pride squeezed her heart once again, hardening it against him.

"You made your choice a long time ago, Sam," she said coldly. "You turned your back on your marriage vows time and again and on your responsibilities to your family. Not one red cent have you sent me to feed your children. If it hadn't been for Papa and my brothers and your brother John, me and these beautiful children that you claim to love so much would have starved to death. You took other women to bed. I know I am still bound to you by my marriage vows and in the sight of God, but I will never live with you again. That's all I've got to say to you. Please leave now. You are not welcome in my father's house."

"You can't mean this, Nola," Sam cried. "You can't be this cold hearted. Think what you're a'doin' here now. I've humbled myself twice to you, and I'll not do it again. If you send me away this time, it will be for the last time. I'll not ask you again. Sam McGinty ain't a-gonna beg no woman again."

Silently, Nola turned and walked out of the room, across the porch that connected the kitchen to the rest of the house, and into the great room. Tears flowed down her cheeks as she heard her son calling after his father.

"Papa?"

"Oh, God, Nola, what have we done?" Sam's voice echoed between the buildings, even as he tried to comfort Jake.

"Jake, I'm sorry that you had to hear all that, son. Maybe someday you'll forgive me for bein' such a fool." Sam leaned down and pried the child loose. He held him up and looked into his eyes, then hugged him fiercely to his chest before setting him down again.

Nola clutched Samantha tighter, and her stomach was in knots as she listened to Jake's plaintive cries.

"Don't go, Papa. Please don't go," he sobbed.

Sam climbed into the buggy, where he sat for several minutes, hands dangling loosely between his knees.

Nola's head throbbed, and she almost went after Sam. But he's shamed us! she thought desperately. No matter what I feel, he cannot stay here. Someday Jake will understand. He has to!

Nola flinched as Sam finally slapped the buggy's reins across the horse's back. Then she heard the horse step into a lively trot and speed away from the house.

She walked to the door, watching the buggy until it was only a puff of dust on the horizon. Her marriage was over. All that was left was the grief of her small son, who was also watching the buggy disappear.

Jake turned and ran into the barn.

Nola watched Jake's flight, quelling an impulse to follow him.

"Better he gets it out of his system now," she muttered. "This may not be the end of it, I'm afraid, but he'll have to learn to live with it, just like I have."

Samantha looked at her mother out of solemn, bewildered eyes. Nola had stopped shaking, and she stroked Samantha's hair, feeling suddenly cold and alone.

"What else could I do?" she demanded, more of herself than of Samantha. "How could I ever take him back after the way he shamed me with all those women? How could I hold my head up again and look anybody in the face? What would Papa have thought of me if I'd taken him back? If I could forgive him the grief he caused me, I could never forgive him for the hurt and embarrassment he's caused my family."

A whimper from Samantha caused her to turn the child loose, and Nola cried out in dismay as she realized how tightly she had been clutching her daughter.

"I'm sorry, baby," she cried. "Mama didn't mean to hurt you. Mama would never do anything to hurt you or your brother either."

Crying again, she rocked the child in her arms, her tears streaming down her face and falling into Samantha's hair.

"Nola," Ellen said, "is there somethin' the matter? Did I hear one of the children cryin'?"

"No, Mama," Nola said softly. "Nothing's wrong. Don't worry, Mama, it's nothing for you to worry about."

"That's good," Ellen murmured. "They're such good children. They should be happy, not sad. Will Sam be stayin' for supper?"

"No, Mama, Sam won't be staying."

"Well, that's too bad. It was kind of him to come," Ellen said. "I like Sam. He's a good boy."

Nola looked sadly at her mother, then resolutely dried her eyes and set about preparing the evening meal. She heard a noise and looked up as Jake came into the house and started helping her set the table. She reached down and hugged him, and then they continued their silent preparation.

THIRTEEN

The next morning, Nola climbed wearily out of bed and prepared herself for another day. She stood brushing her hair, and, as she looked into the mirror at herself, pondered what had happened to her life.

"Is this all there's going to be for me?" she asked her reflection. "What's going to happen to me and my babies? How will I ever raise them by myself? And poor Mama, what's going to become of her? Oh, dear Lord, what have I done to deserve all of this? If only Papa was here, he would tell me what to do. Oh, Papa, I miss you so."

"Mama, Mama, come quick!" Jake called as he burst into her room. "Grandma is up, and she wants you to come fetch her some water. She said she's goin' to fix breakfast, and she needs water."

"What?" Nola exclaimed. She and Jake rushed from the room. "You mean your Grandma's out of bed without someone making her get up? Why, that's wonderful! Come on, you're big enough to fetch the water yourself. I'll go and help her."

Her heart was warmed as she entered the kitchen and found her mother busy at the stove preparing breakfast.

Perhaps there's hope after all, she thought.

Ellen turned as Nola entered the room and said, "Well, it's about time somebody got up around this house. You know it's a sin to lay in bed past sunup. Somebody go fetch that water so we can have some breakfast. I know these children are hungry, and I am, too. David and Joseph will be through with the milking any minute now and you know how them boys are. Both of 'em's got hollow legs."

"Oh, Mama," Nola said happily, "it's so good to see you up and around like this. I was beginning to think I'd lost you, too."

She put her arms around Ellen, and the two of them hugged. Then

68

Ellen turned away and picked up her old black skillet and set it on the stove.

"I'm done with mournin'," she told Nola. She continued with the breakfast preparations as she talked, more active than Nola had seen in months. "I know it's been hard on you, but it seemed like I just couldn't help myself. I gave myself a good talkin' to last night, and I just come to know Will wouldn't want me to give up. I remember how it was when little Tildy died. I never forgave myself for what I put him through then. I picked up the Bible last night before I went to bed and my eyes fell on the passage that says, 'To everything there is a season, a time to be born and a time to die,' and it said too, 'There is a time to mourn and a time to dance.' I don't reckon I feel like dancin', and probably never will, but I do know it's time I set my grief aside and got on with life. I thank you for bein' so patient with me, daughter, just like Will was the other time, but now it's time to get on with other things. Let's stir up a pan of biscuits and cut off some of that ham and put it on. Them boys do love my biscuits."

Nola happily set about helping her mother prepare breakfast for the family, giving silent thanks to God for the transformation in Ellen.

"You know, Nola, I think I might start a new quilt top today," Ellen said as she rolled out her biscuit dough. "I been thinkin' about a new pattern I seen over at Mrs. Cole's last quiltin'. I think the name of it was Flyin' Geese. I aim to ask her for it. I been thinkin', it's been too long since I last put a quilt in the frames. I reckon somebody in the family can always use a new cover for their bed."

Ellen's recovery was the lift Nola needed, and she threw herself into helping Ellen get a new focus for her life. In doing so, she found a new direction for herself. Instead of looking with suspicion at every overture her friends made to her, she began accepting them at face value. She began attending church services again and accepting invitations to social gatherings.

As much as she could, Nola put Sam out of her mind. She heard nothing from him, and several months passed before word of him surfaced. She and Ellen had taken a new quilt top to Martha's, planning an afternoon of sewing and talk. After they had been there a few minutes, Martha told Nola that John's sister Pearl had heard from Sam.

"He wrote Pearl all about what's happened to him since he left," Martha told Nola. "He said that he started from here not knowin' where he was headin'. Said he just kept goin' south. He thinks he was somewhere in Georgia when the buggy lost a wheel. After that, he rode his horse. He slept anywhere he could—in barns, on the trail, anywhere he could lay his head. He ended up in Jacksonville, Florida, takin' whatever work he could find to feed himself."

"I guess he did a lot of fiddling," Ellen said drily. "That's about the only thing he ever cared about doing."

"Well, I think he did some of that," Martha answered. "But he also mentioned he did some work in a blacksmith shop. Said he always hated it when Papa McGinty made him do it but was real grateful for the skill when he was in trouble. Anyhow, he said he got in a card game one night, and when the game was over, he'd won some man's barber shop. That's what he's doin' now, runnin' a barber shop. Don't that beat all? Who'd have ever thought Sam would end up cuttin' hair?"

Nola had made no comment during Martha's recital. Her heart was pounding so hard, she was sure everyone could hear it. I will not let this hurt me again, she told herself. I am not going to let this make one bit of difference to me.

"I don't suppose he said anything about me or the children, did he?" she asked.

"No, I'm sorry, Nola, he didn't mention any of you," Martha answered quietly. "He asked Pearl to write to him and to tell his ma and pa he was sorry for the worry he'd caused them."

"What did they say?" Ellen asked.

"She hasn't got up the nerve to tell them yet," Martha replied. "She only told John, and he told me. They're still awful mad at him for the way he's done you and the children."

"She ought to tell them," Ellen said. "No matter what Sam's done, he hasn't stopped bein' their son. You tell John that. Tell him, as a mother, I know how Louisa has been agonizin' over Sam. It's not fair to make her keep on worryin' about him."

"I'll tell him, Mama," Martha said. "I told John I was goin' to tell Nola. He agreed she had a right to know."

"Well, now I know," Nola said shortly. "Can we talk about something else?"

Martha and Ellen exchanged looks, then bent to their sewing. Before Ellen and Nola left for home, they had completed the quilt top and had made plans for a quilting bee at Ellen's house the next week.

"What can I do to help?" Martha asked. "Do you want me to cook something? I could get Mother McGinty to help me make a pound cake."

Ellen and Nola both laughed. Martha had a reputation for being a terrible cook, and they both knew that Louisa McGinty would bake the cake. Martha grinned and ducked her head at their good-natured teasing.

Ellen kept Nola busy the next week, cleaning and preparing for the quilting bee. Nola was not fooled by her mother's energetic spurt of cleaning. She knew Ellen was trying to keep her mind from thinking about Sam.

The day of the quilting was warm and sunny. Counting Ellen and Nola, a dozen women gathered around the quilting frame. Samantha and Lucy were seated near their mothers, diligently working on a doll's quilt Ellen had put together for them. Ellen smiled at them, remembering how Martha and Nola had sat at her feet when they were the same age. It's like a never-ending circle, she thought, a never-ending circle of love between mothers and daughters. Maybe I'll just write me a poem about it, she thought and smiled to herself.

The talk rose and fell as the women worked on the quilt. Shortly before noon, Ellen and Nola excused themselves and went to the dining room, where they laid out the noon meal. Ellen had baked a ham and made two large pans of biscuits, which she had kept warm in the warming ovens over the stove. A large pot of green beans, seasoned with a slab of side meat, had been simmering on the back of the stove. A heaping bowl of cole slaw and platters of red tomatoes were added to the table along with Martha's pound cake and other delicacies the women had brought with them.

"Looks like enough to feed an army," Ellen observed contentedly. "Why don't you tell everybody to come on and eat, Nola. Them that can't set around the table can take their plates out on the porch. I'll pour the milk and lemonade while they're gatherin'."

Nola looked at her mother and laughed. "Mama, you never look as happy as when you're feeding a bunch of people."

As Nola entered the room to call the women to their meal, she was struck by the sudden silence that fell over the group. She looked at Martha, whose face was flushed and angry.

I don't have to ask who they were talking about, she thought. Well, if they think they can get my goat with their gossip, they've got another think coming.

"Dinner's on the table," she announced. "Mama says for everyone to come on and eat."

As Martha started by her, Nola held her back for a moment. "Don't let it bother you, Martha," she said. "I'm not going to let it upset me."

"It was that gossipy old . . ." Martha started.

"Never mind, I don't want to know. Besides, I can guess by the way she wouldn't look me in the face," Nola answered. "I'm just glad Lucy and Samantha had already left. I wouldn't want Samantha to hear anything that would hurt her feelings."

"I don't see how you can be so calm, Nola," Martha said. "It makes me mad as fire when people start askin' their nosy questions."

"What makes me mad is they upset you," Nola said worriedly. "Your face is as red as a beet. You know Doc Hall said you shouldn't allow yourself to get overwrought."

"Oh, I'm all right," Martha said hastily. "I just wish Mother McGinty had been here. She'd a'told them off in a hurry."

"I doubt that they'd have had the nerve to say anything if she'd been there," Nola laughed. "We all know Mother McGinty's temper. Come on now, let's go eat. I'm dying to taste that pound cake you baked."

"Oh, you!" Martha exclaimed. "You know as well as I do who baked that cake."

With their arms around each other, the two sisters went to the dining room to eat. Nothing more was said about the incident. By the time the afternoon was over, the quilt was almost half finished. After everyone left, Nola and Ellen pulled the quilting frame back up to the ceiling and tied it securely.

"Well, that was a right nice day," Ellen said happily. "We got a lot of work done on the quilt too. I think we can finish it off the next time they come."

"Who are you going to give this one to, Mama?" Nola asked her. "You never have said who you were making it for."

"Oh, I don't know," Ellen answered. "I wasn't makin' it for anyone in particular. Maybe I'll save it for Samantha or Lucy. I had a thought while we was settin' there quiltin' about how life is just like a big circle, goin' from one generation to another, just repeatin' itself as it goes."

Nola thought no more about the unpleasant incident at dinnertime until she went to bed that night. After the noise and bustle of the day, she felt suddenly lonely and vulnerable.

I will not let them make me feel this way, she thought. I will not feel sorry for myself, nor will I play the part of the abandoned wife. I've got too much to be thankful for, and that's what I'm going to think about.

Turning over, she began her nightly prayer. "Thank you, God, for my many and wonderful blessings. For my children and my family. Forgive me for dwelling on life's gloom without seeing its brightness—the brightness of my children's faces and my mother's love. Forgive me for complaining about my problems instead of doing something about them. Open my eyes and my heart to all that is good in my life. Help me be strong and take control of my life again. In the strong name of Jesus, I pray. Amen.

FOURTEEN

Nola's presence, and the presence of Jake and Samantha, in the household helped Ellen establish a new routine for herself. The constant activity revolving around two active children helped ease the loneliness that had threatened to engulf her after Will's death. She and Nola shared the housekeeping chores, and she depended more and more on her sons David and Joseph to manage the farm duties.

When the quilt was finally finished, Ellen and Nola wrapped it carefully and stored it in the quilt chest until Ellen could decide what to do with it. Two months had passed, and Ellen suddenly realized that she had not made her usual trip to town for supplies.

"I don't know where my mind has gone," she fussed. "I've just about let us run out of everything. Tomorrow mornin', if the weather holds good, we better get ourselves into town."

The next morning she confessed, "I dread ridin' that wagon all the way to town, but with all we need, I reckon there's no other way."

"Why don't you let David and Joseph drive the wagon and me and you can go in the buggy," Nola suggested. "We can travel together and keep an eye on the boys. Jake will want to ride in the wagon, but Samantha could go with us."

"Well, I hate takin' everybody away for the day, but that sounds like the best thing to do. I'll go tell the boys. I reckon they won't mind missin' a day's work," Ellen laughed. "Be sure and put in that pound cake that was left from supper last night, and you better add some more biscuits and ham if the boys are goin'."

Nola followed Ellen's instructions, making sure there was a bountiful basket of food to take with them. When she had finished, she went to find a bonnet for herself and one for Samantha.

The children were excited at the unexpected trip and raced around, gathering up their belongings in preparation for the journey. Samantha had to have her favorite doll to take along, and Jake declared he couldn't go without his slingshot.

Finally, all were ready and the little family started out on their trip. Once they got out of the cove where they lived, the road was in better condition and they made good time. The mules were not as swift as the mare pulling the buggy, but with two under the harness, they managed to keep pace fairly well.

Waynestown was a good fifteen miles from the cove where Ellen and Nola lived, and the trip took almost three hours. The much traveled road was packed hard from all the traffic between Waynestown and Asheville. Although they were surrounded by mountains, the area they traveled was relatively flat, and they passed the depot as they approached the town, climbing a gentle hill up to the main street.

When they arrived at their destination, Ellen gave her sons a list of supplies needed from the grain and livery stable and she, Nola, Samantha, and Jake made their way to the general store in the middle of town where they stocked up on sewing and cooking supplies. The store carried everything from groceries to clothing, with a long counter down the middle of the store separating the dry goods from the groceries. Several men sat around the stove at the back of the store swapping tales and whittling.

Nola had been eyeing a beautiful pitcher on the shelf as she made her purchases and when they had finished, she went over and picked it up. She traced the shape of the pansies that were molded on the side of the pitcher, running her fingers over the petals and down the stems. She looked at the deep wine color of the spout and the rich purples and yellows of the flowers. She thought to herself that it was about the most beautiful thing she had ever seen.

"Nola, you've been lookin' at that pitcher for the last six months," the proprietor said to her. "Why don't you go ahead and buy it before somebody else gets it? You know how much you want it."

Nola sighed as she carefully placed it back on the shelf.

"Wantin's not the same as gettin', Mary," she said. "I've got more important things to put my money on. What little there is of it. It's hard enough to stretch it far enough to keep Jake and Samantha in shoes. Better give me another spool of that white thread. I've got to let the hems down on Samantha's dresses again. That child is growing like a weed."

"Here you go," Mary said, handing her the thread. "That'll be three more cents. Sure you don't want me to wrap that pitcher up for you? Somebody's goin' to buy it soon if you don't."

"Where did you get it, Mary? I declare, I never saw anything so pretty,"

Nola said, looking again at the pitcher. "Can't you just see it full of black-eyed Susans?"

"It says on the bottom it was made in France," Mary answered. "Papa bought it off a drummer that come through here last winter. He was wantin' to sell out his wares so's he could go back to farmin'."

Nola took a deep breath and stood a little straighter. "Well, no use longing for the impossible," she said briskly. "Here's your money, Mary." Nola looked around, searching for her children. "I wonder where that Jake went? I can't let that boy out of my sight for a minute. If you see him, tell him to come on to the wagon."

Nola had no more than cleared the doorway of the store, when Jake emerged from behind a barrel.

"Miz Francis," he whispered to Mary, "I got somethin' to ask you."

Mary was startled by Jake's sudden appearance. "What in the world are you up to, Jake McGinty, a'slippin' up on a body like that? Yore mama's lookin' all over the place for you."

"Yes'm, I know," Jake said. "I heard her. First I got to ask you somethin'. How much is that pansy pitcher Mama fancies? I been thinkin' I'd like to get it for her. I know how took she is with it. I got me some money, and I figger if you'd save it back for me, I could, maybe, pay it off by Christmas."

Jake dug in the pocket of his knickers and pulled out some coins and laid them on the counter. Mary sorted out the money and counted it. There was a nickel and seven pennies. She looked into Jake's shining eyes, smiling at the serious expression on his face.

"Well, Jake, I don't know no reason why I can't put it back for you. They ain't nobody I'd rather have it than your ma. Want it for Christmas, do you?"

"Yes'm, I reckon, if it ain't too costly, I can manage it. I been workin' some for Uncle John and he pays me. Give me this nickel yesterday," Jake said proudly.

"A whole nickel, huh?" Mary smiled. "You better run on now and not keep your mama waitin'. I'll put it aside, and we'll talk cost some other time."

She shook her head and laughed as Jake tore out the door.

Every trip they made to town, Jake came in and proudly laid his offering on the counter for Mary, always being careful to conceal his dealings from his mother.

"My goodness, Jake, where you gettin' all this money you been layin' out?" Mary asked him one day. "You must have a right big job, the way you been payin' on that pitcher."

"Been workin' for my Uncle John," Jake declared proudly. "My grandma give me ten cents for pickin' blackberries for her, and my Uncle Willie paid me a nickel for helpin' him clean out his barn. All the rest of it I earned helpin' Uncle John."

"Well, you keep this up, and you'll have that pitcher paid off in no time," Mary smiled. "You sure you don't want to hold out a penny for some candy?"

"No'm, I don't reckon so," Jake said.

Mary saw him looking longingly at the candy counter as he started out.

"Hey there, you, Jake," she called gruffly. "Come back here a minute."

She reached in the glass jar that held the peppermint sticks and handed him one.

"I got a policy of rewardin' my best customers," she said. "That way they'll keep comin' back."

"Thank you, Miz Francis," Jake grinned. "I reckon I better go now, Mama'll come lookin' for me in a minute."

Then one day as Christmas approached, John McGinty came in to do some shopping for his wife, Nola's sister Martha.

"Howdy, Mary." He nodded in greeting. "I wonder if you've got some of that stick candy like Martha bought last Christmas. She said for me to tell you she wanted the same thing she bought last year."

"Why, shore, John. How is Martha? I ain't seen her about lately. Is she still feelin' poorly?"

"I'm afraid so." John sighed. "Seems like she just never got her strength back after havin' the babies. I told her I'd come in and pick up a few things for her. She wanted to come herself, but she just wasn't up to it. While you're at it, look and see if you got a good pocketknife for a boy. I've been thinkin' I'd get Jake one for Christmas. He shore has been a help to me this fall and winter. I swear, they ain't many men that could've worked any harder than he has. Jest pesters me all the time for somethin' to do. Like to of tore him up yesterday when I told him not to worry about comin' back till the weather warmed up a little. He was so upset, I give him an extra penny. I don't know what he spends his money on. He's too young to have a girl."

"I know what he's doin' with it," Mary said. "He gives it to me. Every penny he can rake and scrape up."

"Gives it to you?" John exclaimed. "What on earth for? I know I don't pay him much, but what on earth is he buyin'?"

"Well, I guess it's all right if I tell you, but don't let it go no further," Mary said. "I wouldn't want to spoil his surprise. He's buyin' a pitcher for his ma for Christmas. Leastways he's tryin' to get it paid off by then.

He's still got a'ways to go though, and even with me lettin' him have it for half of what I was askin' for it, it's gonna take him another year to pay it off the way he's goin'. He's gonna be mighty disappointed if he can't give it to Nola for Christmas though."

"A Christmas present for his mama, is it?" John asked. "If you don't mind, let me look at it, Mary."

Mary took the pitcher out from under the counter where she had put it, carefully unwrapped it, and held it up for John's inspection.

His eyes lit up as he took in the rich colors.

"Looks like somethin' Nola would like, don't it? Tell you what, Mary, when the boy comes in again, tell him you made a mistake on the price of it and be sure he gets it in time to give his mama for Christmas. I reckon I'd like to jest pay it off for Jake. He's worked hard, and I probably ain't been payin' him what he's worth. 'Course, you know, this little transaction is jest between me and you. No need for anybody else to know anything about it."

"Why, that's right generous of you, John," Mary said. "I reckon, like you said, we can jest keep this between you and me. It's good of you to look after Jake like this. I'm sure Sam'd be beholden to you."

"I ain't doin' it for Sam," John said shortly. "I'm doin' it for the boy. It ain't easy bein' without a pa. He could be doin' other things a lot worse than lookin' after his mama's wants. He's a good boy, and I aim to do everything I can to see he stays that way. Now, let's look at them pocketknives. A boy needs him a good pocketknife."

Christmas morning dawned cold and crisp, with a weak sun reflecting off the snow. Jake and Samantha tumbled over the top of each other in their eagerness to see what Santa had left for them. Nola and Ellen smiled at their childish squeals of delight as they pulled stick candy and apples from their stockings. Nola had made new clothes for both of them with Ellen's help, and they exclaimed over everything, declaring they were the finest clothes they had ever seen. David and Joseph stood back, grinning at their enthusiasm. They quietly thanked Ellen for the knitted socks and shirts she had made them. In addition, she had found a new knife for Joseph and a set of writing pencils for David. After the excitement had died down, they took their pails and went to the barn to do the milking.

"If yore papa had been here, he'd of made some toys for Samantha and Jake," Ellen said sadly. "Never a Christmas went by that he didn't make somethin' for you young'uns. Seems like I miss him more and more every day I live."

"Now, Mama, we're not going to be sad today," Nola said briskly. "Besides, you did a fine job on the doll for Samantha, and we did manage to get the sled for Jake. He's pleased as punch with it. Willie was kind to let us fix it up for him. By the time his boy is big enough to use it, Jake will be done with it. Everything worked out good."

Suddenly Jake was tugging at Nola's apron and extending a crudely wrapped package to her. Nola looked down in surprise.

"Well, what on earth is this?" she asked. "Do you mean old Santa left something for me? Don't he know I'm too old for such?"

"It ain't from Santa, Mama," Jake said shyly. "It's from me. Open it, please."

Nola smiled at Jake and carefully unwrapped the package, curious as to what childish gift he had made for her. When she pulled the last piece of paper from it, she stared in amazement at the pansy pitcher.

"What on earth?" She was stunned. "Jake, how on earth did you manage to get this? Miss Francis didn't give it to you, did she? You know we don't take charity. I know how costly this was. Where on earth did you get enough money for it?"

"I worked it out," Jake said proudly. "I been workin' for Uncle John ever since last summer, and I saved up and paid on it every month. I paid for it all by myself. I thought you'd like it, Mama. You said it was the prettiest thing you'd ever seen. I just wanted you to have somethin' pretty all for yourself. Don't you like it?"

"Like it? Why, I reckon it's about the prettiest pitcher in the whole wide world," Nola said softly. "Oh, Jake, you spent all your money on me. I reckon I must be about the luckiest mama on the face of this earth. My pansy pitcher! Why I never dreamed I'd own anything this fine."

Putting her arms around her son, she said tearfully, "Jake, if I have a hundred more Christmases, none of them will ever be as fine as this one."

"Yes'm, thank you," Jake said. "I just wanted you to be happy today, Mama, and not be sad."

"How could I ever be sad with two fine children like I've got?" Nola asked, wiping the tears from her eyes. "Now, look under the tree again, Jake, there's a little package under there that your Uncle John left for you. I don't know what it is, but he said to tell you it was from one farmer to another one, and that you must promise to be careful with it. There's an envelope under there, too, that came from your papa. Your Aunt Pearl sent it over. It's meant to be for the both of you."

Jake found the package and quickly tore the paper off of it. He whistled softly to himself when he saw the pocketknife. The handle was black bone with shiny metal trimmings around the edges. He opened it carefully, exclaiming over the double blades that folded neatly back into itself.

"I don't reckon anybody ever had as fine a knife as this one," he marveled. "I reckon, maybe I'll just learn to whittle like Grandpa did. Might be I could make some of them animals like he used to make."

"Might be you will," Ellen declared, eyes shining with tears. "Guess he'd be right proud of you today if he was here, Jake, and not just because you got a new pocketknife for Christmas either."

"Open your letter from your papa, Jake," Nola said.

Slowly Jake picked up the envelope and turned it over and over in his hand. He gave it to Samantha. "Here, you open it," he said.

Samantha pulled out a card with a picture of Santa Claus on it. Inserted in the card was a silver dollar. Samantha looked at the card, then silently passed it over to Jake. He looked at the card briefly, then handed the money to Nola.

"Here, Mama, you take it. I don't have no need for it," he said.

"No, Jake, it's yours and Samantha's. If you want, I'll keep it for you till you find something you want to spend it on," Nola said gently.

Jake nodded, then shouted, "Come on, Samantha, let's go out and ride the sled. That snow ought to be just right."

Nola helped them bundle up and watched out the window as they started off for their ride. She turned and picked up the pitcher, holding it close to her breast, then turned to the fireplace.

"Look, Mama, don't the pitcher look fine on the mantle? When spring comes, I'm going to fill it with black-eyed Susans!"

FIFTEEN

N ola lifted the two letters and turned them over, looking at them curiously. She recognized Cassie's writing on one envelope and smiled in anticipation. She felt an urge to tear it open at once. It had been months since she had heard any news from her friend. Curiosity compelled her to examine the second letter first though. Receiving mail was a rare occurrence for her and to receive two at a time was almost unthinkable.

The return address of the second letter was Jacksonville, Florida, and her heart skipped a beat as she looked at it. Recalling a conversation with Pearl when she told Nola that Sam was living in Florida, she laid Cassie's letter aside and quickly tore the second letter open.

She paused and clasped it to her bosom, waiting for her heart to stop its excited racing before she read it. I should just tear it up, she thought, but I won't. I'll see what he has to say. Oh, why should I let him make me feel this way after all this time? It's been nearly five years now since I saw him last, and I still feel like that silly girl that had no more gumption than to fall in love with him.

Finally, she unfolded the letter and started to read the contents. Her face paled, and her hand shook so that she could hardly hold the papers still. The single horrible word leapt out at her. *Divorce*. She was suddenly dizzy, and her knees were weak.

"Nola, what on earth is it?" Ellen asked in alarm. "What's in that letter? You look like you're a'gonna faint. Here, sit down and let me see what's got you so upset."

Ellen pushed a chair up under Nola, and she sank limply into it. Wordlessly she handed the letter to her mother.

Ellen looked in bewilderment at the legal documents and then, when it sank in on her what it was, she stared in concern at her daughter's bowed head.

"It says here that Sam's divorced you, Nola," she said slowly. "But how could that be without you knowin' about it? Can he do that? How could he divorce you? You never gave him any reason to do such a thing. Can he do this just because you've been separated these five years? I thought it had to be because of adultery. Lord knows, there was none on your part, only his. I just don't understand."

Nola shook her head numbly. "It's different laws in different states," she said. "I guess in Florida you can get one on separation. Anyhow, that's what it looks like he's done."

She grabbed the papers from her mother and ran out of the room. She went into her bedroom, closed the door, and sank down weakly on the bed. She opened the papers and stared at them until her eyes were so tear-filled that she could no longer read the words. Turning her face into the pillow, she cried heartbrokenly, muffling the sounds of her sobbing in the pillow.

Nola cried until she felt there were no more tears left in her. The word *divorce* echoed in her head until she thought she would surely go mad. Faces swirled around her, pointing fingers jabbing at her, and she put her hands over her ears, trying to shut out the hateful word.

Late that afternoon, Nola finally emerged from her room. Her dress was smooth, and she had put on an apron over it. She had brushed her hair back from her face and pinned it tightly on top of her head in a bun. Her eyes were red but dry.

"Oh, Nola honey, what can I do to help you through this?" Ellen asked. "Just tell me what you want me to do that'll make it easier for you. You know I'd do anything I could to help you."

"There's nothing to be done, Mama," Nola replied woodenly. "He's made this same choice over and over. I don't know why I'm surprised at what he's done. I can tell you this though. He can send me a dozen divorce papers, and it won't change anything. We were married in the sight of God, and a paper won't change that. It won't change the vows we made to each other. We said we were married till death parts us. We didn't say till some paper of divorce parts us. What he's done is a sin, and he's the one who'll have to live with that, not me. He can divorce me all he wants to, but I'll still be his wife 'till the day one of us dies."

"Oh, Nola, don't let this harden your heart," Ellen exclaimed. "Let him go his own way, and you go yours. You're too young to condemn yourself to a life alone."

"Mama, I'm surprised at you," Nola said heatedly. "You know what the Bible says about divorce as well as I do. I believed it when I married, and

I believe it now. I *won't* go against the things Papa taught me. I know what he would have wanted me to do." She took a deep breath. "Now, I will hear no more about it. I never want this mentioned again, especially in front of the children. I couldn't ever hold my head up again if people knew he'd divorced me. Nobody in our family or his has ever divorced. I won't have people gossiping about me and my family behind my back."

"Oh, Nola," Ellen said sadly, "you can't say what your papa would have wanted for you. I know he would have wanted you to be happy. He would never have wanted to see you so bitter and hard. If you'll remember, there was a time when he urged you to divorce Sam. Let this be a chance for you to start over again and put all of these unhappy memories behind you. These children need a father, and you need a husband to help you."

"No! No more men," Nola said bitterly. "Nobody will ever hurt me again like Sam did. I made my mistake when I didn't listen to Papa. He told me not to marry Sam, that he'd bring me nothing but heartache. I wouldn't listen, so I'll just have to suffer the consequences. Now I'm going to fix supper, and I never want to talk about this again. It's over and done with, and I don't care if I never have to hear his name again."

Nola turned and went into the kitchen. Ellen could hear her poking up the fire in the stove and pulling out pots and pans in preparation for the evening meal. Sadly, she shook her head and followed Nola into the kitchen. Silently, she began to set the table.

SIXTEEN

T he next week was one of soul-searching agony for Nola. She had spent the days walking the trails where she and Sam had courted, recalling their happiness and agonizing over broken promises. She visited the farm where they had spent their married life and where Jake and Samantha were born. She finally sat at the oak table in the kitchen where she had spoken the words that had sent him away for good.

Was it false pride that turned him away? she asked herself. Should I have put my pride aside and taken him back for the sake of the children? Would it have done any good, or would it just have prolonged the inevitable? She asked herself these questions over and over as she tried to make sense out of the mess her life had become. Finally, she had to admit that much of her hurt stemmed from her injured pride over Sam's infidelity to her. This admission was almost as painful to her as their initial separation had been.

Ellen had done all she could to reassure the children, who were confused by their mother's withdrawal from them. With the help of David and Joseph though, she had maintained as near a normal atmosphere as possible. She was relieved when Nola seemed ready to join the family circle again.

"Mama, do you know what happened to Cassie's letter? I don't remember what I did with it. I know I didn't read it. I hope you put it up somewhere. I'd hate to think I lost it," she said to Ellen.

"Yes, I know where it is," Ellen replied. "I put it in a safe place for you. Here it is."

"Thank you, Mama," Nola said quietly. "And thank you for not asking me any questions this week and for looking after Jake and Samantha. I know it's been hard for you, but I think I finally have been able to make some sense from all of this, and I'm going to be all right now."

"No thanks necessary," Ellen said gruffly. "Come on and open that letter. I haven't read it, and I been dyin' of curiosity to see how Cassie's getting along. It's been close to a year since we heard from her last."

Nola opened Cassie's letter and read aloud to Ellen:

Dear Nola,

Well, it's been a time since I rote you last, but things have been real busy for me and I just couldn't find time to put pen to paper, what with trying to help out on the farm and keeping the house going. We have another son. Named him Jeremiah. I had a right hard time the whole nine months, and the doctor said I mustn't have any more babies. We'll see.

Good news for Joshua. He's teaching school again. His brothers are old enough to take over most of the farm work now, and Joshua is so happy to be back teaching again.

Mother Perkins has married again and moved into her husband's house. Aunt Jenny died nearly a year ago, and her and Uncle Grover just up and married. Surprised all of us. We didn't even know they was courting. The girls, except for Lottie, are living with her. Course it's just down the road a piece, so they're here most as much as they're at home.

Nola, I got a favor to ask of you. I been thinking about my sister and brother that I left when I come to your house, and I would deem it a favor if you could find out where they are now. I worry a lot about what's happened to Anne Marie. I reckon you know why.

Write me all your news and give your Ma a hug and a howdy for me.

Your friend,
Cassie

"Well, that was a lot of news for such a short letter," Ellen observed. "We must see what we can do about finding out about Cassie's family for her, Nola."

"Yes, Mama, of course we will," Nola replied thoughtfully. "Don't you think it was strange that no one ever looked for Cassie? Everyone in the community knew she was with us. You would have thought someone would have come around looking for her, wouldn't you?"

Ellen nodded. "'Course, given the way her pa treated her, her ma probably was glad to see her go away. I just hope he ain't been doin' Anne Marie the same way."

Nola looked grim. "I guess we need to ask Sheriff Tate first."

Before Nola and Ellen could launch their search for Cassie's family, however, they were caught up in their own family problems. Martha's poor health suddenly worsened. John came to seek Nola's help one morning. She was sitting on the porch stringing beans when John's buggy drove into the yard at a fast pace. The haste of his arrival alarmed Nola.

"What on earth's the matter, John?" she asked as she started down the steps. "Is something wrong with one of the children?"

"No. Nothin's wrong with either one of them," John said as he stepped out of the buggy. "It's Martha. She just ain't doin' no good at all. I don't mind tellin' you, Nola, I'm mighty worried about her."

"Yes, we have been too," Nola replied. "It's funny, but I was just thinking about her and planning on when I could go see her. I've missed seeing her at meeting this past month. What with one thing and another though, I hadn't done anything about going."

"She got up this mornin' and nothin' would do her but I come and get you," John said worriedly. "Ma took the children and went to Pearl's to help her with some cannin' this mornin', and Martha said it would be a good time for you and her to have a quiet visit. I think she's got somethin' on her mind she wants to talk to you about. You know, that ain't like her, to say she needs somebody."

"I'll go get my things together," Nola said hastily. "Does she want Mama to come too?"

"No, just you, she said. I'll put Goldie in the barn and use your Ned, if it's all right. I can swap when I bring you home tonight," John said.

Without wasting any more time on conversation, Nola went into the house to tell Ellen where she was going. John went to the barn to exchange horses.

"Mama," Nola called as she entered the house, "John is here. He says Martha wants to see me. Can you do without me for the day? I'll likely be back by suppertime."

"Is she worse? What's happened?" Ellen asked. "Should I go with you?"

"No, not now, Mama. Let me go see about her, and then we'll decide what to do," Nola answered, putting her arms around Ellen. "You know she gets upset if she thinks she's worried you. Try not to worry, I'll tell you everything when I get back."

"Why don't you take your papa's medicine bag," Ellen suggested. "It's still got all his herbs in it. Maybe there'll be something there that will help her."

"Good idea," Nola said as she pulled her shawl around her shoulders. "There's John now. I'll be back quick as I can."

Nola climbed up beside John, and they drove off at a brisk trot. Thoughts of Martha whirled through Nola's head as they rode down the trail. She thought of how Martha had looked on her wedding day.

Happiness had radiated from her face as bright as the summer sun, until everyone around her was caught up in her joy. Since her illness, the light had faded from her until she was a dim reflection of the girl who had promised herself so fervently to her husband that day.

Why haven't I been more mindful of her? she thought. I've been so caught up in my own problems that I couldn't see that she was gettin' worse. I've let nearly a month go by without going to see about her.

"I hope we haven't worried your ma, Nola," John said. "The last thing Martha said to me was, 'Don't upset Mama.' It's been so hard on her with Will's death and all, and we just didn't want to add to her burdens. I know we haven't been as much help as we should have been, but seems like we been so busy with our own worries, we couldn't do nothin' else."

"Nonsense," Nola replied. "We've been managing just fine. It's me that should feel guilty, not you. Martha's the only sister I have, and I should have paid more attention to her. I was just thinking how happy she was the day you married. It seemed like nothing bad could ever happen to any of us then, didn't it, John?"

John glanced over at Nola, his face flushed. "I'll never forgive Sam for what he did to you, Nola," he said grimly. "Someday he'll have to account for all the misery he's caused you and the children. To say nothin' of Ma and Pa's heartache. I know that just before Pa died, he said he forgave Sam, but I get mad all over again at him every time I look at Jake and Samantha."

"Hush, John," Nola said sadly. "Getting yourself upset won't solve anything, and it sure won't change Sam. Tell me now about Martha. What does Doc Hall say? Can't he help her at all? What does he say is wrong with her?"

"Just the same old thing he always says," John answered despondently. "He says her blood is thin. He gave her a new tonic the last time, but it's so bitter that she can't keep it down. Nothin' he's given her has helped. Maybe you've got somethin' in your pa's herbs that'll help her."

"I'll look," Nola said, "but I doubt I've got anything that Doc Hall hasn't already tried. How's her spirits? She must be getting discouraged."

"That's what's got me so worried," answered John. "Through all this time she's been sick, she's always talked about gettin' well, but lately she's took to talkin' about dyin'. I don't mind tellin' you, Nola, it's breakin' my heart."

With this declaration, John could no longer hold back the tears that had been welling up in him. He dropped his head in his hands and broke into sobs.

Nola watched helplessly, at a loss to find words of encouragement for John. A cold fist seemed to grip her heart as she faced the possibility of losing her only sister. Awkwardly, she patted him on the shoulder, her own tears coursing down her face.

"Here now," she said huskily. "This won't help Martha for me and you to break down. We've got to be strong for her sake."

"I know," John said, wiping his eyes, "but sometimes it seems like it's more than I can bear. I'm sorry I burdened you, Nola. It's just that sometimes I get so filled up with sorrow, it's just got to spill out. Usually I just go off to the barn by myself."

"If I can be of any comfort to you, John, I'm glad," Nola said quietly. "We've been friends for a long time, and I guess I'll be leaning on you through this too."

They rode the rest of the way in silence, both lost in their own thoughts.

"Well, here we are at last," Nola said briskly. "Let's try to be cheerful for Martha's sake. I hope I can at least lift Martha's spirits while I'm here."

SEVENTEEN

John let Nola out at the footbridge and went on to the barn with the horse and buggy. Nola crossed the bridge and went up the path to the steps of the porch that spanned the front of the house. She paused and looked at the long, rambling structure. At a time when the architecture of the countryside favored two-storied houses, the McGintys' home was decidedly different. It was long and spread out over the spacious green yard, surrounded by large willows and walnut trees. A stream flowed down the hillside at the back of the house and disappeared in the springhouse, then emerged again and ran into the creek in front of the house.

Nola thought sadly of the times she had come here as a part of the family, a daughter-in-law, come to bring her children to proud grandparents to make over and admire. She still came occasionally, but she never felt quite as comfortable as she had when Sam had been with her. She tried to send the children often, usually arranging for John or their uncles to bring them.

Straightening her shoulders and putting a smile on her face, she went into the cool dimness of the kitchen, calling out to Martha. "Hey, lazy bones, where are you? Don't tell me I've come all this way, and you're still lying in bed! Martha, Martha, where are you?"

"Nola, is that you? Is it really you?" a soft voice responded. "I'm here, in the bedroom. Come on back if you don't mind. I'm just restin' for a few minutes."

Nola took off her shawl, draped it over a kitchen chair, and followed the sound of Martha's voice. The house was laid out so that one room merged into another, with the living room on one end and the kitchen on the other. The bedrooms were strung out in between. The only outside entrances were from the porch into the two rooms on each end, except for the back door off the kitchen, which went out onto the back porch. Several smokehouses and storage sheds fanned out from the back yard.

Nola had asked Martha once how anybody ever had any privacy with such an arrangement. "Oh, if we don't want anybody comin' in, we just close our doors," Martha said. "That way they know to go down the porch to get where they want to go. It's not bad, and, of course, they built it this way so Papa McGinty could get around easier. He never had very good use of his leg after his fall. Until the day he died, he told us regularly how Papa saved his life. He said Papa sat up two days and nights with him a'doctorin' him and holdin' him down when he was out of his head with fever. Said if it hadn't been for Papa, he'd a'lost his leg for sure and probably his life, too."

Nola went through two bedrooms and into John and Martha's room. She was startled at the change in her sister since their last visit. Martha was lying on the bed, and her dark hair was fanned out around her pale, colorless face. She smiled tremulously at Nola, her pale pink lips quivering as she put her arms up to her sister. Nola leaned down to embrace her, then stared into her eyes, thinking they looked feverish to her.

"Well, now, what's this?" Nola asked gruffly. "John tells me you've been feeling poorly. We'll just have to see what we can do about this. We've got to get you well so you can keep up with those two wild Indians of yours. Where are they anyway?"

"Mother McGinty took them and went to see Pearl," Martha replied. "You know how wild Pearl is over them. They'll be rotten when they get back. She spoils them somethin' awful. I guess it's because she don't have any of her own. They should be home before long, but I'm sort of glad they're not here now. I wanted some time with you all to myself, and when they're here they're bound to get all of the attention."

"Well, first thing let's do is get you up and outside for a little fresh air. I do love to sit on your front porch. Seems like there's just something special about being able to sit out there and look up at the mountains," Nola said briskly. "Here's your slippers. I'll get your blue shawl for you just in case you get chilly."

She turned away quickly, afraid that Martha would see the alarm in her eyes as she helped her sit up. She felt as if a tight fist had gripped her heart and was wringing all of the blood out of it. She knew then with a terrible certainty that her sister would not get well, and hot tears welled up into her eyes. She brushed them away as she busied herself at the dresser looking for the shawl.

Nola put her arm around Martha, half supporting her as they made their slow way to the porch. She helped Martha settle herself in one of the cane-bottomed rockers that lined the porch. She put a cushion behind her back as well as under her, thinking of the thinness of her body against the chair.

"This is nice," sighed Martha. "I don't remember when I've felt like gettin' out here, and I hate to ask Mother McGinty to help me. Lord knows she has her hands full keepin' up with the twins and doin' all the cookin' and cleanin' without havin' to pull me around."

"Martha, why don't you come home and stay with me and Mama for a while, just till you get to feeling better?" Nola asked her impulsively. "You know how Mama would like having you there. She hasn't had anybody to fuss over in a long time. Samantha is so independent she won't let anybody do anything for her. You could bring the children with you. Jake and Samantha would love having them there, and so would we."

"Oh, I couldn't do that, Nola, much as I'd like to." Martha smiled. "I just couldn't leave John here by himself. He'd work himself to death if I wasn't around to remind him to stop and rest awhile. As much as I love Mama and Papa's home, this is my home now. I want to stay here as long as I can. Besides, I don't want Mama to worry about me. She's had enough to worry about these past years."

"I brought Papa's medicine bag," Nola said. "We'll just look through it and see if we can't find one of his tonics to help you. I bet that stuff he used to mix up for us in the spring would get you right on your feet."

"Yes, or put me in my grave, one," Martha laughed. "Oh, Nola, do you remember the time when we were all so ornery and ill with each other? Papa said we had the springtime janders, and he gave us all a dose of sulphur and molasses that like to have killed us all. Whew! I never tasted anything so bad in all my life. We were afraid to look cross-eyed at each other after that for fear he'd dose us again. Even old Willie behaved himself."

"Law, yes, I don't guess any of us will ever forget that," Nola laughed. "If you remember, he gave all the dogs a dose, too. Them old hounds like to have run themselves to death. I never saw anything so miserable in my life. Old Blue slunk around for a month after that and every time Papa came near him, he dove under the house."

John smiled as he approached the house, listening to the sound of the sisters' laughter. "I see I brought you the right medicine this time, Martha," he observed. "Nola, I haven't heard her laugh like that in a month of Sundays. I guess you can manage without me for a while, honey, with Nola here. I think I'll just go and finish that row of corn I was hoein' on this mornin'. When I get that done, I'll be through with that field for the rest of the summer. It's goin' to be too big to hoe anymore. I'll be back directly."

The sisters watched John as he strode off to the garden behind the house. Martha smiled, thinking that he held himself a little straighter than he had in a good while.

"John's a good husband to you, Martha," Nola said softly. "And I never saw a man as proud of his children as he is. I hope you know how lucky you are."

"Oh, I do, Nola," Martha said. "I'm just sorry that I haven't been a very good wife to him lately. You know, life turns out funny, don't it? John was so much in love with you, and you turned him down for Sam, then me and him got married. I knew I was second choice for him, but I guess I don't have much pride, 'cause I wanted him no matter what. Now the way things has turned out, with Sam runnin' off and me bein' so poorly, it looks like you'd a'both been better off if you'd just a'married him like he wanted."

"Martha! Don't you ever say such a thing again. John would never have married me. He might have thought he wanted me once, but he knew it wasn't right, just as much as I did. I'm too ornery for somebody as steady and even tempered as John is. He knew who was right for him. It just took him a little while to realize it. I never saw two people as well suited as you are. Listen here to me, John loves you, and don't you make any mistake about it. What you've got to do is get yourself well, and you will be well again, Martha, I tell you. You *will* get well," Nola said fiercely.

"I wish I could believe that," Martha said sadly. "You and me both know it's not true though. I saw in your eyes that you knew, too, when you looked at me this mornin'. We both know there's somethin' wrong with me that herbs and tonics won't cure, so let's stop wastin' time pretendin' that I'm goin' to get better. I asked John to bring you over here this mornin' 'cause there's somethin' I've got to ask of you. I've put it off as long as I can."

"I won't listen to any such nonsense," Nola protested. "You can't give up, Martha. You just can't."

"Shh," Martha said gently. "Please, let's not waste what little precious time we have. Just listen to what I've got to say, Nola. I don't know how much longer I've got, but I do know that every day I lose a little ground. Last week I could walk all the way through the house. Today I had to stop three times before I could make it. Tomorrow I may not be able to get out of the bed. I've had to accept it and make peace with myself. I want you to do the same. I tried to talk to John about it, but it distressed him so that I just didn't have the heart. I know that deep down he knows it as sure as I do. He just can't accept it yet."

"Oh, Martha, what are you saying?" Nola cried.

"I'm tellin' you that I don't have much longer to live, and there are some things that only you can do for me. I know you will, Nola, because I know how strong you are. Look how you've took care of Mama and how you've stood up under all the trouble with Sam. I can depend on you to help me, can't I?"

"You know you can ask anything in the world of me, Martha," Nola said tearfully. "But I'll not listen to any more talk of dying."

"All right, have it your own way," Martha said sadly. "Just hear me out. Now, the one thing I can't reconcile myself to is the thought that my children are goin' to grow up not knowin' their mother. I know Mrs. McGinty will take good care of them. I got no worry about that, and Lord knows John loves them more than life itself, but it saddens me to think they'll forget about me and never know how much I love them. What I want you to promise me is that you'll look after them and see that they don't forget me. Just come when you can and tell them stories about things we did when we were girls. Tell them how much I love them and how proud I was the day they was born. Don't tell them any of the bad things about me. How selfish and vain I was when I was a girl. And when it's time for Lucy to be told woman things, Nola, I want you to tell her for me. John can talk to Charles, but Lucy'll need a woman she can talk to and one who will tell her things she'll need to know."

Martha reached into her apron pocket and took out a small package wrapped in paper. Carefully, she undid it and handed it to Nola.

"When we went to town last month, I got this made. It ain't a real good likeness, but, at least, maybe it'll help them remember what their ma looked like. I want you to keep it and show it to them when you talk about me. I got one made for John, too. I've put it where he'll find it when the time comes."

Wordlessly, Nola stared down at the small photo of her sister. The stern-faced woman that looked back at her bore little resemblance to the fun-loving girl she knew and loved.

"I'll do what you ask, Martha, if it becomes necessary," she promised huskily. "But I'm telling you right now that I think you'll be here to do your own talking. I'm going through Papa's satchel and mix you up something that will help you and drive all this nonsense out of your head."

Martha smiled sweetly at Nola and sat back, spent from her emotional declaration. "Whatever you say, Nola," she said softly. "Just remember your promise."

A noise from across the creek caused them both to end their conversation as Lucinda McGinty and the twins returned from their visit. The children squealed in delight as they recognized their Aunt Nola and pounded noisily across the bridge toward them. Nola rose and started down the steps to meet them.

Old Tom, the turkey, self-appointed guardian of the yard, saw them, too. He rounded the corner of the porch just as the children started up the yard. With tail feathers fanned out to their most impressive width and wings dragging on the ground, he launched his attack toward the intrusive racket. His red head and wattle looking for all the world like a bullet, he aimed himself for the shins of the children.

Lucy spotted him first and squealed in fright, then doubled her speed as she ran to her aunt. Charles froze where he was, sure he would get flogged within an inch of his life, but unable to move. Nola picked up a stick and ran toward the turkey, brandishing it and shooing at the bird as she went. Tom stopped and looked at this new adversary, then finding himself outnumbered when Lucinda turned toward him also flapping her apron, he turned and, with the utmost dignity and disdain, strutted back around the house and flew up into the walnut tree to resume his watchful vigilance.

Laughing at the sight of his mother and sister-in-law preparing to do battle with a turkey, John came down the yard, swooped up both children, and carried them to their mother.

"I vow, Ma, if that wasn't the funniest sight I ever seen," he said, laughing. "You and Nola gangin' up on old Tom. It's a good thing he knows enough to quit when he's ahead. I've told you children not to run when he does that. If you'll just stand still, he'll leave you alone."

"The only thing that keeps that old turkey out of my pot is he's too mean and tough to make a decent meal," declared Lucinda. "If he gets after these children one more time, though, I'm goin' to wring that scrawny red neck of his.

"Howdy, Nola," she continued. "You're shore a sight for sore eyes. How long has it been since you visited? Must be a month or more. Did you bring the children?"

"No, Mrs. McGinty, I left them at home with their grandma. I just wanted to look in on Martha and see how she's doing." Nola smiled.

Lucinda looked toward the porch where Martha was sitting with the children, one on each side of her, encircled by her arms. "I sure am worried about her, Nola," she said quietly. "It don't seem like anything Doc Hall does for her helps. She's so patient and sweet. She never complains, and I have to insist on doin' for her. She never asks for anything for herself, just for the children. Lord knows I'd do for her just like I would for my own girls if she'd just let me."

Nola laid her hand on Lucinda's arm and said softly, "I know, Mother McGinty. You've been an angel to her. I tried to talk her into coming home with me so we could take care of her for a while, but she says this is her home and she doesn't want to leave it. I just don't know what any of us can do anymore."

"Well, we can pray," Lucinda said shortly. "That's all that's left, I'm afraid." Impulsively she embraced Nola and said gruffly, "It makes me feel good to hear you call me 'Mother McGinty' again, Nola. I miss you. Enough of this talk though. When John told me he was goin' after you, I put a pound cake in the oven and made some of my fried chicken I know you're fond of. It won't take me but a few minutes to stir up some biscuits and have dinner on the table. You visit with Martha and the children. I'll manage in the kitchen."

Martha was right about the twins monopolizing the attention. They chattered continuously, basking in the undivided attention of three adults. Nola found herself spending the rest of the afternoon playing with them and telling them stories. Martha watched quietly from the lounge that John had pulled out on the porch for her after lunch, smiling and enjoying the stories as much as the children.

The lengthening shadows brought John to stand quietly by Martha and signal to Nola that he was ready to take her home. Reluctantly, she told the children good-bye, hugging each of them fiercely as she promised to return soon and bring Jake and Samantha.

When she turned to tell Martha good-bye, she looked at her sternly and said, "Now, I mixed up some boneset and burdock for you to take. I told Mrs. McGinty about the dose, and I want you to promise me you'll take it like she says. Papa wrote in his book that the boneset was a good tonic and the burdock root is good for cleansing the blood. I'll be back in a day or two to see if it helps. If it does, I'll go to the woods and find some more."

"I promise I will, Nola," Martha said quietly. "And I want you to promise you'll remember what we talked about."

"I remember," Nola said quietly as they embraced each other. "Good-bye for now, Sister. Take care, and you remember what I said."

John was so encouraged by her visit that Nola did not have the heart to voice her fears to him. He chatted on about the children and his crops as they rode across the mountain, not noticing Nola's preoccupation with her thoughts. As he changed horses, harnessing his own back to the buggy, he said, "I think your visit did Martha a world of good, Nola. She seemed better than she has in a long time. I know the tonic will help her, too."

"I hope so, John," she answered quietly. "I'll come in a day or so and check on her. You be careful going home. It's going to be dark by the time you get there."

"Oh, don't worry about me," he laughed. "This old mare knows the way home. I might just take me a little nap on the way. Good-bye, Nola, and thank you."

Resolutely, Nola went about preparing the evening meal with Ellen, sharing her concerns as they worked. Finally, after the children were in bed and they were all talked out, they clung to each other, sharing their tears as they had so many other times.

EIGHTEEN

Nola and Ellen made countless trips over the mountain between the two homesteads during the next two months. They had to watch helplessly as Martha steadily weakened. Nothing seemed to stem the tide of the inevitable.

Leaving Martha became harder and harder for them, and finally, after one particularly painful farewell, Ellen told Nola, "When we get home, I'm goin' to pack me a bag and tomorrow I'm goin' back to Martha's and stay with her till this is over."

She held up her hand as Nola started to protest. "Now, I know what you're goin' to say, Nola, but my mind is made up. The Lord has always given me the strength to do what I need to do, and I know that my place is with Martha now. I know that John and Lucinda are both good to her, but there are things a mother can do and say that nobody else can. I'm goin' to leave first thing in the mornin'."

Nola knew her mother would not be dissuaded, so she did not protest. When Ellen had her clothes packed the next morning, she hitched up the buggy and they began their trip. Ellen clutched her worn Bible in her hands as they rode in silence back to Martha.

When they arrived, Ellen went straight to Martha's bedside and took her hand. Martha looked up at her mother and said, "I knew you'd be back, Mama. You're goin' to stay with me now, aren't you?"

"Of course I am," Ellen replied calmly. "Now, I'm goin' to wash your face and brush your hair just like I did when you were little. Everything will be all right now. Mama's with you."

John told Nola later, "Everything was all right with Martha after Mother Johnston came to stay. I don't know what they talked about, but she never left Martha's side except to eat a little and rest for a while. I do know she read to Martha from the Bible a lot. Toward the end, when

Martha didn't wake up anymore, she just sat and held her hand. She was holding it when Martha died."

They buried Martha on a warm October afternoon. The clear sky was blue, and Nola thought that she had never seen such a beautiful day. Only the raw earth of the grave marred the scene, until a stray breeze covered the ugly scar with a blanket of fall colors as the leaves rained down from the trees.

As they drove back home that afternoon, Ellen told Nola, "I prayed that I would never have to bury another one of my babies, but it wasn't God's plan for me to be spared this sorrow. Every child makes their own place in a mother's heart, and when one is gone, that place can never be filled again. I have two empty places now. First Tildy and now Martha, but there's an emptiness that Will's death left that has made me feel like half my strength was taken from me when he died. I had him to comfort and help me when Tildy died, but now he's gone, too. I feel like an old, useless piece of plunder, with no purpose in life."

Nola was dismayed by her mother's words. "Oh, Mama, you have a purpose. You have the rest of your children. Where would we be without you? We'd be just like ships with no anchor if we didn't have you. You know your place in our hearts is just as important to us as our place is to you. We all depend on you, just like Martha depended on you right up to the end. You keep us on the right paths. I don't know how I would have made it these past months without you. Think of all your grandchildren that look to you, especially Lucy and Charles now. Martha made me promise her that I wouldn't let them forget her and that I would tell them stories about her so that they'd know what she was like. You will have to help me with this. I can tell them about things that a sister knows, but only you can tell them things that a mother knows. Like what she looked like when she was a baby, and how you felt the first time you held her, and the little girl things she did that made her so special to you. Most of all, though, how much you loved her."

"You're right, of course," Ellen sighed. "I reckon I've still got a lot to be thankful for. I'd better stop feelin' sorry for myself and get on with the business of livin'. We'll have to bring Lucy and Charles home with us for a few days as soon as things settle down and John can spare them. I know they will be what he's goin' to live for now. Maybe I'll even make up a foolish rhyme or two for them like I used to do for you children. I can even show them the book you girls fixed for me that Christmas with all of my poems and stories in it. I haven't looked at it in a long time. Well, get this old horse to movin'. You know David will want a good meal before he starts back to school, and that Joseph was born hungry. Maybe Willie and Nancy will come by on their way home, too. You know it won't take much persuadin' to get Willie to put his feet under his ma's table. Jake, you and Samantha pay attention now, I want to tell you a story about your Aunt Martha and your mama and Uncle Willie when they was about your age. It happened this a-way. . . . "

They made their slow way back across the mountain, with Nola driving the buggy and Ellen sitting beside her with a grandchild on each side, snuggled in the warm circle of her arms.

The October blue of the sky deepened as the sun began to dip behind the mountains, casting an aura of color through the reds and golds of the fall leaves on the mountainside. The sound of Ellen's voice mingled with the rustle of the leaves in the path, until everything blended together like the sound of wings ascending to the heavens.

NINETEEN

Trrue to her promise, Nola kept in close touch with Martha's children, inviting them to spend weekends with them and seizing every opportunity to keep their mother's memory alive. Ellen fell into her role of storyteller and the act of recalling happier times when her children were little seemed to give her a measure of comfort also. She would tell the four children stories about their grandfather and their mothers as long as they would sit still for them. When their attention wandered, she sent them off to play.

Martha had been dead for almost a year, and the visits to their grandmother's had become a natural part of the children's lives, when John brought them over the ridge on a Saturday morning in late August. He smiled at their eagerness as they piled out of the buggy and ran to find Samantha and Jake.

Ellen came out on the big broad porch and motioned John to come in. He tied the horse to the rail and went slowly under the rose arbor and up the path to the house.

"I've got a fresh pitcher of cold buttermilk that I just brought from the springhouse," Ellen told him. "Set for a while and cool off."

"I thank you, Mother Johnston. It will taste good today. Can't remember when we've had a hotter August. Look at them young'uns go. You'd think they hadn't seen each other in a month. They shore love to come, and I'm obliged to you and Nola for all you do for them. It's hard for them without a mother." He sighed. "Ma does a good job and Lord knows Pearl dotes on 'em, but it jest ain't the same. I know you keep Martha's memory alive for 'em, and I'm grateful."

"It helps me just as much as it helps them, John," Ellen replied. "I look at Lucy and see Martha as she was at her age. There's somethin' about the eyes of a child. If you look deep enough, you can see generations in 'em.

Sometimes somethin' Samantha does puts me in mind of my mother so much that I catch my breath. Same way with David. Some of his ways is so much like Will's that it hurts me to watch him sometimes. And then there's Willie, who's always been his own special person. I look into them black chinquapin eyes of his, and it's just like lookin' back into his childhood. I can still see that mischievous little boy lookin' out at me through his man eyes. Same way, I look at his little Thomas when he's cuttin' a rusty and I recall all of Willie's antics when he was little. I tell you, John, these grandchildren are the sunshine of my life. I reckon that's why the good Lord give 'em to us. Goodness knows, we got to do somethin' to brighten up all the shadows we've had to endure." She shifted in her chair, suddenly aware of how long she had been going on. "Oh well, you'll have to excuse an old woman. Sometimes I get to carryin' on and I forget myself."

John reached over and squeezed his mother-in-law's hand. "One of the special blessin's I got when I married Martha was havin' you and Will become part of my family," he said quietly. He straightened as if embarrassed by his display of affection. He looked around for his children. "Well, I got to go now. I'll pick these wild Indians up after meetin' Sunday, if you can stand 'em that long."

"John, why don't you come on home with us for dinner Sunday?" Ellen asked impulsively. "It's been too long since you've eat with us. That is, if it don't pain you too much to be here," she added quickly.

"I think I'd like that," he replied quietly. "I'll see you Sunday."

Ellen watched John as he drove off, thinking how sad and alone he looked. He had always been a big, strapping man, but the weight of his loss had bowed his shoulders, making him appear diminished in size.

Ellen was shaken out of her melancholy mood by the shouts of the children as they ran through the yard shouting, "Grandma, Grandma, are you goin' to tell us a story today?"

"Why, yes, I reckon I am. Now just what sort of tale do you want to hear?" she asked them.

"Tell us about how the deer got his horns," Jake said. "I tried to tell Charles about it, but I always get it mixed up. Besides, he didn't believe me anyhow."

"Well, I reckon you'll have to decide for yourselves if it's true or not," Ellen chuckled. "Anyhow, my ma said the old Indian woman who told it to her shore believed it.

"It come about this way, or so she said. In the old days, the animals was right fond of gettin' up big meetin's and contests of various kinds. They always wanted a prize for the winner, too. On one occasion a prize was offered to the animal with the finest coat. The otter deserved it, but the rabbit, who was always schemin' and cheatin', stole his coat and almost got it for hisself. I tell you this so's you'll understand what a sly sort of animal the rabbit is.

"One day the animals got together and made a large pair of horns to be given to the best runner. The race was to be through a thicket, and the one who made the best time with the horns on his head would get them for keeps. Everybody knew from the first that either the rabbit or the deer would get them, 'cause they was the fastest runners. Most everybody was a'bettin' on the rabbit though, 'cause they considered him the best runner. 'Course you know the rabbit had no tail and had to always travel by jumps, and his friends was afraid the horns would overbalance him and make him fall over in the bushes unless he had somethin' to balance hisself with. So they fixed up a tail for him with a stick and some bird feathers.

"'Now,'" says the rabbit, 'let me look over the ground where I got to run.'

"He took off into the thicket, but he was gone so long that some of the animals got suspicious and went to see what had become of him. They found him a'gnawin' down bushes and cuttin' off the hangin' limbs of trees, makin' a road for hisself clear through to the other side of the swamp. They slipped back, not lettin' the rabbit see 'em, and told the other animals what he was doin'. Pretty soon that old rabbit came out again, ready to start the race. When the animals told him they suspicioned he'd been a'cuttin' a road through the bushes, the rabbit denied it up and down. They sent a delegation into the bushes to see if he was tellin' the truth, and when they come back and said that, sure enough, the rabbit had cut a road clean through the thicket, the chief of the animals got real mad and said to the rabbit, 'Since you are so fond of the business, you may spend the rest of your days gnawin' twigs and bushes.' So to this day, that's what the rabbit has to do.

"The animals wouldn't let the rabbit run a'tall now, so they put the horns on the deer, who run into the worst part of the thicket and made his way to the other side. Then he turned around and come back again a different way in such a fine style that everyone agreed he should have the horns."

"What happened to the rabbit, Grandma?" asked Charles. "Did the animals run him off?"

"Oh, no, they thought what they'd done to him was punishment enough. How-some-ever, he was awful mad at the deer for showin' him up and winnin' them horns, so he plotted how he could get even with him. One day he went out into the woods and pulled a big thick grapevine down and gnawed nearly through it. Then when he knew the deer would come by and see him, he commenced jumpin' up at the vine, until the deer come up and asked him what he was doin'.

"'Don't you see?' says the rabbit. 'I'm so strong that I can bite through that grapevine at one jump.'

"The deer couldn't hardly believe this and wanted to see it done. So the rabbit ran back, made a big jump, and bit through the vine where he had gnawed it before. The deer, when he saw that, said, 'Well, I can do it if you can.'

"So the rabbit stretched a larger grapevine across the trail, but without gnawin' it in the middle. Then the deer run back as he'd seen the rabbit do, made a big jump and struck the gravevine right in the middle, but it only flew back and threw him over on his back. He tried again and again, until he was all cut up and bleedin'.

"'Let me see your teeth,' says the rabbit at last. So the deer showed him his teeth, which were long and sharp, like a wolf's teeth.

"'No wonder you can't do it,' says the rabbit. 'Your teeth are too blunt to bite anything. Let me sharpen them for you like mine. My teeth are so sharp, they're just like a knife.'

"The deer thought that was a fine idea, so the rabbit got a hard rock with rough edges and filed and filed away at the deer's teeth until they were filed away almost to the gums.

"'Now try it,' says the rabbit. So the deer tried again, but this time he couldn't bite at all.

"'Now you've paid for your horns,' said the rabbit as he laughed and started home through the bushes. And ever since then, the deer's teeth are so blunt that he can't chew anything but grass and leaves."

"Oh, Grandma, you're the best storyteller in the world," Lucy exclaimed, throwing her arms around Ellen. "I bet nobody knows as many stories as you do."

"Run along now and play," Ellen said with a smile. "I reckon that's enough stories for one day."

She watched her grandchildren as they scattered across the yard, seeing in them her own children when they were little. She sighed and turned to the doorway, smiling as she went back into the house.

A little later Nola came across Ellen going through her scrap bags, laying out bits and pieces of material.

"I think I'll make up a quilt top for Lucy," she smiled up at Nola. "I was just reminded of how much sunshine these grandchildren of mine have brought into my lives. I think I'll just make up that Sunshine and Shadow pattern like I sent Cassie and Mrs. Perkins. Somehow that just seems to suit Lucy."

TWENTY

John came home with Nola and Ellen after the church meeting on Sunday, but he seemed a bit ill at ease for a time. Martha had always been a buffer between John and Nola. Now he felt awkward and tongue-tied whenever Nola was around. When he married Martha, he put aside his memories of courting Nola. He thought he had been able to put her out of his mind, but now he felt some of the same old feelings when he was near her.

Ellen had prepared a bountiful meal, frying up a large platter of chicken and cooking heaping bowls of potatoes, green beans, stewed corn, and summer squash. Nola sliced a plate of luscious red tomatoes and cucumbers while Ellen quickly patted out a pan of biscuits and stirred up gravy with the drippings from the fried chicken. When they sat down to eat, the children squirmed in anticipation, eyeing the drumsticks and counting to see if there were enough for all of them to have one.

Ellen grinned. "Now, children," she said, "you can just hold your horses for a minute and stop countin' those drumsticks. I found a pullet that had enough legs for all of you. First though, I'd like for John to say the blessin' for us."

The children shouted with laughter at the thought of a four-legged chicken, but, after admonishments from John and Nola, finally settled down for the blessing, squirming in impatience until John's "Amen." Ellen laughed at the sight of four plates extended eagerly in her direction. She beamed as her family enjoyed the food she had prepared for them. When she topped off the meal with generous slices of apple pie, everyone sighed and sat for several minutes, too full and content to move. One by one the children drifted off to various favorite spots on the farm.

John trailed the two boys to the barn at Jake's request for some advice on a harness he was repairing.

"Remember, Jake, this is the Lord's day," Ellen admonished him. "Your grandpa never allowed any farm work on the Sabbath."

"I know, Grandma," Jake replied. "I just want Uncle John to show me how I can get that harness to hold."

Nola smiled as she watched the three cross the yard to the barn, then shook her head sadly.

"Poor Jake. He does miss out on having a father to turn to. I'm grateful that John has the patience and is willing to fill some of that void," she said to Ellen.

"Yes, John is a fine man," Ellen said thoughtfully. "It's a puzzle to me how two men raised in the same family by the same standards can be so different as him and Sam are. It just don't seem fair that Martha was took from him so young. John has so much love in him. I hope he can find him somebody else to fill Martha's place some day. I know he ain't ready yet, but he's a young man and it just goes against nature for him to go through life without a helpmate."

"He's got his ma," Nola said quickly, "and Pearl. She just dotes on them children. They sure don't want for lack of a woman's attention. And, of course, me and you, too. I reckon John is doin' all right."

"That's not what I meant, Nola, and you know it," Ellen told her sharply. "A man needs a wife, and all our good intentions don't warm his bed at night."

"Oh, Mama, there's more to life than that," Nola said.

"I ain't sayin' there's not," Ellen responded. "But I do say it ain't a natural way for a man to live. Nor a woman neither," she muttered under her breath.

"I heard that, Mama," Nola said drily.

Dishes washed, table cleared and food put away in the cupboard and springhouse, Ellen and Nola went to the front porch and settled themselves in their rocking chairs. Nola was staring absently toward the barn when John, having solved Jake's problem with the harness, joined them in companionable silence on the porch steps.

"John, come up here and make yourself comfortable," Ellen urged him. "That step's as hard as a rock."

"I'm afraid if I get too comfortable, I'll fall asleep," he said, laughing. "I tell you, Mother Johnston, that was a right fine meal. Don't know when I've enjoyed your good cookin' any more. It's a good thing I don't eat that way every noon meal. I sure wouldn't get much work done if I did."

They sat there quietly for a time, then Ellen said, "Nola, why don't you show John them fancy hot pepper plants Willie brought us. I never saw anything grow like they have. We'll have enough hot pepper to give the whole cove indigestion the way they're growin'."

"I doubt if John is interested in looking at gardens on his only day of rest," Nola said drily. "He'd probably welcome the chance to sit and rest while he can."

"Well, I reckon I'd be glad to look at them," John said. "I'm always interested in something new. Maybe you'd better give me a few to take to Ma for her chow-chow. My hot pepper didn't do much good this year."

"Well, if you'll remember, Cassie said you had to be bad tempered to get pepper to bear," Ellen laughed. "I reckon that means you're just not ornery enough, John."

"I guess we'd better get you some then, John," smiled Nola. "We all know you're not bad tempered. Wait a minute, and let me get my bonnet. I got blistered picking beans yesterday, and I sure don't need to get burned on top of that."

John waited at the bottom of the steps while Nola went in the house and pulled her blue calico sun bonnet on her head. He gave her a hand as she came down the steps, which she took reluctantly, then dropped quickly as she stepped into the yard. She chattered nervously as they walked around the yard to the garden behind the barn. John listened to her, giving an occasional nod or grunt in reply.

Nola showed John the row of blood red-hot peppers, and he was appropriately impressed with the bunches of pods on each plant. They forgot their nervousness as they talked about their gardens and, eventually, the children.

Nola snipped off a generous bag full for John's mother, and they placed it in the buggy.

"It's been nice bein' here today, Nola," John said quietly. "I didn't realize how much I'd missed comin' here before. I know I come and bring the young'uns, but it's different from settin' down to a family meal like today. Aside from the fine cookin' Mother Johnston does, I guess I've just missed this part of my life that I had with Martha. I'm glad I can feel that I haven't lost our friendship, too. I wouldn't want to lose that. It's always meant a lot to me."

"Why, thank you, John," Nola said. "I reckon it's meant a lot to me, too. Especially the way you try to help Jake. It's been hard for him since his Uncle David went off to school. Joseph don't have anything on his mind these days except that little Davis girl from the other end of the cove. We only see him at mealtimes, and I'm not sure he's with us then in any way except body. His mind and spirit is shore occupied elsewhere." She laughed. "I expect it won't be long till he'll be wanting to get married. He's so young though. I hope he'll wait awhile."

"Anyhow," she continued, "it was nice to have a man to cook for. That is, I mean for Mama. She misses Papa so, it's good for her to have somebody to fuss over. I hope you'll feel welcome to come whenever you want to."

She felt suddenly awkward with John, afraid that she had revealed too much of her feelings to him. She turned hastily toward the house, and as she turned, her foot slipped. If John had not caught her, she would have fallen. He pulled her tightly to him for a moment, and she felt her heart racing wildly as she looked up into his eyes. They stood for a long moment, then she righted herself and pulled away, pushing stray tendrils of dark hair back up under her bonnet.

"My goodness," she said, laughing nervously. "I don't know what got into me. I'm not usually so clumsy. I must have stepped in a hole or something. I'll have to get Jake to fill it in tomorrow."

John only looked at her, his face flushing.

"Nola . . ." he began tentatively. Before he could say anything more, she turned her back and fled toward the safety of the house.

Ellen looked curiously at Nola's flushed face as she and John returned to the porch, but before she could ask any questions, Nola went into the house and the children came trooping out, energized from their rests.

"Papa, Papa, can we go to the creek and wade, please? Please?" Lucy begged. "It's so hot today."

John laughed and put his hand on her head, smoothing her blonde curls down.

"Now, who could refuse such an earnest request like that?" he laughed. "Go on now, and cool yourselves off. In fact, I think I'll just go with you. But soon we have to start for home. I know your grandma is chompin' at the bit for the two of you to get home, and I wouldn't be surprised if your Aunt Pearl isn't settin' there waitin' for you, too."

The group trooped to the creek and were soon splashing and wading through the clear stream. Ellen watched them, smiling and content with her yard full of happy children.

"Are you up there watchin', Will?" she murmured. "Do you remember when it was like this with our own babies? Oh, I do miss you so."

Nola stared out the window, slowly untying the strings of her bonnet and pushing her hair back from her face. She felt hot and strangely unsettled.

When John and the twins packed up to start their ride home, she did not come out but waved at them from the doorway. Ellen looked at her thoughtfully, but kept her silence.

Nola went to the back porch and poured a dipper full of cool water in the wash pan and bathed her face. She patted it dry as she gazed thoughtfully at the ridge that separated the two farms.

TWENTY-ONE

T wo weeks passed before Ellen and Nola saw John again. On a warm, sunny Saturday morning, the sound of a buggy in front of the house brought Nola and Ellen to the front door. At the sight of John getting out of the buggy and tying the horse at the hitching post, Nola's eyes lit up.

"Howdy, Nola, Mother Johnston," he greeted them. "I was goin' into town and wondered if any of you wanted to go along or if you needed anything. Seemed a waste just to go by myself."

His eyes lingered on Nola as he proffered the invitation. Nola dropped her eyes, feeling suddenly shy under his gaze.

"Why, that's mighty thoughtful of you, John," Ellen exclaimed. "As a matter of fact, I stand in need of some sewin' supplies. I'm plumb out of thread. Nola, why don't you go along, and maybe you could find that piece of goods you wanted to make Samantha a new dress. Mrs. Cole told me they had a new shipment of piece goods at McCracken's store."

"Oh, Mama, there's too much to do here for me to go traipsing off. Besides, I'm not dressed to go, and I'm sure John is in a hurry," Nola protested.

"Nothin' here to do that can't wait," Ellen said shortly. "And I reckon John won't mind waitin' for you a minute, will you, John?"

"No, ma'am, I sure won't," John assured her. "I got an early start a'purpose in case you wanted to go. This mare is right swift of foot, so it won't take us no time to make the trip if you're a mind to go. And that new road they've cut makes the trip a sight shorter than it used to be."

"Well, I guess I'd like to go if Mama thinks she can do without me for a while," Nola said. "If you're sure you don't mind waiting for me to change. I'll hurry."

"Done told you I don't," John replied. "While I'm waitin', I'll just water the horse. That way she'll be fresh for the trip."

Nola went to her room and selected a blue print gingham dress with a tiny flower in it. The lace collar framed her face and brought a sparkle to her eyes. Impulsively, she searched out two turquoise combs and put them on each side of her hair, picking up the color of her dress. She took her Sunday shawl from the chest and draped it across her shoulders, then went out to meet John as he returned from the barn.

John made no effort to hide the admiration in his eyes as he gave her a hand up into the buggy. "You look mighty pretty, Nola," he told her quietly. "Them combs sure bring out the sparkle in your eyes."

"Why, thank you, John," she said, ducking her head to hide the blush she felt heating up her face. John took a basket of food from Ellen, then climbed in the buggy and clucked the horse into motion. Ellen stood watching them ride away, a happy smile on her face.

Once they were off the mountain and turned into the hard-packed dirt road going into Waynestown, the trip to town went quickly. They passed several other buggies on the road, and John remarked at how much the area was changing.

"Seems like just yesterday that it took us more'n two whole days to make this trip," he mused. "Things are sure changin'. I'm glad we still live out of town a ways though. I don't think I'd be cut out to live where things are so close and with all them people around me all the time."

"Oh, I think it would be exciting to live in town," Nola protested. "There's always something to do and new people to meet. They say since the railroad is finished that a whole load of people come in every weekend to drink the sulphur water and sit on the porches at the big hotels they've built."

"Beats me how anybody could be content just to set and look at the trees," John laughed, shaking his head in disbelief. "Looks to me like that's sort of sinful, just wastin' your time like that."

They rode on in silence until they reached the outskirts of Waynestown.

"Oh, look, John, the train's just pulling into the station," Nola said excitedly, pointing at the train. "Goodness, look at all the black smoke. It looks like an angry bull sitting there."

"Just look at all the people," John said. "I bet there's fifty or more. That's the most buggies I ever saw in one place. I reckon they're from the hotels, waitin' to pick up folks. There's McCracken's wagon pullin' up to pick up supplies."

"I wonder how all these people make a living here?" Nola mused. "I guess some of them clerk in the stores, and the others must work at the hotels."

"They say the livery stable does a good business," John said, "keepin' all these horses shoed and the buggies and wagons repaired. I heard that they got two blacksmiths goin' full time now."

Before Nola could reply, the engineer blew a loud blast on the train's whistle and started to pull slowly out of the depot. The horses reared and some of the women squealed in alarm. John was hard put to control his frightened horse. Finally, the train made its slow way out of the station. The wagons and buggies began pulling out, taking their reluctant leave. John turned his horse up the hill toward the main street.

Main Street was a hard-packed dirt road, marked with an occasional mud hole. Ducks paddled about in the pools of water, quacking loudly in protest when the buggies and wagons splashed through the holes. John pulled up in front of McCracken's store and helped Nola down.

"I'll get the things Mama needs here at McCracken's, John," Nola said, "and then I reckon the only other thing I need is a harness that Joseph wanted me to get for him."

"I'll get the harness," John volunteered, "if you could just pick up these things for me that Ma wants. She wanted me to pick out a dress length or two for Lucy, too. I'd sure be obliged if you'd do that for me. I ain't much at pickin' out things for girls. Also, Charles is in need of a new shirt or two, if you see anything suitable."

"I'll be glad to, John," Nola answered as he passed her his list. "Maybe we could go over to the springs and eat the food Mama packed when we get through, if you want to."

"That sure sounds good to me," John smiled. "If it's not too late, maybe we could ride up and see that new hotel they've built up there, too. I hope she remembered how much I admire her fried pies when she was packin' that basket. I'll go on and get back as quick as I can."

Nola filled Ellen's list first, then started on John's. When she had everything on it, she turned to the bolts of cloth. A piece of rich brown with tiny yellow flowers in it caught her eye, and she thought it would be perfect with Samantha's red hair. She selected a deep wine print for Lucy, then found a soft blue that she thought would be good for new shirts for the boys. Wistfully, she fingered a piece of grey print with tiny pink flowers in it, thinking how much Ellen would like it. John came in while she was admiring it.

"Don't you want that?" he asked as she returned it to the table.

"I was just thinking about Mama," she answered. "Just thinking it would look pretty with her white hair. I've already spent more than I meant to though. Maybe he'll still have it when I come next time."

"Well, would you let me get it for her then?" John asked. "I'd like to get somethin' to show my appreciation for all she's done to help me with Lucy and Charles."

"I don't know, John. It's right costly," Nola said. "This piece is twenty-five cents a yard. It's nice of you to offer though."

"Just tell the clerk how much you need, Nola," John said firmly. "Have him add it to my bill, and tell him to hurry. I've been thinkin' about them fried pies ever since I left here, and I'm near about starved."

Nola bought the cloth, and they began carrying their purchases out to the buggy. John helped Nola in, then put the packages to the outside of the buggy, forcing her to move over in the middle closer to him.

As they rode down the street, Nola became acutely aware of John's body pressed against hers. As the buggy swayed around the corner and started down the hill toward the depot, John put his arm around her shoulder, holding her back from the tilt of the buggy. Nola felt John's thigh pressed against hers and the weight of his arm as it encircled her shoulders. She was so absorbed in the intensity of her emotions, that she barely noticed the depot and surrounding area as they made their way up the well-traveled road to the springs. She was aware that they had left the incline, but John made no effort to remove his arm from around her shoulders.

"Nola," John said, "we're here."

With a start, she realized the buggy had stopped, and they were in the grassy area surrounding the springs. John stared down into her eyes for a moment, then reluctantly dropped his arm and climbed out of the buggy. He offered his hand up to her, and, wordlessly, she reached out and placed her hand in his. Before she could step down though, he dropped her hand and lifted her easily to the ground. He held her for a long moment, hands encircling her slender waist, then flushing, released her.

Nola turned and busied herself getting the basket of food from the buggy, fumbling and delaying until she could compose herself.

"Here, John," she said brusquely. "Take this cloth and spread it out over there beside the spring. Then we'll open this basket and see what Mama packed for us."

"I hope there's a jug of water in there," John said. "I sure don't hanker to drink any of that sulfur water. They say folks pay a heap of money just to come here and drink it, but I tasted it one time, and I reckon there ain't enough money to pay me to drink it again."

They settled on the grass around the cloth and ate hungrily from the well-filled basket, enjoying the ham and biscuits, still warm beans, and sweet juicy tomatoes that Ellen had included. They topped their meal off with the spicy fried apple pies.

John lay back in the warm fall sunshine, looking up into the clear, deep blue sky and following the mountains' sharp outlines against the horizon. Here and there a bit of color was beginning to appear on the mountainside, promising that cooler weather was not far away. He inhaled the heady odors of the lush green grass he lay in and began to drift into a light sleep.

Nola sat, thinking about the strange feelings she had experienced that morning. She was able to look, unobserved, at John as he lay dozing in the warm sunshine.

Was it because he reminds me of Sam? she wondered. Is that why I felt so excited and strange? But he doesn't look anything like Sam. He's so dark and Sam had that wild, curly red hair. How could I be feeling like this about my sister's husband—my husband's brother?

As if he sensed that she was looking at him, John opened his eyes and stared into hers. Neither of them said anything but sat locked in a look so intimate that she felt as if his arms were around her again and his body pressed against hers.

"Nola," John began huskily, "what is it? You're lookin' at me like you've never seen me before. Am I such a stranger to you?"

"I feel so strange," she murmured, unable to take her eyes away. "I don't know what's come over me. What's happening to us, John?"

"Nothin' that shouldn't be," John answered her softly. "Maybe you're just beginnin' to feel for me what I've felt for you for a long time. I loved Martha. You know that, but you know, too, that you were my first love. I never made no bones about it. Martha knew it, too, but she knew that when we married, I put all of that behind me. If Martha had lived, I'd a'kept it in the past. But she's gone, and I can't deny anymore that it's always been there."

"Oh, John, how could we think of each other this way? Martha was my sister, and I'm married to your brother. It's wrong, and we both know it," Nola protested weakly.

"Nola, I know Sam divorced you," he said quietly. "He wrote Pearl all about it. He wrote her that he was fixin' to marry again. I never said anything to you because you've never mentioned it to me, and I knew it was still causin' you pain. But you're free of Sam. You don't owe him any loyalty anymore. What's to stand between me and you findin' happiness with each other? How could it be wrong?"

The mention of Sam's name was like a dash of cold water in Nola's face, and she moved away from John, trying to regain her composure.

"Oh, I'm so confused, John," she cried out. "Everything I've ever believed in tells me that you marry for life, till one of you dies. You're free, but I don't think I can ever be free of Sam, no matter how many divorce papers he sends me or how many other women he marries." She paused and looked away from John. "I'm so ashamed. I wonder how many other people know he divorced me."

John moved to her side and took her hands in his. "Don't do this to us, Nola," he said. "Why should you condemn yourself to a life without love just because of Sam's mistakes? Let him go. Let him have his life in Florida or wherever he wants to go. Don't deny your need to have a home and a husband who loves you. Let me be that man, Nola. Marry me. Marry me like you should have done years ago."

"I don't know, John. I just don't know what to do," she said miserably. "My heart wants to say yes, but there's something inside me that says it's wrong."

"Don't listen to that," he said. "Listen to your heart. Listen to mine."

He took her hand and placed it on his chest, and she could feel his heart beating as strongly and as wildly as her own was. Suddenly, nothing else mattered, and she was in his arms, returning his kisses with a passion that matched his. He caressed her and pressed kiss after kiss on her throat until she felt she would faint with the heat of her emotions. She lay back in his arms, surrendering herself to the sensuality of the moment, closing her eyes and feeling his hands on her body. Then, just when she thought that everything else was blotted out of the world except the two of them, she saw Sam's face smiling mockingly at her. She gasped and pulled away from John, thrusting him from her with a strength that surprised both of them.

"Nola, what is it? What happened?" he asked her in surprise.

"I—I don't know. I mean, we mustn't," she stammered. "What—what if someone saw us?"

"I'm sorry," he muttered. "I just let myself get carried away. I meant no disrespect to you, you know that. It's just that I love you so much. I've always loved you."

"Oh, John, it's me who's sorry," she cried out in dismay. "I should have stopped this before it went this far. You'll just have to give me some time. Time to sort things out in my mind. Please, could we go back home now? I've just got to get my head straight before things go too far. I hurt you enough the first time, and I could never live with myself if I ever hurt you again. You are the kindest, most gentle man I've ever known, and the last thing on earth I want to do is to hurt you again."

"The only way you'll hurt me is to turn your back on me," he said huskily. "I couldn't stand it if you did that, Nola."

"Dear, sweet John," she murmured.

When he would have taken her in his arms again, she hastily moved away from him and began gathering up the picnic things and packing them in the basket. Silently, John began folding up the cloth and putting things in the buggy. Nola pushed everything over into the middle of the seat so that they were between them, then before John could help her, she climbed into the buggy.

John got in, then reached over and squeezed her hand. After a moment, he dropped it and snapped the reins across the horse's back, turning her toward town.

There was little conversation between them on the ride home. Both were absorbed in their own thoughts. John kept wondering what Nola was thinking, and she kept listening to the kaleidoscope of thoughts that kept tumbling over and over in her mind.

She kept hearing a passage from the Gospel of Matthew that Preacher Abernathy had quoted one time. She could hear him again now as he declared in his authoritative voice, "It says right here in the book of Matthew, 'That whosoever shall put away his wife, saving for the cause of fornication, causeth her to commit adultery; and whosoever shall marry her that is divorced committeth adultery.'" The remarks about divorce made around the quilting frames and the social gatherings also ran through her mind, and the contempt and scorn with which divorced women and their children were treated in the community rose up to mock her.

When they finally pulled up in front of Nola's home, she would have fled without further conversation, but John would have none of that. As she moved to leave the buggy, he reached out and grabbed her arm.

"Nola, what I said to you today, I meant with all my heart," he said earnestly. "I want an answer from you, and I want it soon. We've wasted too much time as it is, and I don't mean to waste any more worryin' about Sam or what anybody else thinks about this. I stepped aside for Sam before, but I'll not do it again. I want you, and I think you want me just as strong. Don't take too long."

"I won't, John," she said quietly. "I promise you, when I see you again, I'll have an answer for you. I tell you right now, though, I've got to do a lot of praying over this decision."

"I pray it's the right one, Nola. I love you," he declared.

Nola watched the buggy drive out of sight. Sighing, she picked up the basket and her parcels and started up the path.

Ellen watched her as she approached the porch, wondering what could have happened to make her look so forlorn. When Nola saw Ellen watching her, she burst into tears.

"What on earth is the matter?" Ellen asked.

"Oh, Mama, John asked me to marry him," Nola sobbed.

"Well, what on earth are you cryin' about, then?" Ellen asked, bewildered. "I should think that would make you happy, not sad."

"You don't understand," Nola said. "How can I marry him and go against the teachings of the Bible? How can I live in this community and go against people's moral values, their feelings about divorce? Oh, Mama, I don't know what to do."

"Do what your heart tells you," Ellen said sharply. "You're the only one that knows what's right for you. Stop worryin' about what everybody's goin' to say, and do what you know is right."

"That's just the trouble," Nola sighed. "I *don't know* what is right or wrong anymore. I'm so confused. I feel like I'm being pulled in ten different directions."

"Listen, Nola," Ellen said. "There's just one question you've got to ask yourself, and that is, Can you put Sam aside and be a real wife to John? That's all you have to decide. Everything else is unimportant."

"You're right, Mama," Nola said. "And that's the question I've asked myself over and over. Can I put Sam aside?"

"Pray, Nola," Ellen said quietly. "Just put it in God's hands."

TWENTY-TWO

Nola slept fitfully that night. John's pleas kept echoing in her mind, repeating themselves over and over until she finally drifted off into a restless sleep. She began to dream.

She dreamed she was in an alien land and couldn't find her way home. She looked around her and saw that she was in the midst of a wasteland of salt. It was a drab, colorless land from the barren earth to the dull, grey sky. The land was monotonous, an unending flat skyline.

She was sitting in the middle of this wasteland, rocking endlessly in her mother's old cane bottomed rocking chair. There seemed to be no purpose for her rocking. No child was in her arms, but she rocked on with a frightening and constant speed.

"Why am I here?" she cried out. "How did I get here? Where is my family? My children? What has happened to me?"

"Nola! Nola!" a voice called to her.

She looked all around, but saw no one.

"Who is it?" she asked. "Who is calling me? Where are you? Come closer, so I can see you."

"I am here," came the reply. "Look deep inside yourself, and you will see who I am."

She stood up and thrust the chair from her, turning in every direction. Still, she could see no one.

"Who are you?" she cried again. "How can I look inside myself and find you? Let me out of this place! I want to go home."

"You can't go home until you answer the question," the voice said. "You have to find out for yourself. You are the one who has to decide."

Nola tried to run, but she was rooted to the place where she stood. The sand became deeper and deeper. The harder she tried to run, the more she mired down in the sand.

"Help me, someone!" she cried. "Help me out of this terrible place."

"No one can help you," came the answer.

Nola agonized over her situation. Never to be united with her loved ones again, to exist in a void, the hell of monotony and loneliness never ending. Suddenly she saw herself as if she were a stranger looking on the scene. She saw years of isolation and loneliness, cut off from everyone and everything that was dear to her.

"Oh God," she cried out in desperation, "Let me go and be with my people. I can't endure this isolation. I want to hold my children again and see my mother again. Tell me how to get out of here."

Her words echoed back hollowly. She raised her head, and in the distance she saw the pleading arms of her family reaching for her, clutching at the empty air. Nola reached for them, but then she found herself chained to the chair. She felt herself beginning to slip away, fading into the wasteland.

Suddenly a figure emerged from the mass of entreating arms, and a young man stood tall and distinct from the rest. Only his face was concealed from her, hidden in a smoky mist.

"Nola, don't you know me?" he asked. "Can't you look at me and recognize who I am?"

Nola slowly turned her face toward the figure and raised her head, looking him full in the face. Suddenly the mist dissipated, and she knew at last who he was.

"Yes," she whispered. "Oh yes, I do know."

"And who am I?"

"You are Sam," she said. "You are my husband."

Then she slumped over, and the salt of her tears mingled with the salt of the ground and ran like a river through the wasteland.

The sky was split with a bolt of lightning, and where there was wasteland and drabness, there was now green grass and flowers. Lush, green trees dotted the landscape, and mountains rose majestically against the blue of the sky. Nola felt herself shedding the encumbrances of the wasteland. A great weight lifted from her heart as she walked into the outstretched arms of her husband and her loved ones.

Nola turned in her sleep and sighed. A single tear rolled down her cheek and was absorbed by the pillow that had already soaked up so many of her tears.

When she woke the next morning, she remembered her dream as vividly as if she had really lived it. She knelt by her bed and prayed before she began to dress.

"Father," she prayed, "now I know what I must do. I was so confused and lost, but you have led me in the path that I should take. You gave me a sign, so that I know thy will for me. Amen."

Nola rose and went about her morning chores, secure in the knowledge that the question had been resolved. Now she must make John understand.

TWENTY-THREE

Nola got up early the next morning and, before she lost her resolve, she wrote Ellen a short note telling her mother that she had gone to John's. She hitched up the buggy and rode over the mountain trail to the McGinty farm. She rehearsed what she would say to John over and over as she rode, but when she came in sight of the house, everything she had thought out so carefully seemed cold and insufficient.

Nola stopped at the barn and tied the horse to the rail. She got out of the buggy and started for the footbridge, then heard John turning the cows out of the barn. She turned back and met him as he came out.

John's face lit up as he saw Nola, but the light went out of his eyes when he saw her sober expression.

"John," she said hesitantly, "could we talk for a few minutes?"

"I've got a feelin' I ain't a'gonna like what you've come to say to me," he said sadly.

"John, please, just hear me out," she begged. "This is just as painful for me as it is for you. I want you to know I have searched my soul harder and longer than I ever have about anything in my life. It would be so easy to just say yes to you. It would solve all of my problems. You would be a wonderful father to my children, and I know you'd be a wonderful husband to me. I know you'd take care of us and that I'd never have to worry about anything again.

"The only thing wrong with this is it wouldn't be fair to you. Wait, just hear me out," she said hastily as he started to protest. "The truth is, John, I could never give myself fully to you as I did to Sam. I know this now. Sam would always be there between us, because in my heart I know he will always be my husband and I will be his wife. You deserve better than I could give you, and someday you'll find someone who will be the kind of wife you deserve. Someone who will love you unconditionally, the way Martha did."

"Oh, Nola," he said brokenly, "don't do this to us. Don't fool yourself that Sam is ever comin' back to you. You know he ain't. I love you, Nola. I know you don't love me as much as I love you, but I can love you enough for both of us. Just give me a chance to show you."

"Please, John," she cried. "Won't you just try and understand that I have to do this because I do love you? A part of me always has, and a part of me always will. But you deserve a whole woman, not just somebody who can only give you half a heart. Can't you understand that I still feel married to Sam? I know you could live with that now, but eventually you'd resent it. It just wouldn't be right for me to marry you. I'm so sorry I've hurt you again. I'd give anything in this world to take that hurt away."

"Is this your final word?" he asked hoarsely. "Are you sure you don't want to give this more thought? I'll not ask you again."

"Yes, John, I'm sure," she answered sadly. "I'm sorry that I've hurt you. I should never have given you false hope. Can you understand that I truly wanted to believe we could be happy together? Deep down, though, something told me it wouldn't work, and I should have listened to that voice instead of to my physical nature. I'm sorry, and I'm ashamed of myself for not facing the truth earlier."

John's shoulders slumped, and he picked up his milk buckets and started to walk away. He turned back and looked at Nola, knowing this would be the last time they ever spoke of this.

"You've laid yourself out a hard path to follow, Nola," he said bitterly. "You're goin' to have a lot of empty hours to fill one of these days. Jake and Samantha will be grown and out on their own before many more years, and you're gonna end up with nothin' but some old memories to keep you company and some of them ain't too wonderful.

"I don't want you to waste any time feelin' sorry for me though, 'cause I aim to get over this. I'm gonna take care of my children and go on about my business. If there is somebody for me to marry and make a life with, then I guess in God's own good time I'll find her. If not, then I'll live by myself. Don't worry about my hurt. It'll go away in time."

John crossed the footbridge into the yard. He went on up the path and into the kitchen without looking back.

Nola stood for a long minute looking at John's cold back. Then she got back in her buggy and turned the horse up the mountain trail. The tears that ran down her face fell unheeded on the reins she gripped tightly in her hands.

"Oh, dear God!" she cried out. "Did I do the right thing? How could I have done anything else? Sam, Sam, will I never be able to forget you?"

No answer came for Nola. The mountains absorbed her words and gave back only silence.

John went woodenly about his work that day. Lucy and Charles looked at the stony face of their father when he came in at suppertime, and their excited greetings died on their lips.

"Tell your Aunt Pearl I won't be home tonight," he said abruptly. "I'm goin' to take the dogs and go up the mountain. Tell her she's not to worry. I'll be home in plenty of time to do the milkin' in the mornin'."

John picked up his gun, whistled the hounds around him, and set off up the mountain trail. He climbed without resting until he reached the crest of the mountain. Then he turned the dogs loose to start their hunt. Perspiration was pouring down his face, and his clothes were soaked from the swift climb.

He sat slumped against the trunk of an oak for a while, then rose and began to load the double-barreled shotgun he had brought with him. He made out the silhouette of a poplar tree several hundred yards away and began firing into the trunk. He fired both barrels, then reloaded and shot again. He continued until he ran out of shells. Then, crying out in rage and frustration, he took a fallen limb and began hitting the tree until only a shred of the limb remained. Then he pounded the tree with his fists until the pain stopped him.

He cried out in frustration to a God who denied him the woman he loved, and he shook his fists at the heavens shouting, "Damn you, Sam! Twice you've stole her from me."

Finally he sank to the ground and slept, exhausted from his outburst. He was awakened the next morning by the whimpering of his dogs, who looked as spent as he did from their night of running. He picked up his gun, whistled up the dogs, and slowly set out for home.

Pearl took one look at him when he arrived home and quietly began putting his breakfast on the table from the warming oven where she had saved it.

"I know you don't want to hear this, John, but you're better off without her. She would never have belonged to you. Sam would have always been there between you. Now that she's out of your life, you'll find somebody else. I know you will."

Tiredly he shoved the food from him. Picking up the milking pails, he walked to the barn.

TWENTY-FOUR

Nola and Ellen talked far into the night about her decision to turn down John's marriage proposal. When they finally went to bed, Nola still did not know what she would do with her life now. She did know that she had cut the ties to John and that option was no longer open to her.

Ellen's parting words to her were "Nola, what you must do now is put your life in the hands of the Lord. He will lead you in the way you have to go. When you can do that, you will find some peace, but until you can let go tryin' to shape your own life and put it in His hands, you're never goin' to have any peace of mind."

On that note, they went to their own rooms, Ellen to rest peacefully, knowing in her wisdom that Nola would eventually find her own path, and Nola to toss and turn all night, waking periodically worrying about her future.

Events of the next day drove all thoughts of personal problems from Nola's mind for a time though, and, although she didn't realize it at the time, gave her time to sort through her feelings and find a new direction for her life.

Nola was in the back yard, shucking corn for a run of pickled beans when she was startled by a rustling in the weeds behind her. Half expecting to see a deer or some other forest animal, she looked up and instead encountered the frightened eyes of a very dirty child.

"Yes?" she asked the girl. "Are you looking for someone?"

The girl shrank back into the bushes and seemed on the verge of flight, then made an obvious effort to gather courage and timidly approached Nola.

"Air ye Miz Johnston?" she asked in a low voice.

"I'm Mrs. Johnston's daughter," Nola replied. "Why are you looking for my mother?"

121

"I hear tell she might know somethin' about the whar-abouts of my sister, Cassie Martin," the girl replied. "If'n ye could tell me whar she is, I'd be much obliged."

Startled by the request, Nola looked more closely at the child. She appeared to be in her early teens, thin almost to the point of emaciation and extremely dirty. It was hard to tell what color her hair was, but there was no mistaking the color of her bright blue eyes.

"My heavens!" Nola exclaimed. "Come here, child, and I'll call my mother."

Nola drew the girl across the yard and to the back porch, keeping a wary eye on her, fearful that she might bolt any minute. When she reached the back stoop, Nola called out to Ellen.

"Mama, come here, please. There's someone to see you."

Ellen came through the back door, expecting to see one of the neighbors. She stopped abruptly at the sight of the girl.

"My stars," she said, "who are you, child? What brings you to us?"

"I air hafsister to Cassie Martin," the girl answered, "and my name be Anne Marie Martin. Most calls me Annie, though. I hear'n tell you might tell me whar Cassie is. I'd be might' obliged to ye, if'n ye could."

"Why are you lookin' for her after all these years?" Ellen asked sharply. "Who sent you here?"

"Nobody sent me. I come on my own," the girl replied. "And as to why I come, well, my ma told me if somethin' happened to her, I was to come here to the Johnston place and ask for Cassie. My ma died awhile back, and I figgered hit was time for me to find her. If ye'll tell her I'm here, I'd count hit a favor."

"Cassie isn't here," Ellen said. "She lives a good far piece away from here in another state. What do you want from her?"

The girl's face crumpled, and her shoulders slumped. She sat down abruptly on the stoop. The news deflated her as surely as letting the air out of a balloon.

"Gone? She's gone?" she asked confused. "I never thought on that. Jest s'posed she'd be here like Ma said."

Observing the effect the news had on the girl, Ellen spoke more kindly to her.

"Perhaps if you'd tell us why you're lookin' for her, we could help you."

"I jest didn't know what else to do," the girl mumbled. "He was after me harder ever day since Ma died, and I knowed I'd have to go. I didn't know what else to do," she repeated.

"Who was after you?" Nola asked sharply. "Was it your father? Was he trying to do to you what he did to Cassie?"

"Yes'm, it was Pa," she said. "After Cassie run away, Ma swore she'd kill him if he touched me. He let on like he wasn't a'skeered of her, but he never had the nerve to test her. Then after she died, he set in on me."

"You poor child," Ellen said. "Don't worry. We'll help you. You will not have to go back to that man. How did your mother know where Cassie was? I never knew that she made any effort to find her."

"First time Pa went huntin' after Cassie left, Ma come to the settlement a'lookin' for her," Anne Marie said. "When she found out whar she was, she figgered she'd be better off if she just let her be. She heered tell you was good folks. When she took sick with the summer fevers, she told me whar Cassie was. She said if'n she didn't make it, I was to come and find her, quick as I could."

"Well, you didn't find Cassie, but you found us," Ellen said briskly. "Come on in, and I'll fix you somethin' to eat. You look like you're half starved."

"I reckon I could eat a bite," Anne Marie said weakly. "But first they's somebody else ye better see."

Rising, she walked back to the barn where Nola had first seen her and beckoned toward the woods. Two ragged children appeared and walked uncertainly toward her. Taking them by the hands, she led them to the porch where Nola and Ellen were staring in amazement. As soon as they came to the edge of the porch, they pulled back and tried to hide behind their sister.

"This here's Glen and George," Anne Marie said. "I had to bring 'em with me. I promised Ma. 'Sides, they wasn't nobody to look after 'em when I left. Step out here now, boys, and make yore howdys," she urged them.

First one, then the other, dirty face appeared and grinned shyly at the two startled women.

"They're twins," Anne Marie explained proudly. "Glen here, he's the oldest by about five minutes, but George, he's jest a tad bigger."

"Well, my goodness," Ellen exclaimed. "Come on here and wash up, and I'll see what I can find to eat. Nola, show them where the wash pan is."

The three children followed Nola to the back porch where she poured water in the pan with the gourd dipper hanging beside it. They washed obediently and dried their hands on the towel Nola handed them.

Ellen had laid out cold ham and biscuits and baked sweet potatoes. She sliced tomatoes and cucumbers and poured glasses of sweet milk. The children's eyes brightened at the sight of the food, and they quickly began eating. Ellen and Nola looked at each other, remembering the time Cassie had also eaten with the same gusto. They didn't question them any further until they were finished with their meal. When they had finally had their fill, Anne Marie looked up in gratitude.

"We thank ye, ma'am, for them good vittles," she said. "I reckon we was all a mite hungry."

"'Pears you were," Ellen said drily. "Now, I've been thinkin' while you were fillin' your stomachs, and it seems to me, the best thing for you to do is stay here with us until we can get in touch with Cassie. It may take awhile for us to hear from her, but you'll be safe and well fed until she can come."

"I reckon we'd be much obliged to ye," Anne Marie said. "That is, if we wouldn't be puttin' ye out none. We'd make our own way and try not to be no trouble to ye."

Nola wrote to Cassie that same day and sent Joseph into town to mail the letter the next morning. Ellen tried to bed the twins in David's old room, but they insisted on sleeping in the room with their sister. When she saw how lost and frightened they looked, she fixed them a pallet in the room with Anne Marie. When Nola checked on them before going to bed, all three were sleeping soundly in the bed, with Anne Marie in the middle and a twin snuggled up on each side of her.

Almost four weeks passed before Nola heard from Cassie. She wrote:

> Dear Nola,
>
> Your letter came today. I was so surprised to get news from my family after all this time. I reckon I'd tried to put them out of my mind. It saddened me to know my ma is dead. It eases my hurt some to know my ma cared enough to come see about me. I just reckoned she forgot about me.
>
> Joshua says of course we'll take them in. I'll come for them soon's I'm able. We got us a new baby boy. He give me a hard time when he was born, and I ain't got my strength back yet. If you'll just take care of them until I come, I'll be ever so grateful.
>
> Thank you, dear friends, for all your help.
>
> Love,
> Cassie

"Well, that decides it," Nola exclaimed. "I'm going to take them to Cassie myself. You know how hard it would be for her to bring a new baby with her, and anyhow, I've been turning the idea over in my mind that I'd like to get away from here for a while. This is a perfect reason for me to go. That is, if you don't mind me going, Mama."

"I think it's a good idea," Ellen said firmly. "Jake and Samantha are big enough to help look after things here, and I think the change will be good for you. Maybe a little distance will help you decide what to do with yourself."

"Mama, I can always count on you," Nola said. "I'll start packing and as soon as Joseph can go into town and check on the train schedules, we'll go. I know it'll be an unexpected expense, but I've still got some money put back from the sale of the farm."

She turned to the children, who were listening with wide-eyed anxiety.

"Well, what do you say, children, are you ready to take a ride with me?" she asked gaily.

"What do hit look like?" Anne Marie asked fearfully. "I don't reckon I ever seen one of them trains. Air it anything like Pa's wagon?"

"No, nothing like a wagon," Nola laughed. "I can see right now that this is going to be quite an adventure for all of us."

TWENTY-FIVE

T he trip to Cassie's did turn out to be an adventure for Nola. The twins were so excited when they saw the train that they almost exploded. When the big, black engine pulled into the station, they pulled back in fright at first, hiding themselves behind their sister's skirts and peeping out around her in big-eyed wonder. Anne Marie was frightened, too, but held her ground, trying to put on a brave front for the sake of the boys. Once they were all safely on the train, though, they soon overcame their awe and looked around in eager anticipation.

Nola was kept busy answering their questions and trying to keep the twins in their seats. Ellen had found some clothes that David and Joseph had outgrown, and Nola found a dress of Samantha's that Anne Marie could wear that was suitable for traveling.

"I don't want them to look like rag-a-muffins when they get there," Ellen fussed. "It'll be hard enough on them goin' into a strange place without havin' to be embarrassed by their clothes. I found two dresses Cassie left here that will do for a change for Anne Marie until they can do better for her. Poor little young'uns, this'll be a big change for them."

"I know Cassie will make a good home for them, though," Nola said. "From what Anne Marie says, anything will be an improvement over what they've had."

Ellen packed them a generous basket of food to take care of them on their trip, and Anne Marie and Nola were hard put to keep Glen and George out of it until meal times. Sleep was difficult for Nola, but the children seemed able to adapt to their circumstances and slept like puppies, piled up around each other. Nola envied them their total lack of constraint as they slept whenever the need overcame them. She dozed only fitfully, starting awake at every jerk and change in the train's rhythm.

They finally reached their destination two days after they first boarded the train, and it was a red-eyed and weary Nola that strained for the sight of Cassie and Joshua at the station as they pulled in. She almost panicked when she did not spot them right off but sighed with relief at the sight of the unmistakable red hair of her friend.

Anne Marie and the twins were overcome by a sudden fit of shyness when they finally stepped down from the train, awed at the sight of the fine-looking lady who rushed up to greet them. They cowered behind Nola at first, but soon recovered and stepped out to be caught up in an ardent embrace by Cassie. She looked first at one, then the other, shaking her head in disbelief at how much they had grown in the years since she had last seen them.

"You was just babies," she said over and over to the twins. "You was just babies. And you, Anne Marie, wasn't bigger'n a minute, and look at you now, 'most growed up."

Cassie turned to Nola. The two friends stood and drank in the sight of each other for a long moment before they embraced.

"Oh, Nola, at last," Cassie sighed. "I thought this day would never come when I would see you again. Oh Lordy, but you look good!"

"Oh, Cassie," Nola laughed through her tears. "You haven't changed a bit, except to get more beautiful."

The ride to the farm was filled with talk as the three friends talked about all that had happened to each other since Cassie and Joshua had left the mountain cove. When they drove up to the front porch, Anne Marie and the twins were awestruck at the sight of the huge house.

"You live in a castle!" Anne Marie whispered.

Cassie laughed. "I remember how I felt when I first saw it, too. I thought I'd never seen anything so big in all my life. You get used to it though. It seems to shrink a little more with every baby. Come on now, I know you're all wore out. I told Lottie and Belle to have you some supper ready when we get here. We'll eat, then I know you'll want to lie down in a real bed for a change. Nola, you can't know how much we thank you for bringin' them to us."

"Well, I guess I was sort of looking for an excuse to get away for a while myself," Nola said quietly.

"What's wrong?" Cassie asked sharply. "Has somethin' happened?"

"We'll talk later," Nola replied. "There'll be plenty of time."

The next few minutes were taken up with introductions to Cassie and Joshua's children and family. A smiling Belle ushered them into the dining room where she had prepared a table full of food for them. Nola was so tired she barely remembered putting food in her mouth and could not have told anyone what she ate. She felt great relief when she finally lay down on the bed, and she didn't even hear Anne Marie crawl in beside her.

A soft knock woke her the next morning, and she opened her eyes to see Sue Ellen, Cassie's eldest, bringing in fresh towels for them. Nola lay, confused for a moment, thinking it was Cassie, so strong was the girl's resemblance to her mother.

"Sue Ellen, you are the image of your mother when she was young," Nola smiled at her. "How lucky you are to have her red hair. I always envied her. She made the rest of us look drab in comparison."

"Oh, thank you, ma'am," Sue Ellen blushed. "I don't mind the color, but sometimes the curls are an aggravation. It gets so tangled sometimes. It must be nice to have straight hair like yours."

"Well, I guess we're never satisfied, are we?" Nola laughed. "I've heard my Samantha say the same thing. She has red hair and curls, too. She got them from her father though, sure not from me."

"I almost forgot to tell you," Sue Ellen said. "Mama says breakfast is ready whenever you are."

"Thank you. We'll be down in just a few minutes. I didn't realize we had slept so late. I guess I was a lot tireder than I realized."

Nola and Anne Marie rose and dressed quickly, then made their way down the stairs to the dining room. The twins were already seated at the table eating, with Cassie hovering around urging food on them. She looked up as Nola and Anne Marie entered and rushed to embrace them.

"Oh, Nola, I can't believe that you're really here," she said. "I've dreamed of this ever since we moved here, a'havin' you here like this. I wish you'd a'brought your ma and your children. I'd give anything to see them."

"I know what you mean, Cassie. I can't believe I'm here either," Nola replied. "You know Mama would never leave the cove, and I thought it best for Samantha and Jake to stay there and help her. Mama said, 'If the good Lord had a'meant for people to ride on them rails, he'd a' give 'em wheels instead of legs, and I have no intention of ever getting on one of those contraptions.'"

The two friends laughed together, delighted to be with each other again and to share their memories of Ellen.

"Hurry up and set down and eat, so we can start talkin'," Cassie said. "I'm hungry to hear everything that has happened to you. You, too, Anne Marie, I want to know about Ma and everything that's happened."

Tears welled up into Cassie's eyes as she said this, and she turned away and busied herself with filling their plates and seating them at the table.

Glen and George had finally filled their stomachs and came up to Anne Marie, pulling shyly at her dress tail.

"William Taylor said he'd show us where there was some horses when we finished," Glen said. "Can we go? Please, Anne Marie?"

"Well, I don't know," Anne Marie said hesitantly, looking at Cassie. "It's whatever Cassie says, and if you'll promise me you'll behave yourselves and not get into somethin' you ain't supposed to."

"It'll be fine," Cassie smiled. "There's nothing they can get hurt on, and Joshua will be there to see after them."

"Can I go, too, Mama?" Sue Ellen asked. "I helped Belle carry the food in and washed up part of the dishes."

"Go on then," Cassie laughed. "She's more boy than girl," she said, as Sue Ellen tore after the boys.

"Oh, Cassie, your children are so beautiful," Nola said. "I can't believe they're as big as they are. It makes me sad to think I didn't get to see them until they're half grown. I don't know why I should be surprised though. They're about the same age as my Jake and Samantha."

While they ate, Anne Marie told Cassie about their mother's illness and death and her instructions to find Cassie. It was very emotional for both of them, and Nola found herself weeping with them.

"Well, that's enough of this cryin' and carryin' on," Cassie said, finally. "I'm just grateful to find out that Ma did care enough about me to see that I was took care of and that she knew I'd look after you'uns. It's give me a lot of comfort to know she didn't forget about me. From now on, Anne Marie, you ain't goin' to have nothin' to worry about. I'll look after all of you, just like Ma wanted."

The two sisters embraced and smiled tearfully at each other, then the three of them began clearing the table and carrying the dishes to the kitchen. Belle shooed them out, declaring, "I done had more help than I can stand today," and they went back to the living room where they met an eager Sue Ellen, who had come for Anne Marie.

"Come on, Anne Marie," she begged her. "Let's go to the barn. Star has foaled, and she's got the cutest little colt you ever saw. I want to show it to you."

After the two girls left, Cassie and Nola settled down and tried to catch up on all that had happened to them during the years since Cassie left the cove. They talked for two hours, laughing, then crying over all that had transpired in their lives.

"Oh, Cassie," Nola said, "do you remember that barn dance we sneaked out and went to? Papa was so adamant about us going to barn dances unless he and Mama were there. I just knew he'd catch us for sure."

"Yes, and thanks to that mean old Willie, he almost did," Cassie said. "He blackmailed us for a month to keep him from tellin' on us. You'd a'thought your papa would have wondered why me and you got so fond of milkin' all of a sudden, wouldn't you?"

"I can hear Willie yet," Nola giggled. "'I don't know why, Papa, but Nola and Cassie insisted that I let them milk for me tonight. I reckon it's some girl thing they got goin'.' Papa would look at him, then look at us, and just shake his head."

"We wouldn't have done that except for that Sam teasin' you into it," Cassie laughed.

"Of course, you knowing Joshua was going to be there didn't have anything to do with it, did it?" Nola teased her.

"I vowed that some day I'd get even with Willie for the way he used us," Cassie said. "I wish I still lived in the cove so I could fix him up good."

"Don't worry," Nola laughed. "He's paying for his raising ten times over with that oldest boy of his. He keeps old Willie hopping trying to keep him on the straight and narrow. I just sit back and laugh at him when he comes around complaining to me and Mama about his shenanigans."

When they finally stopped talking, Nola felt emotionally drained. Cassie's final question to her, "What will you do now, Nola?" hung between them.

"I don't have it all worked out in my mind yet," Nola said, "but I know I have to do something completely different with my life now. I can't stay on at Mama's like a girl anymore. It's time I found something that's mine. Something that I've made for myself and that belongs to me. John was right. Jake and Samantha will soon be ready to strike out with their own lives, and I can't depend on them to be there forever. I've been thinking about moving into town and starting a boarding house. The town is growing, and I've heard there's a need for a good boarding house where working people can live and get decent food. I don't know yet, but right now that's what I'm thinking about. There's not many things a woman can do to earn a living, other than sewing and cleaning houses, and I don't fancy doing either one of them. You've got to be certified to teach school now, and I can't spare the time nor money to get certification. It seems to me that this is my best course."

"I think it's a fine idea, Nola," Cassie said. "Do you know how you'll get started? Seems to me you'll have to have some money to start out with, to get you a house and get set up."

"Joseph has offered to buy out my share of Papa's place," Nola said quietly. "You know, Papa's will said everything was to be shared equally among us after Mama dies. Joseph is happy to farm the place, and he and the little Davis girl are talking about getting married. That's another reason I need to move out. Three women in one household would just be too many. She and Mama get along fine, so I'm not worried about that. Anyhow, it will be enough to make a down payment on a house and get me started."

"If that's what you want, I'm happy for you, Nola," Cassie said. "Maybe you'll meet somebody someday that'll make you forget about Sam. I hope you will. I don't think you know just what a hard row you've laid out for yourself, not marryin' again. It won't be easy."

"I know," Nola sighed, "but if I'd wanted to marry again, I'd have married John. Lord knows, there's never been a better man. It's just something that I know in my heart would have been wrong, and I just couldn't live with that on my conscience. It wouldn't have been fair to John."

The two friends talked on until Cassie realized with a start that it was almost time for dinner. They rushed to the kitchen and found that Belle had everything under control. Cassie tried to apologize to her for not helping, but Belle would hear none of it.

"My goodness, Miz Perkins, it warn't no trouble to me. I knew you and Miss Nola had lots to talk about. Now you just g'wan 'bout yore business and leave me to finish," she told them. "I'll call you when I'm ready to put it on the table."

Cassie took advantage of the time to show Nola around the house. She could not keep the pride out of her voice as she took her through the rooms. Nola was suitably impressed with everything.

"Who would have ever thought I'd end up in such a fine house?" Cassie sighed. "Sometimes I just have to pinch myself to believe it's true. I'm glad I can share it with my sister and brothers. I wish Ma could have known how well I made out. I know she'd have been proud for me."

Wordlessly, Nola reached to embrace her friend, and they both wiped tears from their eyes. Belle called from the dining room that she was ready for some help, and they went arm and arm down the staircase, giggling like girls again.

TWENTY-SIX

N ola stayed a month with Cassie and her family before she went back home to the mountains. It was a busy time, with many parties and days filled with laughter and conversation between the two friends. All the ladies in Cassie's quilting club wanted to entertain this friend from the mountains whose mother had come to mean so much to them. The most eager of all, though, was Joshua's mother. She plied Nola with questions about Ellen and her quilts.

"You can't know how much your mother has come to mean to me," she told Nola. "Her quilt patterns and her letters to me have opened up a whole new world for me. I would give anything to be able to sit and talk to her in person. I think she must be the wisest lady on the face of this earth. Did you know that she sent me a copy of the poem that she wrote about quilting? I treasure it above anything."

"You have been so kind to me while I've been here," Nola told her. "I can't wait to get home and tell Mama all about the party you had for me and how nice everyone has been to me. I wish I could have persuaded her to come with me, but I don't think anything could pry her away from the mountains. Maybe some day you can come with Cassie for a visit."

Elizabeth had been in her element as she entertained in Nola's honor. "You will not tell me I cannot have a party for Nola," she had told Joshua. "If I have to sell some of my jewelry, I intend to have the grandest party this town has ever seen."

Grand it was, too. For days Elizabeth had Belle and all the girls in the family polishing silver and getting out her finest china and crystal in preparation for the party. They stored furniture in other parts of the house and opened up the living room, dining room, and library into one large party area. She secured a string quartet for musical entertainment and, in deference to Nola's and Cassie's mountain background, a square dance band also. The dancing alternated between elegant waltzes and foot-stomping square dances.

Nola told her mother later that the food was beyond belief. "There was enough food to feed Pharaoh's army," she declared. "And fancy dishes that I had never seen nor heard of before. Belle cooked for two solid days."

Nola had brought a pale blue voile summer dress with her, and with some alterations of the neckline and the addition of a deeper blue sash, it made a very attractive gown. Cassie sent to town for a piece of deep wine satin and made a simple but elegant dress for Anne Marie. Sue Ellen and Cassie had dresses of emerald green that set off their red hair. Elizabeth chose a flowered chiffon in pastel shades of rose.

"This is the most beautiful bunch of women I have ever seen in one place," Joshua said admiringly as they all stood for his inspection before the guests began arriving. "I want a dance reserved for me from each and every one of you."

Nola was dazzled by all of the attention she received that evening. Her dance card was filled all night, and she was complimented and admired by every man she danced with. Anne Marie was too timid to try the waltzes, but she joined in with enthusiasm when the square dances were called.

"Tell me to shut my mouth every once in a while," she told Cassie. "I know I'm a'standin' here with my eyes bugged out and my mouth wide open. I never seen so many fine dressed folks in all my life."

After the party was over that night, they sat for some time talking about all that had happened, reluctant to end the evening. Cassie beamed at Nola and Sue Ellen, so filled with pride that she felt she would burst.

After everyone had gone up to bed, she told Joshua, "I think this was one of the happiest times of my life. Next to when we got married, of course. It sure did my heart good to see how excited and happy your mother was over the party. I am so glad that she liked Nola."

"I think you can take credit for the change in my mother," Joshua said. "Since you came into our family, she's a different person. You can't have forgotten that first night when we came home."

"I was thinkin' about that tonight," Cassie smiled. "Things have changed, haven't they?"

"Yes, and all for the better," Joshua grinned. "Now, if we don't get to sleep, I won't be able to get up in the morning."

"I don't want this night to ever end," Cassie yawned, as she snuggled up against Joshua. "It's just about the best time I ever had."

Joshua smiled at Cassie and smoothed her hair back from her face, noting that she had already gone to sleep.

*   *   *

Eventually, the time came when Nola knew it was time for her to get back home. She declared to Cassie that she would never forget her visit, but she confessed that she was beginning to be homesick for the sight of her mother and children.

Glen and George were perfectly happy in their new home, loving the animals and the farm. They had not even balked too much at Joshua's lessons. He knew that if they were to go to school that winter, they needed much help in catching up to an age group that they wouldn't feel embarrassed to be in. They had come to depend on Anne Marie less and less as the days had passed.

When Nola began making plans to return to the mountains, Anne Marie became quieter and withdrawn. Two days before she was to leave, Nola was awakened by the quiet crying of the girl.

"Anne Marie, what on earth is wrong with you? Are you sick?" she inquired anxiously.

"I reckon I am in a way," Anne Marie snuffled. "I'm jest so sick for the sight of the mountains, sometimes I feel like I could just die. This is a nice place and all, but I just can't hardly stand the thought that I'll have to look at this old flat land from now on. Oh, Nola, I'll miss you, too."

Nola put her arms around the girl and patted her, murmuring comforting words to her.

"Why haven't you said anything, honey?" Nola asked. "The boys seem so happy, and I thought you were having a good time, too."

"I have had a good time," Anne Marie said. "And I've been so happy to find Cassie again, but I jest don't feel right in this place. People talks different from me. I know Sue Ellen don't mean nothin' by it, but she laughs at me sometimes, at some of the things I say. I told her the reason Jeremiah couldn't larn to swim was because they never made him swaller a fish bladder. Everbody knows a boy young'un can't larn to swim if he ain't never swallered a fish bladder, but she jest laughed fit to kill. Said they wasn't nothin' to that, that she knowed lots of boys that had larned and hadn't et no sech a'thang. Called it a 'stition or some sech. I tell ye, Miss Nola, hit hurt my feelin's somethin' awful."

Nola was glad for the darkness that hid her smile. "I'm sure Sue Ellen meant no unkindness to you," she said gently. "She shouldn't have laughed though. People are different and hold different beliefs, but it doesn't necessarily mean that one's beliefs are right and the other's wrong. Now, you go to sleep, honey, and tomorrow you and Cassie and I will talk and see what we can work out."

As they did their chores the next morning, Nola talked to Cassie, explaining Anne Marie's feelings.

"Poor child!" Cassie exclaimed. "I know how she feels, 'cause I can remember how I felt too when people laughed at the way I talked when I first came to live with your folks. I am so sorry that Sue Ellen was so thoughtless. I don't want Anne Marie to be unhappy. What can we do?"

"I've been giving it some thought," Nola answered, "and if it's all right with you and Joshua, why don't you let Anne Marie go back home with me? She would be a great help if I start my boarding house. Samantha and Jake loved having her with us, and I would see to it that she goes to school. I could tutor her and get her ready before it starts."

"Nola, are you sure?" Cassie asked. "It seems to me that you'll have burden enough takin' care of your own two without addin' another one. 'Course, we would provide clothes and such for her. You wouldn't have to worry about that."

"She'd earn her own way helping me," Nola reassured Cassie. "I think it would be a perfect solution for all of us. Of course, I don't know how this will affect Glen and George. I'm sure they'd miss her. They were so dependent on her when they first came, although they do seem to have transferred some of that to you since they've been here."

"Yes, I feel that we're getting closer every day," Cassie smiled. "They're so sweet, and they've taken to Joshua, too. They were a little stand-offish with him at first, but that's understandable. They never had any reason to trust their father, so I guess it stands to reason they'd have trouble trustin' another man. I think seein' how William Taylor and Jeremiah worship him helped."

You are very lucky, Cassie," Nola said wistfully. "You have a fine family and a loving husband. It's everything we ever longed for when we were girls."

"Oh, Nola, I wish you could be happy, too!" Cassie exclaimed.

"I *am* happy, Cassie," Nola protested. "I have my children, and I know where my life is going. You can't know what a sense of peace I have now that I've made a decision about what I'm going to do. It's like I've been living in a horrible empty void all of these years, just marking time. Now I have a purpose, and I feel stronger and more content than I have in a long time."

When Cassie and Nola approached Anne Marie with their plan, she accepted Nola's offer with enthusiasm once she saw that Cassie was not going to be hurt by her leaving. After an initial flood of tears, George and Glen accepted that Anne Marie would go back to the mountains with Nola, and they would stay with Cassie. Promises of visits and letters helped ease their fears.

"I want you to know that I will be a good sister to you," Cassie assured them. "Me and Joshua will do the same for you that we do for our children. If you stay with us, you will be as much a part of our family as the others are."

The next day Nola and Anne Marie began packing for the trip home. Late that afternoon, when they thought they had packed everything, Joshua's mother appeared with a package for Ellen.

"My dear, I would appreciate it if you would take this little gift to your mother," Elizabeth said to Nola. "Her letters and quilt patterns have meant so much to me, and I've been hurryin' to finish this for her."

Nola unwrapped the package and found a beautifully constructed quilt. It was done in shades ranging from a pale yellow to a rich brown. The colors were so blended that they gave a new depth of beauty to the Sunshine and Shadow pattern that Ellen had sent them. All the colors were earth tones—yellows, oranges, beiges, tans, browns, and burnt umbers. As Nola looked at the quilt, she was reminded of the colors of the trees in the autumn and the ways they changed into the dark browns of winter. She felt tears welling up in her eyes as she realized how many hours of work had gone into the quilt.

"Oh, it's truly one of the most beautiful quilts I've ever seen," she said. "I know Mama will treasure it always. She will appreciate the work that has gone into it, but most of all, she will treasure the love that has gone into it."

Impulsively, she and Elizabeth embraced each other, then Elizabeth left, too moved to say anything else.

The next morning, Nola and Anne Marie left amid tears and promises of future visits from everyone. Cassie clung to Nola and Anne Marie until the last moment, reluctant to give up this link with her mountain roots.

As the train headed back toward the mountains, Nola found herself thinking more and more about the future. She set her eyes and mind on the task ahead of her, determined to find her own place in the world. Fearfully, Anne Marie clung to Nola's hand, wondering what was in store for her now.

"Don't you worry, Anne Marie," Nola assured her. "We'll be just fine, both of us. I've got a feeling we're going to have us some fine adventures."

The trip home was much quieter and more uneventful than the ride with Glen and George. Nola and Anne Marie were both silent for long periods of time, each thinking about the happy times they had shared with Cassie and wondering what lay ahead for them. Nola gave a lot of thought to what effect this move to town would have on Jake and Samantha.

Jake is so caught up in the idea of getting a job so he can buy him a new guitar, she thought. I hope he won't let this fascination he has with music rule his whole life. She smiled, in spite of herself, remembering the nights he had struggled while trying to master the different chords. She could see the earnest expression on his face as he practiced over and over, until Samantha would put her hands over her ears in protest and run out of the room.

As she lay back against the seat, feeling the vibration of the train against her back, she heard Jake begging Samantha to sing with him. After protesting, she usually did, enjoying the praise she received for her sweet voice while protesting what a pain Jake could be.

These episodes were bittersweet to Nola. They brought back memories of Sam and the way he had serenaded her when they were courting.

I hope I never forget the good things we shared, Sam, she thought. I know I'll never forget that these children of mine are a part of you that no one can ever take away from me.

TWENTY-SEVEN

Ellen accepted Nola's decision to move into town, knowing that, right or wrong, it was her right to choose her own course. She rejected Nola's offer to go with her but assured Nola she stood ready to help her if the need arose.

Ellen woke early the morning that Nola was to leave, feeling stronger than she had felt in a long time. The sun had not quite topped the mountain, but it was sending up rays through the early morning mist. She rose and dressed, thinking she would surprise Nola by getting breakfast started. As she started across the porch that connected the kitchen to the rest of the house, she felt drawn by the out-of-doors and, for the first time in months, walked alone in the early morning.

An arthritic hip caused her to be more cautious, and she picked up a cane that Willie had made for her and stepped out into the dew-soaked grass. I wonder how long it has been since I've been out by myself this early in the morning? she thought to herself. It used to be so common for me. Will called it my "day-dreamin' time."

As Ellen strolled across the yard, she gravitated naturally toward her springhouse, almost as if she were pulled by invisible forces to this favorite place.

She opened the door slowly, remembering the time so many years ago when she had found the runaway Cassie sleeping amid the sacks on the floor of the springhouse. She looked around, half expecting to see the tousled red hair of the child.

Idly she picked up a pad and pencil from the shelf by the door, thinking of the times she had stolen off to herself to write down a poem or thought that had come to her.

I used to find so much to write about, she thought. Now it seems like I've been too busy lately to gather my thoughts. Or maybe the sadness

138

that has shadowed our lives lately has just plumb blotted out the sunshine. Maybe since Nola seems to have reconciled herself to startin' a new direction for her life, things will be a'lookin' up.

She walked back out into the sunshine through the grass. The dew soaked her long dress as it brushed against the jewellike droplets, then swished damply against her ankles. The morning was silent, except for the trilling of birds as they roused and began their interminable search for food. She heard a pair of wrens calling to each other across the yard.

She came to the walnut tree that had fallen during a summer storm and, feeling suddenly tired, sat down next to the prone trunk.

Guess Joseph and David will have to get started sawin' you up pretty soon, she mused. Until then, though, you make a pretty nice restin' place for my tired old bones. Reckon I never thought I'd come to this place in life all them years ago when Will first built this house. Ah, Will, I still miss you so!

She looked back at the home that she and Will had built. It was the third house that they had built together. The first one, a simple log cabin, was barely enough to keep the elements out. The second was larger, a more substantial log house; and this one, a two-storied frame house, was built from lumber hauled all the way from Asheville. I've loved them all, she thought. I've loved them because they were houses filled with love and with the laughter of children. I loved them most because they were the places where I knew Will would be at the end of the day. She took the paper and pencil from her pocket and began to write:

I rose from my bed this morning
Before dawn had ever broken.
I looked upon a world so still
Where thoughts were still unspoken.
The world was wrapped in silence
So deep, I feared to move.
All nature slept around me,
Day's beauty still to prove.

I walked alone in the morning dew
And bathed my soul in peace.
I marveled at the stillness
And prayed it would not cease.
I spoke to God and I waited
For Him to speak to me.
He spoke through nature's beauty
And enabled me to see.

I saw his handiwork 'round me
As the world stirred and woke.
I felt His love abounding
In the sun's golden cloak.
I chanced upon a spider's web
Each strand outlined by dew.
I marveled at the beauty there
And watched as patterns grew.

I walked alone this morning
And spoke to no living soul.
I talked to God in silence.
He spoke and made me whole.
He told me that He loved me
With every bird's sweet sound.
He showed me nature's beauty
And there, His love I found.

The effort to write had tired her and she lay back along the broad trunk of the walnut tree, thinking she would rest a bit before she started back. When the pain seared through her temple, she felt slightly surprised, then vaguely annoyed that her peaceful rest had been disturbed. Her annoyance turned to joy as she saw Will reaching out to her, the familiar smile lighting up his face until he seemed to glow inwardly with the light. Eagerly, she reached her arms out to him.

They found her there, thinking at first she was asleep, she lay so peacefully. Tenderly they bore her back to the house and laid her on her bed. They pulled the quilt that had covered her marriage bed up over her and gently smoothed it out.

"It's her Double Wedding Ring quilt," Nola said as she wiped the tears from her eyes. "She told me one time that it was the most precious one that she owned. She said she started piecing it the day after she first met Papa."

The news of Ellen's death spread quickly through the community and caused an outpouring of grief that cast a pall over the whole cove. Neighbors came bringing words of comfort and food until the tables at the Johnston house literally sagged under the weight of it.

Nola knew her mother was respected in the community but was overwhelmed at the expressions of love and revelations of Ellen's kind deeds to her neighbors.

"I'll never forget how she come and set all night with me after they buried my man," one woman declared. "Said she recollected how that first night after her Will was buried was the hardest one of all. We talked till the first rooster crowed in the mornin'. I finally fell asleep in my rockin' chair after that, and she covered me with a quilt and then went home. It was some easier after that, like she said it would be, but they was bad times a'plenty still, and when one of 'em would come along, she knowed somehow. Jest when I'd think I couldn't bear it no more, I'd look up and she'd be there."

"I don't know what we'd of done when Zeb was laid up after he broke his leg if it hadn't been for Ellen," another neighbor spoke up. "She come soon's she heard it and had her boy bring a wagon load of grain and feed for the stock and canned goods for our table. She sent Joseph or David every day till Zeb could manage, to help with the feedin' and milkin'. I reckon we'd of lost everything we had, save for her steppin' in and helpin' out. She even sewed dresses for Frondie and Mary. Said she knew how important it was for girls to have somethin' new ever once in a while. I tried to thank her for it, said I'd be forever grateful for her help, but she just brushed it off, sayin' it wasn't nothin' more'n neighbors ought to do for each other."

One after another people came to testify to Ellen's kind deeds until her children came to know a side of her they had only sensed before, never fully appreciating what a wonderful Christian life she had lived.

Her sons, Willie, James, John, Joseph, and David, and her grandson, Jake, bore her casket to the gravesite. They wrapped her in her precious wedding quilt and buried her by her beloved Will. Reverend Rollins read from chapter 31 of Proverbs, which he said "was shorely written for Ellen Johnston.

> Who can find a virtuous woman? for her price is far above rubies. The heart of her husband doth safely trust in her, so that he shall have no need of spoil. She will do him good and not evil all the days of her life. She seeketh wool, and flax and worketh willingly with her hands. She is like the merchants' ships; she bringeth her food from afar. She riseth also while it is yet night, and giveth meat to her household, and a portion to her maidens. She considereth a field, and buyeth it: with the fruit of her hands she planteth a vineyard. She girdeth her loins with strength, and strengtheneth her arms. She perceiveth that her merchandise is good: her candle goeth not out by night. She layeth her hands to the spindle, and her hands hold the distaff. She stretcheth out her hand to the poor; yea, she reacheth forth her hands to the needy. She is not afraid of the snow for her household: for all her household are clothed with scarlet. She maketh herself coverings of tapestry; her clothing is silk and purple. Her husband is known in the gates, when he sitteth among the elders of the land. She maketh fine linen, and

selleth it; and delivereth girdles unto the merchant. Strength and honour are her clothing; and she shall rejoice in time to come. She openeth her mouth with wisdom; and in her tongue is the law of kindness. She looketh well to the ways of her household and eateth not the bread of idleness. Her children arise up, and call her blessed; her husband also, and he praiseth her. Many daughters have done virtuously, but thou excellest them all. Favour is deceitful, and beauty is vain: but a woman that feareth the Lord, she shall be praised. Give her of the fruit of her hands; and let her own works praise her in the gates.

NOLA

TWENTY-EIGHT

Nola's move to town was delayed by Ellen's death. There were things that needed to be done that her brothers felt they couldn't do without her. She found a list that Ellen had made out among her mother's things designating who was to have certain of her possessions. The last night before Nola left, the family finally gathered around the old oak dining table where they had shared so many meals.

"I've tried to follow Mama's wishes the way she wrote them down," Nola said. "I hope I've done everything she wanted me to. The things she had were not of much monetary value, but they were precious to her, and for that reason I know they'll be precious to all of us."

"What Mama left us couldn't be wrote down on a piece of paper nor put in a box," David mused. "What she left us was the pride and love she had for each of us. I think we're about the richest family that ever was."

Quietly, each added their amens to David's words.

After her mother's wishes were carried out, Nola went to bed in her mother's house for the last time that night. She lay awake for a long time, not because she was restless but because she wanted to enjoy for the last time the feeling of security and love that had always permeated the house. I'll never have this feeling of peace anywhere else, she thought as she drifted off to sleep.

When all of her belongings were finally loaded in the wagon and they were ready to leave, Nola looked back at her home nestled in the shadows of the mountains that surrounded it. Tears welled up as she turned for one last glimpse before she rounded the curve that took her out of sight of her beloved house. Memories paraded through her mind as she took her leave. The faces of her brothers and sisters mingled with childish laughter and youthful pranks and tears. Overriding all of her memories was the image of her parents, the steady, loving force that had always been in her life.

"Why are you crying, Mama?" Samantha asked her. "Remember, you said this was goin' to be a happy day of new beginnings."

"It will be, too," Nola assured her. "It's just that I'm leaving a little part of myself behind. I know I'll come back again, but it will never be the same. The next time I come, it won't be Mama's and Papa's home. It'll be someone else's."

Joseph and David helped Nola get settled in her new home in town. She quickly found boarders as eager to move in as Jake and Samantha were. Her large, two-storied house had six bedrooms. Annie Marie and Samantha shared a room, and Jake found a room behind the kitchen that he declared was just right for him. It was originally meant to be a pantry, but he liked the privacy it gave him from the rest of the household and also the fact that he could come and go through the back door without having to answer to someone everytime he left. Nola rented the other rooms to a young woman who had come to teach in the local school and to six construction workers who were working on the new hotel being built in town.

Nola was preoccupied with getting her household set up and getting used to the experience of having people under her roof with whom she had no real blood ties. She was also very much aware of the responsibility of having two attractive young girls under her care with strange men in her home. For these reasons, she grew lax in keeping tabs on Jake. Samantha brought this to her attention one evening after Nola had caught one of the boarders paying too much attention to her daughter.

"I don't see why you're always after me and Anne Marie all the time, and you just let Jake come and go as he pleases," she protested. "You never say anything to him, and half the time he's not even where he's supposed to be. You'd think he could do no wrong and that we're not to be trusted."

"What on earth are you talking about?" Nola asked her. "I trust you and Anne Marie. It's these men all around you that I don't trust. You just don't understand, Samantha. I'm responsible for you and for Anne Marie. There's no one else around to take care of you.

"And what do you mean that Jake's not where he's supposed to be? He has chores just like the rest of us, and as far as I can tell he takes care of them."

"Yes, he takes care of them, all right," Samantha retorted. "Then he takes off anywhere he wants to. He comes home at night anytime he wants to also. Why don't you ask him where he was until midnight last night?"

"What are you talking about?" Nola protested again. "He knows he isn't allowed to be out that late. Where is he now?"

"That's a good question," Samantha said. "Why don't you ask him when he gets in tonight?"

Jake came in through the back door that night, jauntily sure that no one was about at that hour. He was quite startled when he opened the door and found Nola sitting on his bed.

"Mama, what are you doin' here?" he stammered in surprise. "Why are you in my room? Is somethin' wrong?"

"Yes, as a matter of fact I think there's something very wrong," Nola said grimly. "And don't you ask me what I'm doing here, young man. I'll ask the questions, and my first one is, Where have you been until this hour at night? You know what time you're supposed to be home, and it's not after midnight."

"Well . . . well . . . I was just foolin' around and it got to be later than I thought," Jake stammered. "Gosh, I didn't realize it was this late. I promise you it won't happen again, Mama. Where in the world did the time go?"

"I know it won't happen again," Nola said grimly. "From now on, you're to be in this house by ten o'clock, and you're to come in the front door so I'll know what time you get here. From now on the back door will be locked and bolted as soon as we finish supper.

"If you think I'm going to believe that you just lost track of time, then you don't give me much credit for having any sense, young man. Now I want to know where you've been and what you've been up to, and I don't intend to leave this room until you tell me."

"Good grief, Mama, I'm not a baby," Jake protested. "You can't tell me what to do anymore. I'm seventeen years old, and I've got the right to go where I want to."

"Don't tell me what your rights are, young man," Nola said sternly. "As long as you live under my roof and eat my food, you will answer to me. Now I'm asking you one more time, where have you been?"

"Well, if you have to know, I've been workin'," Jake mumbled.

"Working? Now where on earth would a young boy like you be working this time of night?" Nola said in disbelief. "Most businesses I know of close down at six o'clock. You'll have to do better than that, Jake McGinty."

"I have been workin'," Jake protested. "I got me a job at the Hotel Grainger, playin' in a band. I ain't been doin' nothin' wrong, Mama, honest. It pays two dollars a night, and they give us supper, too. You know how all them city people want some entertainment when they come here, and they like to dance, and we play for them every night from seven till midnight. I was goin' to tell you, Mama, honest I was, just as soon as you got everything settled down here."

"A band? You've been playing in a band?" Nola asked weakly. She felt stunned as old memories of Sam's fiddle playing came back.

"Yeah, and I really like it, Mama. I was afraid if I told you, it'd upset you. I know how you felt about Papa's music, but honest, Mama, there ain't nothin' wrong with what I'm doin',", Jake said.

"A band. He tells me he's playing in a band," Nola repeated, "and I'm supposed to believe this. Maybe you wouldn't mind telling me what kind of an instrument you play in this band. The only instrument I've ever seen you play was the guitar, and the only kind of band I know of that uses a guitar is a square dance band. Does the hotel have square dances?"

"I play the piano," Jake said proudly. "And I'm learnin' the saxophone. Red says as soon as I get good enough on it, he'll let me play it, too."

"The piano!" Nola exclaimed. "Where on earth did you learn to play the piano?"

"Over at Red's house," Jake said proudly. "He showed me a few chords, and the rest was easy. I found out you could put the right chords to any tune and play whatever you want to. I've been practicin' every time we came into town for the past year. Red said I picked it up real easy. He says I'm a natural, says I got a real musical ear. It'd be easier if I could read the music, but I get along all right without it. Same way with the saxophone.

Jake paused, watching Nola closely. "You ain't mad at me, are you, Mama? I didn't tell you 'cause I knew how you felt about Papa's fiddle. I reckoned you'd not want me to make music."

"Oh, Jake, I am mad," Nola said, staring at her son in disbelief. "I'm mad because you've deceived me, and I'm hurt that you had so little faith in me that you kept this hidden from me. Don't you know it wasn't the music I hated? The music didn't cause your Papa to do like he did. It was just one of his excuses, not the cause."

"What are you goin' to do?" Jake asked fearfully. "Are you goin' to make me give it up? I . . . I hope you won't, Mama. I can't explain why it is, but I'd just die if I couldn't play anymore."

"I don't know what I'm going to do right now, Jake," Nola said quietly. "This has all taken me by surprise, and I'll have to take some time and think about it. But I can tell you right now, young man, that this is not the last of it. I won't make you any promises about what I will or won't do until I've investigated everything thoroughly. The first thing I want to know is who is this person you call Red? What's his name, and who are his folks?"

"It's Red Harmon, and I don't know what his name is except Red. I guess they call him Red because he's got red hair," Jake said. "I don't know who his folks are, but they know you. His ma said she went to school with you and Papa."

"Well, that doesn't tell me much," Nola said. "Now suppose you get to bed and let me do the same. We'll talk about this tomorrow. I meant what I said, though, Jake. From now on, you're to come in through the front door. No more of this sneaking in the back."

Nola went to bed, leaving a sheepish and contrite Jake to worry about his fate. She shook her head as she went up the stairs.

"What on earth have I done?" she muttered to herself. "Goodness knows what's to become of us. Maybe I was wrong to move into town."

TWENTY-NINE

Nola spent a restless night, tossing and turning as she wrestled with this new problem with Jake. She rose the next morning, determined to find a solution. As soon as she had breakfast out of the way, she called Samantha and Anne Marie in and gave them a list of the things that needed to be done. She also left a list of things she wanted Jake to do.

"You wake him up right away now," she told Samantha, "and you tell him he's to do these jobs as soon as he has his breakfast. You also tell him that I said he is not to leave this house under any circumstances until I get back."

The Hotel Grainger was within a half mile of Nola's boarding house, and she elected to walk there instead of hitching up the buggy. She carefully picked her way up the rough dirt road, holding her skirts up to keep them clean. The town was growing, and she passed three new homes under construction on her way. She paid particular attention to a big, rambling structure going up. She had heard it would be a boarding house and restaurant.

Hope there's enough business for both of us, she thought.

The Hotel Grainger was a long, straggling building encompassing almost a half acre of land. Nola felt intimidated by the size of the hotel, but she steeled herself and boldly approached the registration desk.

"I wish to speak with the owner," she told the clerk.

"Yes, ma'am," he answered. "Do you want to register? I can do that for you."

"No, I do not," she told him shortly. "I wish to speak with the owner about another matter."

"Just a minute," he mumbled and disappeared into the office behind the registration desk.

A tall, florid-faced man followed the clerk out to where Nola was waiting. He was dressed in a business suit and wore glasses that had no ear pieces but sat on his nose, held there by the pincers that were clamped firmly to the bridge. Nola stared in fascination, wondering when they would turn loose and fall. A long black cord drooped from the corner of one lens, and she supposed that would catch them if they fell.

"Yes, madam?" he questioned her. "You wished to speak to me? My name is George Weathers, and I am the owner of this establishment."

"How do you do. I am Mrs. Sam McGinty, mother of Jake McGinty," she said, "and I have come to inquire about my son playing with a band here."

"Oh, I don't do the hiring for the orchestra," he told her haughtily. "You will have to speak to my manager. He takes care of that sort of thing."

"I am not here to apply for a job," Nola told him, flushing. "I am here because my son has told me that he is playing with your band here, and I want to see what sort of situation he has gotten himself involved in."

"I see," Weathers replied, looking at her fully for the first time. "Marvin," he said to the clerk, "go and call Mr. Jones and ask him to come to the front desk. Won't you please have a seat, er, Mrs. McGinty, wasn't it?"

"Yes, thank you," Nola said coolly.

She looked around and selected a straight-backed chair in the lobby and sat down, arranging her skirts primly over her ankles. Weathers hesitated for a second then, bowing slightly, left.

The clerk returned, followed by a young man in his shirt sleeves whom Nola judged to be in his late twenties. The clerk gestured toward Nola, then returned to his desk.

"I am Christian Jones, hotel manager," he told her. "How can I help you?"

"Are you responsible for giving my son, Jake McGinty, a job with your band?" Nola asked him.

"Jake? Jake McGinty? Oh, the young kid that plays piano for us. Why, yes, I reckon I am," he answered her nervously. "Is there some problem? He seems like a real good kid."

"Well, the problem is that I did not know he was working here," Nola said flushing. "In fact, I did not even know that he could play the piano. I have come to see what kind of place this is and what kind of situation he has involved himself in."

"Oh, I see," Christian said slowly. "I'm sorry, Mrs. McGinty. I had no idea he hadn't told you he was playing here. I sure hope you won't make him quit. We've had a devil—oh, excuse me—a hard time finding a good piano player, and I'd sure hate to lose him. He's got a real talent. That kid can play anything. If you can hum it, he can play it. Listen, why don't you come with me to the restaurant, and I'll show you where they play."

"Yes, I think I would like to see," Nola said, rising to her feet.

Christian led Nola through a hallway and into a large dining room. The tables were grouped around a bandstand, and there was an empty area between the tables and the band, obviously used for a dance floor.

"You can see, we have a nice setup here, Mrs. McGinty," Christian assured her. "The band sits up here and plays for about four hours while people eat dinner and dance."

"Yes, it looks quite nice," Nola said quietly. "I assume, Mr. Jones, that since this county is dry, you don't sell alcohol here, do you?"

"Oh no, ma'am," he said hastily. "It would be against the law for us to do that. I can assure you that this is a reputable establishment. We have people from the best and wealthiest families in the state coming here."

"Well, wealthiest doesn't always mean best," Nola said drily. "Now, if you would be kind enough to tell me where the leader of this band, a Mr. Red Harmon, I believe, lives, I would appreciate it very much."

"Well, let me see, I believe he lives up at the north end of Main Street, right near the Norris house," Jones answered her. "It's a little cottage right behind the Norris's. Has a white fence around it. You can't miss it. You probably won't find Red there though, he works at the livery stable during the day. Only plays here at night."

"Thank you very much," Nola said. "It's really his mother I want to meet. I understand I'm supposed to know her."

By the time Nola walked the length of the town to the Norris house, she had begun to wish she'd taken the time to hitch up the horse and buggy. She was used to walking, and the length of her walk did not bother her. But the roughness of the road through town and the care she had to pay to where she was putting her feet down had begun to wear on her when she finally reached her destination.

She approached the cottage gate and stepped through and up on the porch. She straightened her skirt and raised her hand to knock on the door, but before she could knock, the door was flung open and she looked into the smiling face of a dark-haired woman who was hastily drying her hands on her apron.

"As I live and breathe, if it ain't Nola Johnston," she exclaimed. "I'd heard you was livin' in town, and I been meanin' to come by and see you. But I just ain't had the time to do nothin' 'cept keep this bunch of young'uns fed. How in the world are you, Nola?"

Nola looked at the woman blankly, wondering for a moment who in the world she was. Then suddenly recognizing her, Nola exclaimed, "Why,

Laura Mann! I had no idea you lived here. Are you Red Harmon's mother?"

"That I am," Laura answered her heartily. "His and ten others. Come on in, Nola. I declare it's shore good to see somebody from the cove. I been hungry for the sight of somebody I knowed for ever so long. When Red told me yore boy was playin' with 'em, I vowed I 'us a'goin' to see you. I'm shore glad you come."

Nola followed Laura into the house and looked around at the cheerful room. It was sparsely furnished but clean and bright with stiffly starched curtains at the windows. She heard the sound of children playing in the back yard, and two little girls were giggling in the next room. As Laura and Nola sat down on the clean but worn chairs, Laura called to them.

"You girls go on outside and play now. It's too pertty a day to stay cooped up in the house."

Laura grinned at Nola. "I been so busy talkin', I ain't give you a chance to say why you come, Nola. I bet it's got somethin' to do with that Red and his band though. That's about all he can think about these days. Is yore boy as took with music makin' as Red is? I never seen anybody pick up a'playin' the piano like Jake did. He shore is a natural when it comes to music-makin'. I reckon you already know that without me a'tellin' you though."

"Well, yes, I did come about the band," Nola said slowly. "But I didn't know about Jake playing the piano. This has all been a big surprise to me. Until last night, I had no idea he was involved in a band."

"Well, don't that beat all!" exclaimed Laura. "I swear these boys is somethin', ain't they? Why, Red's been makin' music of some kind ever since he could hold a guitar. 'Course, it ain't exactly the kind of music I like and what we grew up with. He says it's modern stuff, like the city folks wants to hear, but it's right nice anyhow. I shore hope Red ain't got yore boy into somethin' that's upset you, Nola. If he has, I'll skin him alive."

"I'm sure that anything Jake is involved in, he managed it all by himself," Nola said drily. "I just wanted to see for myself what it is he's doing and who he's doing it with. You know Jake is only seventeen, and I don't quite trust his judgment yet."

"Don't I know what you mean," laughed Laura. "Red's near about twenty now, but I remember how he was. Thought he knowed everything and me and his pa didn't know nothin'. You have to keep a tight rein on 'em when they're that age. He's a good boy though, and we're right proud of how he's turned out. You needn't worry about him leadin' Jake astray, Nola. He's so wrapped up in that band and his music, he don't have time to make no mischief. We told him he had to hold down a real job, too, though, and he stays right busy at the livery stable. His pa told him he doubted he'd make a livin' makin' music and he'd better learn an honest trade."

"That sounds very wise of you," Nola smiled. "And you've eased my mind. I can see that Jake is in good company with your boy. I guess I'll let him keep on with this band, at least for the time being. I know he would be hard to live with if I made him quit. I guess what bothered me the most was him not telling me what he was up to."

Nola rose and moved toward the door.

"Do you have to go so soon?" Laura protested. "We ain't had time to visit any."

"I'd better get started back now," Nola told her, "but I'll come back another time when we can sit and talk. Right now I've got six hungry boarders coming in for dinner, and if I don't get home, there'll be nothing there for them to eat. Thank you, Laura, for setting my mind at ease."

Laura followed Nola out to the gate, talking and begging her to come back real soon. Nola started off for home, and as she rounded the corner to go down Main Street, she looked back at the cottage. Laura was still standing at the gate and waved vigorously. Nola waved back, then turned down the street, walking as quickly as she could while avoiding the mudholes and wagon ruts in the road.

An anxious Jake was waiting for her when she got home, hot and tired from her long walk. She brushed off his questions and set about putting the finishing touches on the noon meal. The girls had followed her instructions and had a hearty stew on the stove and the table set. She stirred up a cake of cornbread and sliced the last of the summer's tomatoes. Just as the bread finished baking, the men trooped in, hungry and ready for their meal. Jake waited impatiently in the kitchen for his mother's decision.

When the meal was over and the table cleared, Nola fixed Jake with a stern eye and told him, "Jake, I do not like the way I had to find out about this band, have no doubts about it! My first impulse was to lay down the law to you and lock you in your room if I had to. However, after meeting the people at the hotel and finding out who Red's parents are, I've reconsidered. I have decided to allow you to do this, but only under certain conditions.

"First of all, you are to come home the minute you are through at night, and you are to come through the front door so I'll know what time you get here. Second, if I ever smell alcohol on you, I will withdraw my permission immediately with no discussion. Third, you are not to neglect your duties here, and if I catch you putting your work off on the girls, I'll make you quit. Also, you are to quit this band when school starts and get back to your schooling. Now, do you think you can obey my rules and promise me you will not deceive me again?"

"Yes, ma'am," a relieved Jake quickly answered. "Thank you, Mama. I promise you I'll do everything you want, and I'll work twice as hard here at home."

"Well, we'll see about that," Nola said skeptically. "Maybe you'd better not make me any promises you can't keep. Right now, you'd better pick up that bucket of scraps and take it over to Mrs. Conner's hog pen. It's beginning to smell."

She smiled and shook her head as Jake plunged out the door and grabbed the bucket.

I don't know if I've done the right thing or not, she thought, but I don't really know what else I could have done. Another year or two and he'll be gone anyhow. She sighed. Well, Sam, you certainly had worse faults that he could have inherited.

The strain of running a boarding house, seeing to the needs of three teenagers, and trying to make enough profit on her venture to support all of them began to wear on Nola. She rarely found—or took—any time to herself. If Samantha and Anne Marie had not been there to help her, she could not have managed the enormous amount of cooking and housekeeping. She began to worry about what she would do when school started in the fall and she no longer had the girls' help. She never once considered keeping them out of school. Education was a must as far as she was concerned, and any other course would have been unthinkable. Along with Samantha's help, she had been able to teach Anne Marie to read and write and do simple arithmetic. Fortunately, the girl was bright and eager to learn. By the summer's end, she felt that she had brought Anne Marie to a point where she need not be embarrassed to start school.

Jake, however, was the thorn in her flesh where schooling was concerned. He was so wrapped up in his music that she knew it was going to be impossible to get him interested in going back to school.

"Mama, I've got all the schoolin' I need," he argued with her one evening after supper. "I want to make music, and I don't see how learnin' more arithmetic and history is goin' to help me do that. Besides, you know you need me here at home. How will you get everything done here with Samantha and Anne Marie both in school? Please, Mama, let me stay and help you and keep playin' with the band. We've just now got everything goin' for us. Red's got us booked at the hotel through October, and he says he can get us some bookins' in Asheville, too. Won't you please just consider it?"

"I don't know, Jake," she sighed. "I'll have to think about it. You know how much I've always wanted you both to finish school. Just give me a few days to think it over."

Jake decided his best course was to back off, so he dropped the subject for the time being. He became a veritable whirlwind around the house, helping with even the most menial chores. Nola was not fooled by his tactics, but she decided to take advantage of his help while she could. With his extra help, she took some time to make the girls a few new dresses for school.

While she was shopping at the general store for the dress material, she came face to face with John for the first time since Ellen's funeral. He had Charles and Lucy with him, and they were looking at material also. The twins saw her before she saw them and ran to her in excitement.

"Aunt Nola!" Lucy exclaimed. "How are you? And where's Samantha and Jake? Look, Papa, it's Aunt Nola."

Nola looked up into John's startled face, feeling herself turning red. Before she could say anything, Pearl appeared beside him and smiled tightly at Nola.

"Well, hello, Nola," she said. "It's good to see you again. I hope you are well and that Jake and Samantha are, too. It's been some time since we saw you last."

"Hello, Pearl—John," Nola responded quietly. "We're well, thank you. I hope you're the same. I've meant to have Lucy and Charles in for a visit, but I've been so busy getting the boarding house going. Maybe before school starts they can come for a visit."

Turning to Lucy and Charles, she hugged them both, exclaiming at how grown up they looked. She felt her heart leap when she looked at Lucy. It was like looking at a young Martha, and her eyes misted at the thought that Martha could not be there to watch her children grow.

"She's just like her mother, ain't she?" John said huskily, apparently sensing Nola's sad thoughts.

"Yes," Nola said softly. "Forgive me. It was just seeing her so unexpectedly. It gave me a turn."

Nola turned to Pearl and asked impulsively, "Won't you come by the house and have some apple pie and see Jake and Samantha? It's been so long since we've seen you, and I know how much they've missed all of you."

"We can't, thank you," Pearl said hastily. "We're here to meet the train at two o'clock and thought we'd take this time to come and pick up some cloth to make some clothes for these two. A friend of mine is comin' to visit. She's been twice this summer, and I hope this time she might be persuaded to stay."

John's face flushed darkly, and he dropped his head. The look of triumph Pearl flashed at Nola pulsed between them, and the meaning of the visit was obvious to Nola.

"Well, maybe the next time you're in town," Nola said faintly. She turned and hugged the children again, then took her purchases and left with as much haste as she could. She felt Pearl's eyes boring in her back and stiffened as she went out the door. John's voice stopped her as she reached the street.

"Nola, will you wait just a minute?" he asked her. "There's somethin' I'd like to tell you."

"Of course, John," she replied, steeling herself for whatever he had to say to her.

"First, let me apologize for Pearl's bein' so snippety to you. She means well, but she don't always know when to keep her mouth out of my business. This friend of hers is somebody I hope is goin' to become my wife. We've known each other for a good while, and I think she would be a good mother to Lucy and Charles. I know they're 'most grown now, but they still need a woman's guidance, especially Lucy. I need somebody, too. I've been lonely now for a long time. You know that.

"Daisy—that's her name—is a fine woman who was widowed two years ago, and she's lonely, too. She never had no children of her own and has been livin' with her brother and his wife, helpin' with their children and the housework. She needs somebody as much as I do. Anyhow, I think we could make each other happy and take care of each other. I hope you'll be happy for me."

"Oh, John, how could I be anything else but happy for you?" she said, impulsively laying her hand on his arm. "I can't think of anyone who deserves happiness more than you."

"Unless it's you, Nola," John said quietly. "Are you happy, Nola? Have you found someone who can make you happy?"

"John, I am content," she said quietly. "I have my boarding house to keep me busy and my children to keep me company. You know, I have Cassie's sister, Anne Marie, with me, too, so I have a quite busy and interesting life with all that goes on with them."

"Yes, I know that," he said, "but are you happy, Nola? I hope you aren't just livin' on the fringes of your children's lives. You're too young to settle for that."

Nola smiled at him and shook her head. "Dear John," she said, "you are always looking out for me. Don't worry about me. I am happy. Law me, I'm so busy that I don't have time to wonder if I'm happy or not. This is what I want, though, and I have no complaints about my life."

John looked piercingly into her eyes, then smiled and nodded his head. "I'd best get back to Pearl and the children," he said, "before Pearl busts a gut with curiosity."

They both laughed, and Nola said, "Be happy, John."

"I will," he smiled. "You be happy, too, Nola."

Nola turned down the street and made her way home, thinking about her conversation with John. She felt happy for him, but she also acknowledged that she felt a twinge of jealousy for the woman who had taken her place in John's heart.

How selfish of me, she thought. That's no better than a dog with a full belly begrudging a bone to another dog. I had my chance with John, and it was my own choice to give him up. I will not let myself turn into a jealous, coveting woman.

Perhaps it was the feeling of vulnerability she had after her meeting with John that caused her to give in to Jake's request to stop school. Whatever the cause, when he approached her about it after she returned home, she gave in with no further protests.

"Maybe it would be the best thing for all of us," she told him resignedly. "Goodness knows, I've got to have some help around here when the girls go to school, and we both know you won't have your mind on your studies if you're chomping at the bit to be off making music."

"Thank you, Mama," Jake said, surprised but grateful. "I promise I will help you so good you won't even miss the girls. You've made me awful happy, Mama."

"I hope I've done the right thing, Jake," she sighed. "Maybe I'm just getting old. I don't seem to have much fight left in me anymore. Anyhow, we'll see how it works out."

Jake lived up to his word and helped Nola until the girls got home from school each day, but as soon as they were in the house, he left and was not to be seen again until the next morning. Nola decided that it didn't help her, or Jake either, to nag him about keeping a curfew. After that, he was home most nights on time. When he wasn't, he made it a point to tell her why he was late. It always had to do with playing an extra song for some late customers or working on new music for the next night. When summertime came and the girls were out of school, she expected him to stop helping at the boarding house, but much to her delight, he continued working as hard as ever.

Nola thought to herself, I'd like to tell John what a responsible young man Jake's become and thank him. I know much of it's because of the attention he gave him after Sam left. She didn't want to intrude on his new life, though, with painful memories from the past, since he was newly married to Daisy.

Thoughts of Daisy brought a smile to Nola's lips. She recalled their first meeting and how hesitant she had felt as she went to meet John's new bride. All of her fears were put to rest, though, as Daisy threw her arms around Nola when they were introduced.

"Oh, Nola, I am so glad to meet you at last," she said. "John's told me so much about you and your wonderful family. I know that you and I are going to be good friends."

As Nola looked into the eyes of this open-hearted, genuine woman, she knew they would be friends.

"I am so happy for John," she told Daisy. "I am so happy that he found you. I'm happy that I have found a new friend, too."

Just as Nola was beginning to enjoy her new self-confidence, another worry surfaced. Samantha came to her one day and told her she was worried about Jake.

"What are you worried about?" Nola asked her. "I thought everything was fine with him."

"It's Papa," Samantha blurted out. "He's been writin' to Papa."

"Samantha, you promised you wouldn't tell," Anne Marie said. "Jake'll kill you for tellin' on him."

"I don't care!" Samantha exclaimed. "Anyhow, I ain't scared of him. I think it's disloyal of him, and I don't care if he knows I told."

"Wait a minute, what are you talking about?" Nola asked. "How long has this been going on? How did he know where to write to?"

"It's Aunt Pearl," Samantha said. "She brought us a letter that Papa wrote us. He wanted us to write to him, and he sent his address in Florida. I told her I never would, but Jake said he wanted to know about him— why he ran off—and he's been writin' to him. Papa wants him to come to Florida to see him. I'm afraid he's gonna leave, too, and we won't ever see him again, just like Papa did."

Nola paled to the news but quickly recovered and said in a calm but shaky voice, "There's nothing wrong with Jake writing to his papa, nor would there be anything wrong with you writing to him if you want to. What is wrong is that he has tried to hide it from me. I've never given either one of you any cause to think you couldn't keep in touch with your papa."

"No, Mama, you haven't," Samantha said. "But I just felt like I'd be disloyal to you if I wrote him. 'Sides, I don't hardly remember him anyhow."

"That's not your fault, Samantha," Nola said sadly. "You were just a baby when he left. Oh well, I guess me and Jake had better have a talk when he comes home tonight. We need to get this cleared up before it goes any further."

THIRTY-ONE

Nola's confrontation with Jake was delayed for some time because of a traumatic event that took place the next morning. Anne Marie and Samantha were helping Nola in the kitchen when someone pounded on the front door.

"My goodness," Nola said, "whoever that is must be in a hurry, not to take time to use the knocker. You girls keep on with what you're doing while I go see what they want."

When Nola opened the front door, she was confronted by a tall, dirty man with a wild black beard. He was dressed in a pair of soiled overalls and had a black felt hat jammed on his head. He carried a long barreled squirrel rifle in his hands.

"Yes?" Nola inquired. "What is it you want?"

"I want my girl and my boys. I heared they was here, and I come to fetch them home with me," he said belligerently. He stared boldly in her face.

"Who are you?" Nola asked coldly. "And what makes you think I have your children?"

"I'm Zeb Martin," he said shortly. "And you needn't act like you don't know my girl, Anne Marie. Some of my kin seen her in town and found out she's stayin' at yore boardin' house. Go and fetch her, and the boys, too. I aim to take 'em back home with me where they belong. Don't give me no sass about it neither, or you'll be sorry you did."

Martin brandished his rifle threateningly at Nola as he uttered the last words, and Nola involuntarily shrank away from him. Then stiffening her spine, she stood in front of the door and looked him straight in the eyes.

"I know who you are," she said coldly. "And unless you're off my property in five minutes, I'll have the sheriff after you. I'll not let you put one hand on Anne Marie. Not now or ever! Her mother told her to go to

Cassie, and that's what she did. I intend to honor her mother's wishes. Now get off my porch and leave us alone."

In one motion Nola pushed the front door shut and locked it in the man's startled face, then fell back weakly against the wall, waiting for what she thought would surely come.

"I'll be back!" he shouted through the door. "You can't keep me from what's rightfully mine, and when I do come, you'll be sorry! I'll promise you that!"

He stalked off the porch, muttering as he went. Nola watched him through the window as he stalked down the street. She turned and saw the two girls peering around the dining room door, wide-eyed with fright.

"Oh, I knowed things was a'goin' along too good to be true," sobbed Anne Marie, throwing herself in Nola's arms. "I should a'stayed in Tennessee with Cassie where he couldn't get at me. Now look what's happened. He won't give us no peace till he takes me back again. Oh, Nola, please don't let him take me away."

"Hush, child," Nola soothed her. "I'm not about to let him take you away. You are not to worry. I'll take care of you just like I promised Cassie I would. Now dry your eyes. Then I want you and Samantha to run over to Mrs. Patterson's house and ask her to let her Lucas run an errand for me. Tell him to come here quick as he can. While you're gone, I'll write a note to Sheriff Tate. Then we'll see how brave Zeb Martin is. Don't go out the front door. He might be watching. Go out the kitchen door and through the back gate. Hurry now."

The girls scurried out through the kitchen and across the back yard to the gate in the fence that divided the two houses. They were gone only a few minutes before they returned with Lucas Patterson.

Nola had written a hasty note to Sheriff John Tate, explaining that she needed his help as quickly as he could get there. She sealed the letter hastily and gave it to Lucas.

"Now, Lucas, you take this to the courthouse as fast as you can," she told him. "And be sure that Sheriff Tate gets it. Be sure and come back and tell me what he says."

Lucas left at a full run, sensing the urgency of his errand. Nola breathed a sigh of relief as he rounded the corner out of sight. She latched the back door and left the front door locked. She put her arms around the girls, trying to comfort them.

"We'll just leave the door locked until time for the men to come home to their dinner. Now, I don't want either one of you girls to go outside," she cautioned them. "I don't think he'll come back today, but there's no use taking chances."

"Oh, Nola, what if he does come back before the sheriff gets here?"

Anne Marie asked. "What will we do? He's just as liable to bring some of them Sutton boys with him as not. You don't know how mean they can be."

"Hush now," Nola said sternly. "I'll not listen to a bunch of what ifs. We will just go about our business like nothing's happened. You girls, go on upstairs and start changing the beds. I can manage the rest of the dinner. There's nothing left to do but bake the cornbread. Go on now, and just stay upstairs until I call you."

I do wish Jake was here, Nola thought worriedly as the girls obediently climbed the stairs. That boy is never around when I need him. I know, I'll get Papa's old gun and bring it down here. It won't hurt to have it here just in case. It's been so long since it was fired, it probably won't work, but maybe I could bluff him if I had to.

Quietly Nola went up the stairs and got the gun out of her closet where she had stored it. Slipping out the door, she hastily went back to the kitchen and placed it in a corner near the door. Then she busied herself stirring up the two huge cakes of cornbread she needed for lunch. She looked up in relief when Lucas pecked at the back door, some thirty minutes after he had left.

"That was a quick trip, Lucas," she said. "Did you give the letter to Sheriff Tate?"

"I couldn't," he panted. "He wasn't there. Him and his deputy has gone to take a prisoner over to the Buncombe County jail. They said he probably wouldn't be back before late this evenin' sometime. They said they'd make shore he got your letter soon's he got there though."

"Oh, dear," Nola said, her heart sinking in disappointment. "I didn't think about him being gone. Well, you did the best you could, Lucas, and I thank you for it." She sighed, then reached into the cupboard for some candy. "Here, let me give you a stick of peppermint for your trouble. Thank your ma for letting you go."

Lucas took the candy eagerly and bolted out the back door for home. Nola sank down in a chair, wondering what she should do. A loud banging on the front door jerked her out of her reverie. She grabbed the gun and cautiously slipped through the dining room into the living room and peered out the front door. To her relief, three of her boarders were standing on the porch, puzzled because they couldn't get in. Hastily, she set the gun back in the kitchen and hurried to unbolt the door and let them in.

"I'm so sorry," she murmured to them as they came in the door. "I don't know what I was thinking about, locking the door in the middle of the day. My mind must have been on something else."

"Were you afraid somethin' 'ud come in and git you?" grinned Ezra

Norton. "Course, you ought to be careful with these pertty gals you got here."

Nola looked sharply at him as he eyed Samantha and Anne Marie, who were bringing the bowls of food in and setting them on the table.

"I reckon I'd take care of anyone who offered to cause any harm to either one of my girls," she told him sharply.

"Hey, I was just a'funnin' you," Norton said hastily. "I respect you, Mrs. McGinty, you know that. I'd never do nothin' out of line."

"I'm sure you wouldn't, Mr. Norton," she said, smiling tightly. "Come on now, sit down and eat. Your lunch time will be over before you've had time to eat. That cornbread won't taste too good when it gets cold. Help yourselves. I'll be in the kitchen if you need anything."

Nola went back to the kitchen and sank weakly into a chair. She wondered what she would have done if it had been Martin at the door. Samantha and Anne Marie stood looking frightened and big-eyed at her. With an effort, she pulled herself together.

"Come on now, girls, stop looking so scared. I told you I won't let anything happen to Anne Marie, and I mean it. Go see if the men need something more to drink. Neither one of you are to go outside today, just in case he should decide to come back. Sheriff Tate will be back this evening, and then we'll have some help. Go on now."

After a while, the sounds of chairs scraping on the floor told Nola that the men were through with their meal, and she went in the dining room to follow them to the front door so that she could lock it behind them. As the men went out the door, Trevor McManus dropped back behind the others. He turned to face Nola in the doorway.

"Mrs. McGinty, I think there was more to that locked door than you let on. Your face was as white as a sheet when you came to the door. Is there somethin' wrong? I'd like to help you if there is," he said seriously.

Nola looked up at him and was tempted to blurt out her fears. But thinking how humiliated Anne Marie would be to have them know about her father, she pressed her lips together and shook her head.

"Thank you, Mr. McManus," she said, "but everything is all right. I was just upset with myself for being so absent minded."

"I still think there's more to it than that," he declared. "If you're not willin' to tell me, I'll not press you. Let me just tell you though, if you need me, just send somebody for me and I'll come a' runnin'. Our buildin' site ain't more'n five minutes away."

Nola smiled gratefully at him and nodded her head. As the men left the porch, she closed the door and bolted it behind them.

The day wore on at a snail's pace for Nola. She started at every sound until she was almost at her wit's end. Her heart sank when a boy brought her a message from Jake saying that he had gone to Asheville with the band and would be late getting home that night. Anxiously, she watched out the window for Sheriff Tate. The boarders came in for their evening meal, and still she had heard nothing from him.

"At least we won't have to worry about your father coming back tonight with all of the men folks here tonight," she told Anne Marie. "I'll feel safe with them in the house. Surely by tomorrow morning Sheriff Tate will get my message."

"Guess we'll see you Sunday evening, Mrs. McGinty," Ezra Norton told her as he rose from the supper table.

"Why, what do you mean?" she asked him.

"Hit's Friday." He grinned at her. "We're all a'goin' home for the weekend. Can't wait to see my old woman and my young'uns. I'll be glad when this job's over, and I can stay to home. I don't much like this business of bein' in one place and my family in another."

"Oh, I forgot," Nola said. "I was thinking today was Thursday. Don't know where my mind's been today."

Trevor McManus looked at her thoughtfully, and as the other men trooped upstairs to pack their bags, he lingered behind. Nola was scraping dishes and stacking them when he spoke to her. She jumped nervously.

"Didn't mean to scare you," he said apologetically. "I just wanted to know if you'd rather I stayed here this weekend. You know, I don't have any family much. I was goin' to see my brother, but it can wait till later if you'd rather we didn't all go off. I hope you'll excuse me if I'm buttin' in where it ain't none of my business, but you seemed to be a mite upset when you realized we's all leavin'. I'd just as leave stay as go if you want me to."

"Oh, Mr. McManus, thank you, but no. Please don't change your plans on my account. I have had some unpleasantness to upset me, but I'm sure everything is going to be all right. I do thank you for the offer though," she told him.

"Well, if you're sure," he said. "I'd be glad to stay if it'd ease your mind."

"You are very kind," she smiled at him. "But Jake will be home tomorrow, and we'll be quite fine. Good night, and have a pleasant time with your folks."

Within an hour, all of the boarders had left for their various destinations, and Nola and the two girls were left alone in the house. Samantha and Anne Marie moped around, fuming because they couldn't leave the house. Nola was relieved when Mrs. Patterson sent Lucas over to ask if the girls could come over and help her with party preparations for her twins' birthday the next day.

"Go on," she told them. "Just don't go anywhere else, and be sure that Mr. Patterson walks you home if it's dark when you get through."

"Will you be all right, Mama?" Samantha asked her. "Why don't you come with us?"

"No, I'm afraid I'll miss Sheriff Tate," she said. "I'll be just fine. The doors are locked, and I'm not about to open them for anybody but the sheriff. You two go now. You'll drive me crazy if you don't."

Eagerly the two girls ran across the yard and into the Patterson house, forgetting for the moment their fears about Anne Marie's father. Nola resolutely picked up the week's mending, determined to keep her mind busy and off her worries.

It was beginning to get dark when she heard a noise on the front porch. Cautiously she picked up the rifle she had placed behind the kitchen door and went into the living room where she could see out. She peeked through the curtains but could see nothing. Just as she had convinced herself that she had imagined the noise, the glass in the front door shattered, and she stared in horror as an arm reached in and pulled the bolt back. Before she could raise the gun, Zeb Martin was in the room. He slapped the gun away as if it were a fly. It went sailing across the room and landed with a thud against a table, knocking the lamp over and breaking it.

"Whar's my young'uns?" he growled at Nola.

"You get out of my house!" Nola demanded. "How dare you break in my home like this. I'll have the law on you."

"I don't give two hoots in hell about yore law!" he said. "I want what's mine, and I aim to have it."

"There are other people in this house," Nola said desperately. "I have boarders here, and they'll be here any minute, so you'd better leave while you can."

"No, they ain't nobody else here," he snarled. "I seen 'em all leave more'n two hours ago. I jest been a'waitin' till dark. Now shut yore mouth and go fetch my young'uns before I use this gun on you."

"They're not here," Nola said hoarsely. "The boys are in another state with Cassie, and Anne Marie has gone to stay with some friends. You might as well leave because you'll find none of them here."

"Well, I'll jest see for myself," he said as he grabbed her arm.

He pushed open the kitchen door with the barrel of his rifle, dragging her along behind him. When he saw there was no one in the kitchen, he went back through the dining and living rooms and up the stairs toward the bedrooms. One by one, he pushed open the doors and looked in the rooms. Nola could only follow along helplessly as he held her in an iron grip. It took all of her will power to keep from crying, but she was determined not to let him know how terrified she was. She kept praying silently that the girls would not return while he was there.

He finally gave up in disgust when he could find no one and went back down the stairs, pulling her along behind him. She stumbled on the stairs, trying to keep up with his long strides, and would have fallen if he had not snatched her up.

When they reached the living room, he flung her from him and she fell heavily on the floor. He pointed the barrel of the rifle between her breasts and leaned over her.

"Now, I reckon ye'd better tell me whar my young'uns are, or else I'll blow a hole clean through you," he growled. "Don't tell me no more lies neither, 'cause I've jest about run out of patience with you."

"As God is my witness, I've told you the truth," she whispered. "Kill me if you must, but I can't tell you anything else. Anne Marie came to us with Glen and George and said her mother told her to find us when she died. We took them to Cassie, and the boys stayed with her. Anne Marie has gone to stay with friends. Even if you kill me, I won't tell you where she is."

"You'd rather die than see a gal united with her pappy?" he asked her. "She's my flesh and blood, and I aim to claim her. They ain't nothin' wrong with that. What's wrong is you a'takin' it on yoreself to interfere with a daughter and her father."

"Father!" Nola said contemptuously. "I know what kind of father you are. I know what you did to Cassie and what you tried to do to Anne Marie. You are the vilest creature on this earth."

"Lies!" he shouted at her. "Nothin' but a pack of lies that Cassie told on me! She were as common as a bitch in heat and then tried to lay hit on me. She weren't even my young'un, and I took her in and fed her like she was my own, and that's the thanks I got."

"Cassie is a good and decent woman," Nola retorted hotly. "And she's married to a fine man. No thanks to you, she's made a good life for herself."

Furiously, Martin kicked at her. She tried to move away from him, but his boot landed in the small of her back. She cried out in pain, unable to keep silent. He smiled maliciously at her, then dropped to one knee beside her. He jerked her toward him, then reached for the neck of her dress. With one motion he ripped the front open to the waist, then grabbed her undergarments and wrenched them apart. Her breasts lay exposed, and he stared at her, his eyes filled with hatred and lust.

"I'll jest give you a little somethin' to remember me by," he grinned at her. "That a'way you won't be tempted to interfere again with some other man's kin."

Nola stiffened with fear as she felt his rough hand groping up under her skirt. She tried to struggle as he pulled her underpants down, but he threw his weight on her, smothering her in the rancid odors of smoke, sweat, and corn liquor. She felt the heat of his putrid breath in her face as he half rose to lower his pants. She tried to scream, but he cut it off with a viselike grip around her throat, and she knew with certainty that he meant to kill her when he had done with her.

As his grip tightened, the room exploded in bright bursts of color, then settled into darkness as she gasped for breath. She felt herself slipping into unconsciousness, and she thought with horror that now there would be no one to keep him from doing the same thing to Samantha and Anne Marie when they came home.

Suddenly, she was able to breathe again, and she thought to herself that at least she had passed through the valley of death and would see Ellen and Will again. Then she felt the excruciating pain in her neck where his hand had been and realized that she was still living. Fearfully, she opened her eyes and gazed up into the anxious face of Trevor McManus. He was rubbing her hands and patting her face, imploring her to speak to him.

"Thank God!" he exclaimed when she opened her eyes. "I feared he had killed you."

She tried to sit up but found she was too weak and lay back helplessly. Then remembering what had happened, she looked at McManus with questioning eyes. When she was finally able to speak, she barely recognized her own voice.

"Samantha? Anne Marie?" she croaked.

"They're all right," he said reassuringly. "They've gone back to Mrs. Patterson's to send somebody for the sheriff. Don't worry, they've not been harmed."

Nola tried again to sit up, but the room spun dizzily, and she was forced to lay back down. She realized with a start that she was on the settee and was covered by a quilt.

"What? How?" she whispered.

"I was uneasy about you," McManus said. "You seemed so worried. I meant to leave on the evening train, but when it came in, I couldn't make myself get on it. I know you said you didn't want my help, but for some reason I just had to come back. When I got here, I saw the broken glass in the door and I saw him, and what he was tryin' to do to you. I guess I went a little crazy for a minute, and I just picked up the first thing I could lay my hands on and hit him over the head as hard as I could. I'm sorry, Mrs.

McGinty, but I reckon I shore busted your table up right bad. Anyhow, the girls came in about that time, and I sent them for the sheriff."

"Martin," Nola croaked. "Where is he?"

"He's layin' over there," McManus gestured. "And I reckon he's still knocked out. I tied him up with some rope Samantha found on the back porch. Anyhow, he ain't said nothin' yet."

"Did he—did he rape me?" Nola gasped.

McManus dropped his eyes. "I don't rightly know, ma'am. I was so scared he'd killed you, I just lit in on him. I—I hope I got here in time. It took you forever to get some color back in your face. He'd 'most choked the life out of you. I reckon your throat is goin' to be mighty sore for a few days."

"How can I ever thank you, Mr. McManus?" Nola whispered hoarsely. "If you hadn't come when you did, I'd be dead now. I was so scared. I've never been so scared in all my life."

"No thanks necessary," he said gruffly. "I'm just glad I got back here when I did. The important thing is that you're alive and you'll be all right. Nothin' else really matters. Just remember that. Well, here comes the sheriff. I'll be glad to be rid of this'n. Looks like he's comin' to." He stood up to greet the sheriff. "Howdy, Sheriff, got you a customer here."

Anne Marie and Samantha had slipped in while McManus was telling Nola what had happened. They now knelt beside Nola, patting her hand and crying. Anne Marie turned to look at her father as the sheriff led him stumbling out of the room. He looked back at her as they took him out the door.

"Anne Marie, baby girl," he said. "You know yore pappy loves you. I jest wanted my baby girl back where she belonged. You tell 'em, honey. You tell 'em how that woman stole you away from me."

Anne Marie stared at him for a long moment, then turned her back on him and put her arms around Nola.

THIRTY-TWO

The shock of what had happened to her did not fully sink in on Nola until the next day. After he had locked Martin in jail, Sheriff Tate sent Dr. Hall to see about Nola's injuries. Fortunately, she was not hurt except for bruises around her neck where Martin had choked her and on her back where he had kicked her. However, the injuries were deeper than mere physical bruises.

In all of Nola's life she had never been treated with violence. Her trouble with Sam had certainly been hurtful, but no one had ever lifted a hand to her in anger, nor had she ever been exposed to anything like the savage fury that Zeb Martin had turned on her. Her parents had both been gentle people who had treated their children and each other with respect and love. This experience had been totally foreign to Nola's nature, and it was to have far-reaching effects on her life. Never again would she be able to stand the thoughts of a man touching her or showing any signs of desiring to get close to her. The experience had frozen any desire for intimacy with a man, and she became suspicious of any interest a man might show toward her, no matter how innocent it was.

Jake was late getting home that night and knew nothing of the incident until the next morning. Samantha and Anne Marie told him what had happened. Nola had not risen at her usual early hour and the girls had busied themselves in the kitchen, determined to let her rest for a while. When Jake heard what had happened, however, he rushed to Nola's room. He hesitated at her door, then knocked softly.

"Is that you, Samantha?" his mother's voice called softly.

"No, Mama, it's me," Jake answered. "Can I come in?"

"Yes, of course, Jake. Come on in," Nola answered.

170

Jake opened the door and slipped quietly into the room. He gasped in horror when he saw the bruise marks on Nola's throat.

"Mama, are you all right?" he cried. "How bad did he hurt you? If I'd been here, I'd of killed him."

"Hush," Nola admonished him. "Don't take on so. I'm all right except for being sore and bruised. We were lucky that nothing worse happened. I'm just so thankful the girls weren't here. No telling what he'd have done if he'd got hold of Anne Marie. I'm glad you weren't here, too. He had a gun, and, from the looks of him, he'd just as soon have shot you as not."

"Oh, Mama, I feel so bad that I wasn't here when you needed me," Jake said. "I'll just tell Red I'm not takin' any more trips out of town. I'll stay near so you can send for me if you need me."

"No such thing," Nola said. "If you're going to be part of a band, you'll have to go where it goes. You won't be much help to them if you can't travel. You are not to let this worry you now. It's over."

"What will they do to him?" Jake asked. "I hope they put him where he can't bother anybody again."

"Sheriff Tate said he'd likely get sent to the chain gang," Nola answered. Her voice softened, and it quivered as she said, "For Anne Marie's sake, I hope he does."

In spite of herself, Nola's eyes filled with tears and she began shaking. Jake stood, looking at her helplessly. He had never seen his mother look this vulnerable. He patted her awkwardly on the shoulder.

"Go on now," Nola said shakily. "I've got to get up and see about breakfast. I didn't mean to stay in bed so late, but I guess I was more tired than I realized. Tell the girls I'll be down as soon as I get dressed. Don't worry about me. I'll be all right."

When Jake had left, Nola crawled slowly out of bed, wincing in pain when she stood. She hobbled over to the bowl and pitcher she kept in her room and poured water out into the bowl and washed her face. She dressed slowly, hurting with every movement. She wondered how in the world she would manage to tie her shoes, but the problem was solved for her when Samantha quietly entered the room.

"Mama, can I help you with anything?" she asked timidly. "I didn't know how sore your back would be today. I could help you with your shoes if you'll let me."

"Thank you, Samantha," Nola said gratefully. "I don't think I can manage them today. Do you know where my dress is that I had on last night? I can't seem to find it."

"I put it in with the mending," Samantha said. "He . . . he tore it down the front. Your slip, too. I didn't know if you'd want to mend it or not."

"We'll see," Nola answered. "Did Mr. McManus leave last night? I can't remember if I thanked him properly or not. I shudder to think what would have happened if it hadn't been for him."

"He left this mornin' on the early train," Samantha said. "He was afraid his brother would be uneasy about him if he didn't show up. He said he'd be back tomorrow evenin'. He wouldn't leave until I tiptoed in your room to make sure you were all right."

Nola painfully crept down the stairs to the kitchen where Jake and Anne Marie were waiting. They both rushed to help her sit down at the kitchen table, which Samantha and Anne Marie had set for breakfast.

"Don't fuss over me so," Nola said. "I'm just sore, and I'll be all right after I move around some. Looks like you girls have fixed us a fine breakfast. Jake, you say grace and we'll eat. I know you're all hungry, waiting on me to get up. I didn't realize it was so late."

The meal was quiet, without Jake's usual banter about his out-of-town trip. Anne Marie was especially subdued, looking timidly at Nola and jumping up whenever she thought Nola needed something. Finally, when the meal was almost over, the young woman spoke timidly.

"I reckon it'd be better if I just packed up my belongin's and went to Cassie's," she murmured. "That way Pa wouldn't have no call to come botherin' you all again. I'd of druther cut off my arm than had him harm you, Nola. I don't reckon I'll ever be able to forgive myself for bringin' this trouble on you."

"You'll do no such thing," Nola declared vehemently. "I don't want to hear another word about you leaving. I'm going to talk to Sheriff Tate and make sure he's put where he won't be able to harm you or anybody else. Now I don't want this to trouble you anymore, Anne Marie. You're as much a part of this family as any of the rest of us are, and I'd not even think of sending you away."

Anne Marie cried softly as Jake and Samantha comforted her and added their support to what their mother had said.

"Now, while we're all together, there's something else I need to clear up," Nola said firmly. "Jake, I want to tell you that you do not have to sneak around to write your father. I have never forbidden you or Samantha to keep in contact with him if you wanted to, and there's no reason for you to think I ever would. As for you going to see him, I guess that's for you to decide too. I think you ought to give it serious thought before you take off for a strange place, but as I said, that's for you to decide. I do want to ask you one thing, and that is for you to be honest with me and not do anything behind my back. I've always tried to be honest with both of you, and I think you owe me the same courtesy."

Jake flushed at Nola's words and shot a hostile look at Samantha, who stared back at him defiantly. He finally turned back to Nola and sighed.

"I'm sorry, Mama," he said. "I didn't tell you I was writin' Papa 'cause I thought it would cause you pain. I still remember how hurt you was when he left, and I didn't want to open up old wounds. That's the only reason I didn't tell you."

"It hurts me worse when you deceive me," she said quietly. "You're a grown man, Jake, and you have to make your own decisions, but make them honestly."

"I'm not goin' to see him any time soon," Jake said slowly, "but I think that sometime I will want to go. I promise you that I will tell you when I decide, though. You can believe me, Mama."

"Thank you, Jake," Nola said. "Now. Let's forget this and get on with the day's work. You will have to help the girls today. I just don't quite feel up to it."

Everyone went about their work, very subdued and thoughtful. Not having Nola in the middle of everything was odd, and they felt her presence even more keenly than they would have had she been in the room with them. At lunch time, Samantha fixed a tray and took it up to Nola's room, where she tapped quietly on the door. When Nola didn't answer, she pushed the door open slightly and looked in. Nola was sitting in her rocking chair by the window, looking down on the street below. She started when Samantha came in the room and looked up fearfully.

"Oh, Mama, I didn't mean to scare you," Samantha said. "I thought you might be asleep, and I didn't want to wake you. I've brought you some soup and bread and cheese. You didn't eat any breakfast, and I thought maybe you'd rather just eat in your room and not try to come down the stairs."

"Thank you, Samantha," Nola said. "You didn't scare me. I reckon I'm just a little nervous today. Just put the tray down on the night table. I'll eat in a little while. I think I will stay here for today. I didn't rest well last night, and I might take a nap later. You didn't hear anything from Sheriff Tate, did you?"

"No, ma'am," Samantha answered, "Jake said he was goin' by there later today and see what was happenin'." She set the tray down and went to stand next to her mother. "Oh, Mama, it hurts me to see you so upset. I could just kill that old Zeb Martin for hurtin' you."

"You mustn't talk like that, Samantha," Nola admonished her. "Thoughts like that harm you worse than they do anyone else. Besides, we have to remember that he is Anne Marie's father, and we don't want to say anything to upset her any more than she already is. We mustn't say or do anything that will make her blame herself."

"I would never say anything in front of her," Samantha protested. "She cries everytime she thinks about what he did to you. Mama, she loves and admires you above anyone. You know that."

"Yes, I do know," Nola said, taking her daughter's hand. "And that's why I hope we can put this behind us as soon as possible. I've been thinking, though, Samantha, while I've been sitting here this morning. I want you and Anne Marie to be careful around the men boarders. You mustn't give them any reason to think they could take liberties with you. From now on, I want the two of you to work together or with me and not be alone in the house."

Nola looked intensely at Samantha, then shuddered involuntarily. Samantha looked at her with alarm.

"Mama, you've told us this before. You know we aren't going to do anything to give them the wrong ideas. Besides, they're all nice to us. Mr. Norton teases us sometimes, but we know he doesn't mean half he says. I think he's just homesick for his own family. He told me he has two girls of his own almost as old as we are."

"Nevertheless, you mind what I say," Nola said sternly. "You can't ever know what a man has on his mind."

"All right, Mama," Samantha said placatingly. "I'll remember. Now don't fret yourself so. Eat your soup before it gets cold, then rest."

The boarders came back on the late Sunday train. Sunday supper was always light, so no one was too surprised that Nola wasn't there. Only McManus noted her absence. When he asked Jake about her, Jake told him she was resting on the doctor's orders. He asked McManus if he would tell the other men what had happened so that Nola wouldn't have to make any explanations.

"I can't tell you how much we thank you for savin' Mama from that man," Jake told McManus. "It makes my blood run cold to think what might have happened to her and the girls if you hadn't been here."

McManus shrugged off Jake's thanks, muttering, "I only done what anyone would have."

The next morning Nola was up at her usual early hour and, except for moving a little slowly, seemed her normal self. She wore a high-necked dress that covered the angry bruises on her throat.

McManus lingered behind the other men as they started off for work and laid a solicitous hand on Nola's arm, meaning to express his concern for her. When he touched her, she shrank back in fear, and he hastily withdrew his hand, crushed that he had upset her.

"I'm so sorry if I upset you, Mrs. McGinty," he apologized. "I only meant to say that I was glad to see you was a'feelin' better. Please forgive me for bein' so thoughtless."

"It's all right," Nola said hastily. "It's me that should be thanking you, Mr. McManus. I guess I'm still pretty nervous."

McManus nodded to her and left behind the other men. As soon as they were out the door, Nola pushed the bolt to with shaking hands.

Dear God, what is happening to me? she thought. Am I such a scaredy cat that I'm going to jump every time somebody touches me?

Zeb Martin was sentenced to ten years at hard labor on the chain gang because of his violent acts, and Nola thought that at last she could put the incident behind her. She did heal physically, but the emotional scars stayed with her for the rest of her life. She was never comfortable in the company of men after that, and when time came for her to replace one of the male boarders, she sought out women to take their places until she had only female boarders in the house.

Nola wrote Cassie about the incident after Martin had been dealt with. She wrote as much to reassure Cassie that she had nothing to fear from her stepfather anymore as she did to tell her what had happened. She was surprised that she did not receive a reply from her and began to wonder if her letter had been lost before Cassie received it. Just before she decided to write another one though, she had a letter from Cassie.

> Dear Nola,
>
> I was so upset to get your letter about Zeb Martin. I can't even bring myself to call him my stepfather anymore. I think I'd better come and see about Anne Marie. I hope you won't take it that I don't think you're lookin after her. I know you are. It's just that I think it's my place to come and tell her some things. Joshua agrees with me. Anyhow, I'll be there soon as I can get things took care of here. Besides, I've been longin to see her and you again and finally get to see Jake and Samantha. Seems like life just gets away from us before we do what we want to, don't it? Look for me soon, and till then I remain,
>
> > Your friend,
> > Cassie Perkins

Nola was oddly disturbed by Cassie's letter. There was none of her usual news about the children and the letter seemed to have an air of somberness about it. She kept her reservations to herself though and tried to join in the joy and excitement that Anne Marie was experiencing as she planned for Cassie's visit.

A telegram arrived almost two weeks later announcing that Cassie would arrive the next day. Anne Marie's excitement was contagious, and Jake and Samantha were caught up in the preparations for this visitor whom they had heard so much about over the years. When it came time to go to the train station to meet her, even Jake was dressed and ready to go.

Nola watched eagerly as the train pulled into the station, standing on tiptoe and straining to see over the heads of the crowd at the station. She almost overlooked Cassie, so changed was her appearance. She was shocked when she finally realized that the thin woman standing at the top of the steps was her beloved Cassie.

THIRTY-THREE

"Cassie! Cassie!" Nola cried as she waved frantically to her friend. "Over here, Cassie! Over here!"

A broad grin filled Cassie's face as she spotted Nola. She stepped down from the train, and the two rushed into each other's arms, laughing and crying at the same time. Cassie looked up at Anne Marie, standing quietly behind Nola, and opened her arms wider to embrace her sister as well.

When they finally had a chance to catch their breath, they pulled back and looked at each other. This was a different Cassie from the healthy young woman Nola had bid farewell to in Tennessee, and Nola's heart leaped painfully in her throat as she felt how thin she had become. Remembering the shy mountain girl who had left the cove so many years ago, Nola wondered what her mother would have thought of this Cassie standing before her. She was stylishly dressed in a dove gray traveling suit and was every inch a lady, from the high-buttoned shoes on her feet to the black feathered hat covering her hair.

When they had finished greeting each other, Nola drew Samantha and Jake over and introduced them to Cassie. Cassie gave them both a penetrating stare, then nodded in approval at what she saw.

"I reckon you got yourself two fine-looking children," she told Nola softly. "It's hard for me to think of them as grown-ups. I've pictured them in my mind for so many years as children, I reckon it'll take me some time to get used to them being grown. My, my, Samantha, but you do remind me of your pa. And you, Jake, you remind me of your Grandpa Will. If you're half as good a man as he was, you'll be all right, 'cause no finer man than Will Johnston was ever born on this earth."

"I suppose they'll both do just fine," Nola said quietly. "Now come on. Let's collect your bags. I know you must be wore out with your long trip.

177

Jake, please see to the things on her baggage ticket while we put this stuff in the buggy."

When they got to the boarding house, they were busy for a time bringing in Cassie's luggage and getting her settled, then Nola insisted that Cassie rest for a while.

"I hope you won't mind sleeping with me," Nola said apologetically. "Usually I keep one room for company, but there was a fire at one of the boarding houses, and I had to take two men into my extra room temporarily. Everybody in town that had a room to spare had to help out. It won't be for long, but right now it leaves me without a spare room."

"Oh, Nola, it'll be just like old times!" Cassie exclaimed. "We'll have such fun. We can talk all night long without botherin' anybody." The two friends made their way upstairs, and Cassie sat on Nola's bed. Nola began to unpack some of Cassie's clothes as they talked, marveling at their richness. "Makes me long for the times when we was all here together. Now Martha's gone and your ma and pa. It's so sad. It was always such a comfort to me just knowin' you was all here just like I left you. Now it's all changed, and I miss them all so much. I know you do, too."

"Not a day passes that I don't miss them," Nola said sadly. "I have my memories, though, and we've got Lucy and Charles to remember our Martha by. Lucy is the spitting image of her. Mama used to say it was just like seeing Martha all over again. Now, come on and sit down and let me look at you. Take them feathers off your head so I can see if your hair's still as red as it used to be."

Cassie tossed her hat onto the bed and shook her hair loose. "Well, you sure haven't changed much, Nola," Cassie said. "Your hair's as dark as ever. Mine's showin' some grey, I'm afraid. Course it's time, I 'spect."

Nola looked at her friend. The hair had dimmed somewhat over the years, but the eyes were as bright and clear as Nola remembered. She sat next to her friend on the bed.

"Now, Cassie, you must start at the beginning and tell me everything that's been happening with your family since I saw you. I'm hungry to hear about them and about what's happening with Joshua, too. How are Glen and George? Are they still happy in Tennessee? How about their schooling? Your letters have told me some of this, but I'd rather hear it from your own lips."

"Whoa, slow down!" Cassie laughed. "I'll tell you everything, but let's not do it all in one night. We got lots of time. Sue Ellen finished her schoolin' at home, and then went on to teacher's college. She's teachin' alongside of Joshua and loves it. 'Course she's courtin' right heavy now, and I reckon it won't be long till she'll be talkin' about marryin'. William Taylor is still in school, studyin' to be a doctor. Jeremiah declared he was through with schoolin' when he finished at his papa's school. It's took all this time for Joshua to find somebody to take over the farm for him, but I reckon Jeremiah's gonna be the one. Glen and George help him, and I don't think we'll be able to keep them in school much longer. Jeremiah's talkin' about startin' him a herd of cattle, and when he does, I think that'll give the boys the excuse they need to quit altogether. That's enough about me, though. Tell me how you're a'doin'. Nola, I can't tell you how upset I've been over what happened to you. I can't stand the thought that Zeb Martin put his hands on you."

"That's all behind us now, and he's been dealt with," Nola said hastily. "I sure hope you didn't come all the way back here just because of that trash. I'll admit it shook me up pretty bad, but I'm over it now. We're just going to put the whole thing behind us." She stood up and smoothed her skirt. "Come on now, I've got to get supper started. You come on down to the kitchen with me and keep me company while I cook. Besides, I know Anne Marie is dying to talk to you and find out about Glen and George."

The two friends made their way down the stairs and were met by Anne Marie and Samantha, who bombarded Cassie with a dozen questions all at once. Nola smiled as she listened to their excited chatter.

"How long can you stay, Cassie?" Anne Marie asked. "I hope you can stay a long time."

"Well, Joshua said I was to stay as long as I wanted to," Cassie replied happily. "He said it was to be somethin' called a sabbatical. Whatever that is."

At supper that night Nola delighted in introducing Cassie to her boarders as "my long lost sister, Cassie." She beamed as Cassie charmed them with her straightforward talk and good humor.

Jake was fascinated with Cassie's charm and wit. She teased the three young people and kept them laughing at stories about their mother and their Uncle Willie.

One story in particular that brought gales of laughter from everyone was a story Cassie told about a fictitious uncle of hers.

"I had an uncle that lived in Yancey County," Cassie said. "He always claimed that the mountains where he lived was steeper than the ones around here. He said they was so steep that the cows growed two short legs on one side and two long legs on t'other, just so they could graze the steep pastures. He said them hills was so steep that folks had trouble growin' 'taters. Said the land was a whole lot richer than here, though, and the 'taters three or four times bigger. Maybe more. Once my uncle claimed he planted his rows up and down 'stead of across, and when it come time to dig them, he dug under the first row, and one of the big ones rolled down the hillside and took a great slew of dirt with it. Well, the dirt

dammed up a good-sized stream and made a fifty-acre lake. Then that
'tater bored a hole through a mountain where the railroad was fixin' to dig
a tunnel and went on down a half mile further and dammed up another
stream where a company was fixin' to built a power plant."

By now Jake was laughing so hard he was practically rolling on the
floor. Wiping the tears from his eyes, he said, "I reckon you're gonna tell
us he got paid for all this."

"Why, of course he did," Cassie declared. "With the money he got for
the tunnel and what the power company paid him for savin' them the price
of a dam, you'd a'thought he was settin' on top of the world."

"I'd say he was the world's luckiest man!" exclaimed Nola through her
laughter.

"Well, in a way he was," Cassie continued. "But he didn't always have
such good luck. I mind the time when he was so pore, he couldn't buy a
hen and chickens. Why, he got so down and out, he tried to kill hisself.
He had an old pistol, and he figgered to shoot hisself. But he was afraid it
wouldn't work, so he went down to the store and bought a jug of
kerosene, a piece of strong rope, and some rat poison. Then he went down
to the river and got in a boat and rowed hisself down to where some trees
hung over the water.

"He tied the rope around his neck and to the limb of a tree, soaked
hisself in kerosene, ate the rat poison, and set his clothes on fire, figgerin'
on shootin' hisself soon's he kicked the boat out from under. He was the
sort of man that never done nothin' half way.

"Well, he kicked the boat away and the pistol went off, shootin' the
rope in two. He fell in the water and that put the fire out. When he went
under the water, he got to chokin' and stranglin' so that he throwed up the
poison.

"Now, he wasn't no dumb somebody, so he figgered right away that his
luck had changed. He swum over to the bank and announced to the people
that had gathered around to see what all the ruckus was about that he was
a'declarin' hisself a candidate for the legislater. Got elected too!"

On that tale, the evening ended. Everyone went off to bed, and Jake left
for his job. "I'm sure glad I got to go in late tonight, Cassie," he said. "I
wouldn't have missed your stories for anything. You are just as wonderful
and funny as Mama always said you were."

"That Jake is sure a charmer," Cassie told Nola that night after they
went to bed. "And Samantha, it must tear your heart out every time you
look at her, she's so much like Sam."

"I guess my memories of Sam have faded somewhat," Nola said drily,
"because I just see my daughter when I look at her, not her father. As for

Jake, he's got the makings of a fine man if he just won't let his obsession with music ruin him. Sometime he's going to have to put it aside if he ever settles down and marries. He's going to have to realize he can't make a living at it."

"And Sam, what about him?" Cassie asked. "Do you ever hear from him? Does he ever come to see his children?"

"He's been back here once since his ma died," Nola said slowly. "He brought his wife and children with him. John came and took Jake and Samantha over to see him, but I didn't see anything of him. Didn't want to either."

"And John, did he ever marry?" Cassie asked. "I was disappointed when you turned him down. I felt sad for both of you."

"Yes, he married a nice lady named Daisy Murray. They seem to be very happy. I know that what I did was the best thing for both of us, Cassie. Nobody understood why I wouldn't marry him, but I knew that eventually I'd make us both miserable. Pearl still lives with them, and she and Daisy get along real well. Pearl dotes on Lucy and Charles. Don't know what she'll do when they marry. Looks like Lucy might be marrying soon."

"But you, Nola, what about you?" Cassie asked. "There must be more to life than this boarding house. What makes Nola happy?"

"My children and my church," Nola said quietly. "Don't worry about me, Cassie. I am very content with my life. My days are so full, I don't know how I'd have time for anything or anyone else. Right now we're trying to raise enough money to build a new church, and I've been working on dinners and a quilt with the Ladies Aid Society to raise money to help. Between my church and my neighbors, I have a lot of real good friends. I stay busy."

Cassie looked into her friend's eyes, and what she saw there seemed to satisfy her.

"There's something bothering me, Cassie," Nola said slowly. "You are too thin. Is there something wrong with you that you haven't told me? I watched you at supper, and you just picked at your food."

Cassie sighed and dropped her eyes for a moment. "I don't rightly know what's wrong with me, Nola. I just ain't had no appetite for a long time. Everything I eat seems to disagree with me. One reason Joshua was so anxious for me to come was in hopes the mountain air would make me eat better. I promised him I'd try, but I just don't know."

"Well, we'll just have to see if we can't tempt you to eat more," Nola said brusquely. "If you think of something you want while you're here, just tell me."

The two women talked on into the night, catching up on what had been happening in their lives. When they finally went to sleep, Nola dreamed of pastures of wild flowers and children running barefoot through the grass. It was the most restful night's sleep she had enjoyed in years.

The time seemed to fly by, and before they knew it a month had passed, Cassie said it was time for her to start for home.

"I reckon I'd better get back and see to my family," she told Nola one morning. "I wouldn't want them to find out they could get along without me. There's one thing I'd like to do before I go, though. I'd like to go to the graveyard where your folks are buried and where they buried my baby. I may not ever get back here again, and I want to go there one last time. I reckon all this trouble has made me think about that little baby. It never did seem real to me, and somehow that makes me feel sad now. I'd just like to go see the place one more time."

"Of course we can," Nola said. "I was just waiting for the right time to suggest it myself. We'll pack a lunch tomorrow and drive out there. If you want to, we can go to the rock and eat our dinner, then go by the graveyard on the way back. I've been wanting to go out there for a long time. I haven't been up to the rock since the children were little. Mama loved that place so."

The next morning they were up early and ready to go as soon as they had finished with the breakfast dishes. Nola left instructions for Samantha and Anne Marie to prepare the noon meal, and they hooked up the horse to the buggy and started for the cove.

Nola drove the buggy to the foot of the trail that led to the huge rock that was their destination. This rock had been a place where Nola and her family had spent many happy times picnicking and playing when they were children. It was also the place where Joshua proposed to Cassie. Located at the top of a steep meadow, it was almost a one-mile climb. Nola and Cassie divided up the picnic supplies and started their trek up the mountain slope. They hadn't gone far when Cassie called to Nola, who was ahead of her on the trail.

"I don't reckon there's much traffic on this trail, is there, Nola?"

"No, I don't think so, especially in the middle of the week. Why do you ask?"

"Because I'm tired of this long skirt a'swishin' around my ankles and catchin' on every briar in sight. I aim to fix it a little more comfortable," Cassie said.

With that, she tucked her skirt up into the waistband and stood in her narrow slip.

"There now, that's better," she sighed. "Why don't you hitch yours up, too?"

"What if somebody saw us?" Nola asked. "What on earth would they say, seeing two middle-aged women with their skirts all hitched up half-way to their heads?"

"What difference does it make what they say?" Cassie laughed. "Chances are we'd never see 'em again anyhow. Come on, don't be such a scaredy cat. I bet if old Martha was here, she'd do it in a minute."

"She would too," Nola laughed. "Oh, well, here goes."

They giggled at each other, standing there in their slips, then continued their climb to the huge rock that dominated the meadow above them. When they arrived, they let their skirts down and spread a cloth out on the ground beneath the shade of the rock.

"I remember so many times that Mama used to bring us up here when we were children," Nola sighed. "It was just a good hike from home. She said she loved it up here because she could pretend she was in a different world, but was still close enough to get home if she was needed. Look, you can see the smoke from the chimney of our house, there to the left. Ours used to be the only house in this section of the cove, but Joseph sold off some of the land, and now there's half a dozen more houses.

"Time goes so fast, Cassie, it scares me sometimes. I feel like if I blink my eyes, everything will be over. When we were girls, I fretted because I was in such a hurry to grow up and have everything happen to me. Now I feel like I'd like to take time in my hands and just hold on to it to keep it from running away from me. It was no time ago that my children were just babies and look at them now, all grown up and chomping at the bit to get out on their own. Jake comes home every night with a different scheme that he wants to try. And Samantha—seems like I run a different boy off every day. One of these days soon, one of them's going to take her with him."

"I know, Nola, I'm facin' the same things," Cassie sighed. "Listen, though, let's not spend our last day bein' sad. Who knows, we might not see each other again for a long time. I don't want you to remember our last day together a'cryin' on each other's shoulder."

"Cassie, I've got to ask you one last question, and I promise it'll be the last serious thought I'll have," Nola said quietly. "I want to know how you're feeling. Seems to me you're not eating any better than you were when you got here and if anything, you're even thinner."

Cassie looked at Nola and smiled sadly. "Nola, I've been feelin' a mite tired lately. The doctor said the last baby caused me some problems, and things haven't been exactly right for me ever since. I just leave everything in the hands of the Lord, though. I'll be here as long as He has need of me, I reckon, and when He says it's my time to go, I'll not fault Him 'cause I've had a mighty fine life."

Nola put her arms around Cassie, and the two friends sat for a time clinging to each other. Then Nola brushed the tears from her eyes and spread their lunch out. They ate their simple meal, then, throwing their bread scraps out onto the meadow for the birds, they sat back and watched as a flock of noisy blue jays descended on the unexpected meal. One came and set up a raucous calling until there were a half dozen swooping down to eat. When the scraps were gone, they vanished as quickly as they had come and left the meadow in silence once more.

"Before we leave, I want to pick some flowers for my baby's grave," Cassie said. "I saw a patch of black-eyed Susans just a little ways over there."

Cassie walked through the broom sage and grass until she found the flowers she was looking for. She picked a handful of the bright yellowish orange flowers with dark brown centers and stood for a moment looking at them. Then she buried her face in them, feeling the soft touch of their petals against her face and the sticky stems in her hands. Slowly, she walked back to where Nola was waiting for her.

"I never took flowers to my baby before," she told Nola. "I wonder why—after all these years—I finally can."

As the sun began to slip down toward the mountain, Nola and Cassie gathered up their basket and started back down the trail to their horse and buggy. Then they turned up the trail that led to the old cabin where Ellen and Will had first settled when they came to the cove. It took them fifiteen minutes to reach their destination. There they searched out the burial grounds where Will, Ellen, Tildy, and Cassie's stillborn baby were buried. The area had been freshly mowed, and jars of wild flowers were at each grave marker.

"Some of the folks want us to have them moved down to the church cemetery," Nola said, "but in our hearts we all knew that this was where they wanted to be. Willie and Joseph look after the graves, and I come as often as I can and bring flowers. When I can't come, I know one of them or their children will take care of things."

Cassie knelt down by her baby's grave and laid the handful of black-eyed Susans that she had picked on the grave.

"Good-bye, little baby," she said.

Then she walked over to Ellen and Will's graves and touched their stone markers.

"Good-bye, my dear friends," she murmured. "You were more mother and father to me than my own were. I owe you my everlastin' gratitude. I owe you my very life."

Silently, they left the site and got back into the buggy. They drove home, exchanging very few words, not feeling the need to talk.

Nola took Cassie to the depot the next morning. Her heart was heavy, and she dreaded seeing her friend leave, somehow knowing that this would be the last time they would see each other. They clung to one another, then Cassie broke off and turned to her sister.

"Now, Anne Marie, you write me, hear?" Cassie admonished her sister. "I want to know how things are with you, and if there's any more trouble, you just get on the train and come to me."

"Oh, Cassie, this is my home now," Anne Marie said. "Don't worry about me. I'm gonna be fine. Nola takes good care of me."

"I know she does," Cassie smiled.

The engineer gave two sharp blasts on the whistle, and Cassie hastily climbed aboard.

They waved as long as they could see the train, watching it disappear around the bend, then continued watching until they could no longer see the black smoke belching up from the engine.

Six months later Nola received a letter from Joshua.

> Dear Nola and Anne Marie,
>
> I write you with a heavy heart to tell you that Cassie has died. She was sick from the time she came home from her visit with you. The doctor said it was some sort of female disease that had been eating at her since she had the last baby. I am so glad she had that visit with you. You will never know how much pleasure it gave her and what a comfort it was to her that Anne Marie is with you, Nola. You and your family were so important to her. She felt like she owed all that she was to you and to your mother.
>
> I regret that I could not fulfill my promise to her to take her back to the mountains to live, but circumstances prevented us from returning.
>
> How shall I go on without her? She was the light of my life and my reason for living.
>
> In sorrow,
> Joshua

THIRTY-FOUR

Nola wondered many times how she would go on without Cassie in her life, too. Her death left a void that no one else ever filled. She and Anne Marie became closer as Nola replaced Cassie as an older sister, and Anne Marie came to represent a part of Cassie that was still with Nola.

The next summer after Cassie's death, Samantha met a young man who came to the mountains as an apprentice to the railroad company and fell head over heels in love with him. It was an entirely new experience for her, since she had always been the one to control the tempo of her love affairs. She had held the young men who came courting her at arm's length until she met Jonathan. His quiet good looks and sincere demeanor stripped away all of the pretentiousness of flirtations, and Samantha found herself helpless to resist him. They were married on her nineteenth birthday, and she moved with him to the East Coast where the railroad maintained headquarters. Nola was devastated to have her daughter so far away, but she knew that Jonathan would be a faithful husband to her.

Anne Marie showed little interest in the young men who came around and seemed content in helping Nola run the boarding house for the time being. Jake began spending less time at home, and Nola wondered if there was a special girl in his life. She decided that she would wait for him to tell her and try not to ask him too many questions.

Business was thriving, and Nola began buying up property in the town and investing in rental houses. She soon acquired a reputation as a shrewd businesswoman in the community. By the time Jake celebrated his twenty-first birthday, she had become financially secure for the first time in her life.

Nola felt her life was full and, if not entirely happy, at least reasonably rewarding. She took great pride in the fact that she was independent of any man's help. Since moving to Waynestown, there had been many men who had made the mistake of assuming that she would welcome their attentions. She quickly and firmly dispelled their notions. When she was tempted by her loneliness to become interested in some man, the memory of Zeb Martin's violent attack clouded her mind, and she quickly repulsed all such thoughts. Her only interests, other than her businesses, were her children, Anne Marie, and her church.

The summer of Jake's twenty-first birthday, he finally brought Saralyn home with him to meet Nola. She came from a well-to-do family in Georgia and had come to nearby Lake Junaluska to teach in the summer school sponsored by the Methodist Assembly. Nola liked the gentle, dark-haired girl immediately.

"I want to make Jake a good wife," she told Nola in her soft southern drawl. "I know I'll need a lot of help because I don't know anything about cookin' or keepin' house. I hope you'll help me, Mrs. McGinty. And you too, Anne Marie."

"I reckon we'll be happy to teach you anything we can," Nola assured her. "Our ways are simple, but we will help you in every way we can."

Nola found out that Saralyn was not exaggerating when she said she knew nothing about homemaking skills. Her family had always had servants who took care of their needs, and she knew nothing of what was involved in running a household.

When Saralyn married Jake, she found herself in a situation with which she was unprepared to cope. They were married only a little over a year when their first son was born. They named him William Jacob McGinty, Jr. He was a happy, placid baby, but Saralyn did not have much time to enjoy him because when he was only six months old, she found herself pregnant again. The second baby was also a boy, whom they named John Rogers McGinty after Saralyn's father.

Jake had been raised by two strong-willed women, Nola and Ellen, and he was used to women being able to cope with any situation. Consequently, he was insensitive to Saralyn's inability to cope with her circumstances. Nola tried to act as a buffer when it was obvious to her that Saralyn had reached the end of her patience with Jake. She took Jake to task for his callousness.

"Jake, you must be more sensitive to Saralyn's needs," she told him. "She's not used to the responsibilities of two young children. And besides, she's having to learn how to keep house. You need to help her more, and you need to pay more attention to her needs."

"Mama, I have to make a living for those two babies, and I'm working day and night trying to do that," he protested. "What about *my* needs? I took on this extra job in the daytime, and she ought to appreciate that."

"You have to find some way to work things out so you have more time together. Just remember why you married each other," she told him sharply.

Jake's earnings with the band were not enough to support his growing family, and Nola had helped out by providing a house for them. However, Jake also had to take a daytime job as a desk clerk at the hotel. The extra money eased the financial strain, but the extra time he spent away from home was an added burden on the marriage. Jake stubbornly refused to see what was happening to his marriage.

Saralyn was a gentle, even-tempered person, but finally at the end of a week when she had hardly seen Jake and both babies had been sick, she reached the limit of her patience. At her mother's urging, she packed up both children and went home to her family. Saralyn's mother had opposed her marriage to Jake from the beginning because she did not think he was worthy of her daughter.

"This man will not be able to make the kind of home for you that you are used to," she had warned Saralyn.

Nola was distressed at the development, but she knew this was something Jake and Saralyn would have to work out for themselves.

"I'm only going to say one thing to you," she told Jake. "I want you to remember what it's been like for you to be raised without a father. I can help Saralyn learn how to keep house and take care of the children, but I cannot give her the kind of support she needs from her husband."

A week without his family was enough for Jake. He took the train to Atlanta and then caught a milk truck to the small town where Saralyn's family lived, intent on persuading her to come home with him.

After the first two days under her mother's roof, Saralyn had begun to miss Jake, too. At first she had enjoyed having someone else tend the children and having no housework to worry about, but then she began to chafe under her mother's bossiness. She began to compare her mother's domineering personality with Nola's unobtrusive helpfulness.

When Jake stepped down from the milk truck, Saralyn was sitting on the porch, holding the baby and keeping a watchful eye on little Jake. All harsh words and hurt feelings were forgotten as the two young people looked at each other. Saralyn ran into Jake's arms, and words tumbled over each other as they promised never to be parted again.

Under the disapproving eyes of her mother, Saralyn packed up their belongings and the two young people went back to their home in the mountains. A happy Nola met them at the train station and drove them home.

While she had been busy helping Saralyn with the babies, Nola had turned most of the responsibilities of the boarding house over to Anne Marie. She tried to express her gratitude to Anne Marie.

"If I didn't have you to help me, Anne Marie, I don't know how I would manage," Nola said one day. "Don't let me lean too heavily on you. I don't want you to miss out on your own opportunities because of my needs."

"Don't worry, Nola," Anne Marie answered. "I take as much pleasure as you do in runnin' the house. You just help that little Saralyn all you want. I'll look after things here. Did you get the message that Joseph left for you? He was powerful anxious to get up with you the other day when he come to town."

"Yes, I'm afraid I did," she said wrily. "He needed a loan. Things have got in a bad fix at the home place lately, and he needed to put up a new barn and buy some new equipment and stock. I let him have what he needed."

"I hope you got his note on it, Nola," Anne Marie said quietly. "I know he's your brother, but it's better to keep things businesslike."

"I did," Nola answered. "It's for six months and renewable at that time for six more months if he needs it. He thinks he'll be able to start paying me back by then, though."

When the end of the six months came and passed with no word from Joseph, Nola was somewhat vexed with him but did nothing about it at the time. Jake's second son, John, had scarlet fever, and she was worried about him and was burning the candle at both ends as she tried to care for the older son, William, and the new baby girl, Alma, that had just been born. Consequently, three months passed before she realized that she had done nothing to recoup her money.

When John was better, Nola felt that she finally had the time to take care of the matter with Joseph. She was busy making her plans to go to the farm the next morning when a knock at the front door interrupted her. She went to the door and found a worried looking Sheriff Tate standing there, hat in hand.

"Why, Sheriff Tate, what can I do for you? Is something wrong?" Nola asked.

"Well, Mrs. McGinty, I shore hope not," he mumbled. "But I 'lowed as how I ought to come and tell you that they let Zeb Martin out of prison last week. I just found out about it today. Don't seem like it's been time enough for him to have served his time, but when I looked it up, I found out it shore enough was. I don't know as how he'd try to harm you or nothin', but I thought I'd better warn you about him."

"Oh, my," Nola gasped. "I hoped I'd never hear that man's name again.

I thank you for telling me, Sheriff, but surely the man would have better sense than to come around here again."

"You can't tell what a feller like him might take it in his head to do," Tate worried. "He made some pretty mean threats about you when he left here. It won't hurt for you to keep an eye out for him. I will, too, and if he does come around, you let me know."

"Thank you, Sheriff," Nola said quietly. "You can be sure I will call you if I see anything of him."

Nola went to bed trying not to let the news of Martin's release upset her, but in spite of her good intentions, she found herself reliving the horrible moment when he attacked her. She started to tell Anne Marie that night but decided to wait until morning. She hoped that the news wouldn't seem so threatening in the light of day. It was very late when she was finally able to get to sleep.

Sometime in the early hours of the morning, Nola was wakened by a pounding on her door. When she opened her eyes, she became aware of the choking thickness of smoke that had engulfed the room. Groping her way to the door, she found Anne Marie standing there.

"The house is afire!" Anne Marie gasped. "Help me get the boarders out."

Frantically, Nola and Anne Marie ran from door to door, rousing the boarders and herding them down the stairway. The fire seemed to be coming from the back of the house in the vicinity of the kitchen, so the front door was unaffected for the moment. As soon as they opened the door, though, the air fed the flames, and the whole downstairs became engulfed. Nola counted the people as they fled out the door. When she was sure all were safely out, she turned to look for Anne Marie.

"Anne Marie. Anne Marie, where are you?" she called frantically.

"I saw her go back up the stairs," one of her boarders volunteered. "She said she had to find her cat. I think she called it Prissy. Said it was asleep on the foot of her bed, and she forgot about it when she smelled smoke."

"Oh, no," Nola cried. "I have to find her! How could she have been so foolish!"

If she had not been restrained, Nola would have rushed back into the house, which was now a blazing inferno. Helplessly, they stood back and watched as the flames shot through the ceiling of the house, blowing out windows and licking at the roof. The distant sound of the fire wagon, bell clanging and wheels rumbling, approached the burning house. Nola shivered in her nightgown, crying helplessly and calling Anne Marie's name over and over.

There was nothing that the firemen could do to save the house. They wet down the neighboring houses to keep them from burning and watched as the house was completely engulfed.

Through eyes blurred with tears, Nola looked at the destruction, able only to see Anne Marie's face as it had looked when she wakened her. She turned to Jake, who had just arrived, and buried her face in his shoulder, sobbing heartbrokenly. As she lifted her head and looked around her, she encountered the malevolent stare of Zeb Martin standing on the fringes of the crowd that had gathered.

"You!" she screamed. "You! You did this! You've murdered your own daughter."

Martin's face contorted in rage as he stared in undisguised hatred at her.

"Stop him! Stop that man!" Nola screamed at the crowd. "He did this! He has killed his own daughter!"

Martin started to run, but the crowd behind him was so closely packed that he couldn't get away. Two burly construction workers who had boarded with Nola in the past grabbed him and wrestled him to the ground. Sheriff Tate appeared in the crowd and took over from there.

"You ain't got nothin' on me," Martin snarled. "You can't prove I had anything to do with this fire. She's crazy if she thinks I burnt her house down."

Nola strode over to confront him. "It's not the house I care about," she sobbed. "It's Anne Marie."

"What about Anne Marie?" Martin asked. "She's all right, ain't she? Where is she anyhow?"

"She's in there," Nola said, pointing to the burning house. "She went back in to get her cat, and she didn't make it back out. You've killed your own daughter."

Martin staggered back and paled, then he lunged at Nola and would have struck her if Jake had not stepped between them.

"You better get him out of here, Sheriff," Jake said, "or I won't be responsible for what I do to him."

"Don't worry. If we can prove he did this, he won't be a bother to nobody again," Tate answered.

Jake turned and put his arms around his mother, who had begun shaking with shock and the cold. "Come on, Mama, there's nothin' else you can do here. Come home with me. Mrs. Hoxit and Mrs. Norris said they would find beds for the rest of the people."

"Anne Marie, oh, Anne Marie!" Nola cried. "Why did she go back in there?"

"Shh, shh, come on, Mama. There's nothin' else you can do," Jake soothed her.

Dazed and bewildered, Nola let him lead her away. As they rounded the curve, the roof of the house caved in, sending showers of smoke and sparks up into the air.

When she woke the next morning, it took Nola several minutes to remember where she was. When she did, she got up and pulled on the robe Saralyn had laid at the foot of her bed. She went into the kitchen where Jake and Saralyn were sitting at the kitchen table drinking coffee. They both sprang up when she entered the room.

"Mama, you should have rested longer," Jake protested. "You couldn't have got more than three hours' sleep."

"How could I have slept at all?" Nola asked tiredly. "It's just like a nightmare. I keep hoping it's all a bad dream and it'll just go away."

"I'm afraid not, Mama," Jake said quietly. "I've talked to Sheriff Tate this mornin' and he says he has enough on Zeb Martin to hold him in jail. Two different people saw him around the house last night, and they found a coal oil can near the back porch. The sheriff said that's where the fire started. It looks like he finally got even with us for all the things he thought we did to him. I couldn't help but be glad that Cassie didn't have to know what he's done."

"Anne Marie?" Nola asked quietly. "Did they find her?"

"Yes, Mama, they found her," Jake said. "Sheriff Tate said the smoke probably confused her, and she couldn't find her way back to the stairs. They found her about where her bedroom would have been. They took her body to the funeral home. There's not anything else we can do for her but bury her. I sent Joshua a telegram."

"Oh, poor Anne Marie," Nola moaned. "I wouldn't care about the house, if only she hadn't gone back. It seemed to me it took the fire wagon an awful long time to get there. If they'd come quicker, maybe we could have saved her."

Jake and Saralyn looked at each other. Saralyn raised her eyebrows questioningly at Jake. He shrugged his shoulders and took a deep breath, bracing himself to give Nola more bad news.

"Mama," he said gently, "the reason the fire wagon was so slow gettin' there was there'd been other fires. Martin burned two of your rental houses before he burnt the boarding house. He set a third one, but the Jones boy had been out late to a party and came home before it got a good start. I reckon our house was next, but he just couldn't tear himself away from the sight of the boarding house burnin'. Thank God for that anyway. At least nobody else was hurt. Everybody got out safe, except for Anne Marie. It's ironic, ain't it? Martin ended up killin' his own daughter.

"I'm afraid it's wiped you out except for this house, Mama. He did a thorough job."

"None of it matters," Nola said woodenly. "Nothing matters but Anne Marie. I think I'd better go and lay down now. I feel a little sick."

"That's all right, Mama," Jake said gently. "You rest for a while. We'll call you if we need you."

Wearily Nola went back to the bedroom and crawled into bed. She lay there for a time staring at the ceiling, then she turned her face to the wall and wept.

THIRTY-FIVE

T he next months were nightmarish memories to Nola. Everything she owned, except for the house Jake lived in and the small rental house the Joneses lived in, were wiped out. What capital she possessed, she had lent to Joseph, who declared he could not pay back the loan without putting his own family out of a home. Since Nola had let the note lapse without renewing it, she was helpless to collect from him. Bitterly she had to acknowledge that her own brother had cheated her. She had no money with which to rebuild and could only put the land where her houses had stood up for sale. The only property that was of any value was the one where the boarding house had stood. The rest of the houses had been located in poorer neighborhoods, and the property value was negligible. Nola was living with Jake and his family temporarily until the Jones family could find another house. She planned to move into that house when it was vacant.

Never in her adult life had Nola been dependent on others for her well-being. She rankled under the humiliation of being indebted to others, even if it was her own son. She occupied her days helping Saralyn tend the children and keep house. Saralyn was a gentle, sweet girl who never did anything to make Nola feel unwelcome. She told Nola over and over how helpful she was to her and how much she appreciated having her with them. Even so, Nola felt out of place, like a fifth wheel. There were four children in the family now, two boys and two girls, all under the age of six, and it took both women working from daylight till dark to take care of them. Jake had given up his position with the band and was assistant manager at the hotel. With the extra money the hotel job brought him, he bought a piano, contenting himself with this outlet. On Sundays the whole family enjoyed singing together and listening to Jake play.

Life had become rather routine for the family, and so they were ill-prepared for the sudden death of Jake and Saralyn's youngest daughter, Susan Marie, from meningitis. She had gone from a healthy, happy child one day to a desperately ill one the next day. Nola's strength and faith strengthened Saralyn and Jake, and they learned how to live with their grief.

Samantha's husband had been transferred to Jacksonville, Florida, and they had moved there with their daughter Carol, their only child.

Nola finally was contented with the thought of living with Jake and his fanily until the children were old enough to take care of themselves. When Jake moved to a larger house, she stayed on in the one that finally had begun to feel like her home. Samantha and her daughter, Carol, spent most of their summers with Nola, escaping the heat of Jacksonville in the pure mountain air.

Nola was approaching her sixtieth birthday when Samantha wrote her that she had read in the Jacksonville papers that Sam McGinty had died. The news brought back all of the feelings that Nola thought were buried and forgotten. She decided that the only way she would ever be able to put them to rest was to go to Florida and seek out Sam's grave.

"Mama, I think it's foolish of you to start on such a trip at your age," Jake told her. "What good will it do anyway? I'd think you'd have put all of this out of your mind long ago. Jacksonville's a big city, and you don't even know where he's buried."

"Samantha will help me find it," Nola said firmly. "I know you don't understand my need to do this, Jake, but I have to do it. Just take my word for it. I hate to leave Saralyn now, with her expecting another baby, but I feel like I have to. I know the children are big enough to help take care of themselves, but the washing and ironing are enough to wear her out. Promise me you will help her until I get back."

"Of course, I will, Mama," Jake assured her. "Are you sure you won't change your mind?"

"No, Jake. This is something I have to put to rest," Nola answered quietly.

Sighing in resignation, Jake took her to the train depot in Asheville and saw her off.

Samantha met Nola at the train station in Jacksonville after the grueling fourteen-hour trip. Nola was seemingly unaffected by the trip and chatted on the way to Samantha's house about all of the interesting people she had met. After a light supper, however, she was ready for bed.

"If I can just stop rocking," she told Samantha, "I'm sure I'll sleep like a log. I can feel the train's motion under my feet like I'm still on it. Maybe when I lie down, it'll go away."

Nola did indeed sleep well that night and didn't rouse until the unheard of hour of eight o'clock the next morning.

"I've never slept this late before in my life," she told Samantha. "I've usually got half a day's work done by now."

When breakfast was over and Carol was safely on her way to school, Samantha and Nola set out to find the cemetery where Sam was buried. Samantha tried to persuade her mother to rest for a day before making the trip, but Nola was adamant.

"This is why I came," she declared, "and I won't be able to rest until I do what I came for. We'll rest and visit after this is taken care of."

They found the place where Sam was buried with no trouble, and Nola stood looking at the marker while she held the flowers she had gathered from Samantha's yard.

"If you don't mind, I'll just sit here for a while," Nola told Samantha. "I've come a long way, and there's some things I need to say."

Samantha walked around the cemetery, giving her mother the privacy she wanted.

"Well, Sam, here we are at last," Nola said. "We never thought this would be where we would say our final farewells that day we got married in Papa's garden, did we? I always thought we'd live out our days together with our children around us, just like Mama and Papa did. Instead, here you are, hundreds of miles away from your family and the mountains. And here I am, traveling hundreds of miles to tell you what I should have told you years ago.

"Sam, I love you, and I forgive you for anything you ever did that caused me pain. I know now that it caused you just as much, or maybe more, pain as it did me. I was just too full of pride to admit all of these things then. I suppose we have to do some living before we know what's really important. I know now that all of my reasons for not marrying again boiled down to one thing. I've never found anyone else who I could love like I loved you.

"When I was tempted to get involved with another man, I would remember the day you proposed to me. I would hear you singing that song to me again. Remember? I've never forgotten."

Nola placed the wreath of flowers on Sam's grave and sang softly:

> *I've been gatherin' flowers from the meadow,*
> *To wreath around your head,*
> *But so long you've kept me a-waitin',*
> *They're all withered and dead.*
>
> *I've been gatherin' flowers on the hillside,*
> *To bind them on your brow,*

But so long you have kept me waitin',
  The flowers are faded now.

O many a mile with you I've wandered,
  And many an hour with you I've spent,
Till I thought your heart was mine forever,
  But now I know it was only lent.

Now I will seek some distant river,
  And there I'll spend my days and years;
I'll eat no food but the green willow,
  And drink no water but my tears.

"Good-bye, Sam. Good-bye, my love."

After some time had passed, Samantha looked up to find Nola walking toward her. Silently, the two women left and returned to Samantha's house. Nola did not speak of what had transpired at Sam's grave, and Samantha did not ask her.

Nola returned to her home a month later. She was glad to be back in the cold, crisp mountain air and declared that she didn't think she'd ever leave it again.

"Well, did it help you to go?" Jake asked as he met her at the station. "Do you feel better now? I can't understand why you thought you had to go after all of these years."

"Yes, I think it did help me," Nola answered thoughtfully. "I feel a sense of peace that has always been missing from my life. I think I was finally able to forgive your father for the pain he caused me. More important, though, I was finally able to ask him to forgive me, too. It took me a long time to realize that I needed to be forgiven as much as I needed to forgive him."

"I'm glad that you went then," Jake said. "I've always been sorry that I didn't go to see him when he asked me to come. It was just the wrong time for me. There never did seem to be a right one."

"I'm sorry, too," Nola answered quietly. "I hope that it wasn't my fault that you didn't go."

"You know me better than that, Mama," Jake laughed. "I've never let anyone persuade me to do something or not do something if I really wanted to."

When the new baby came, Nola moved back in with Jake and Saralyn temporarily to help out. It was a difficult birth, and Saralyn was slow in getting her strength back. This last baby, a boy whom they named Charles

Graham, thrived under the attention of his older brothers and sister. There were fourteen years between Jake's first child and his last one.

The years passed too swiftly for Nola. She watched her grandchildren grow up and start families of their own. She suffered as each of her brothers, then Jake and Samantha died. She always seemed to find the strength deep within herself to go on, living by the philosophy that God never gave her a heavier burden than she could bear with His help.

She lived by herself and kept her own household until she was almost ninety-five years old, then she went to live with Alma, Jake's oldest daughter, for her remaining years.

THIRTY-SIX

T he people in the room hovered around the old woman, watching the rise and fall of her breast as her breath became more and more shallow. Her thready pulse was visible through the thin skin of her wrists and neck. One after another, they touched her lightly in gestures of farewell.

Nola's granddaughter, Alma, cried softly, seemingly unaware of the tears streaming down her face. Alma's daughter, Cindy, put her arms around her mother and patted her on the back.

"Please, Mother, don't cry," she said. "You know what she said last week. She told us that she was ready to go on. She said she longed to be with her children and her parents again. You know how lonely she's been these last few years."

"I know," Alma answered. "It's just that she's been so much a part of our lives for so long. I can't imagine what it'll be like without her here. I'm not crying for her. I'm crying for myself."

Nola heard all of the conversations going on around her with a clarity that she had not experienced in years. Somehow she was able to see what was going on, too, but not from her bed. She was observing everything from above the crowd, looking down on the scene in the room.

Is this what it's like, this dying? she wondered. Somehow I thought it would be different, a sort of fading away.

As she watched the people in the room, she became aware of the presence of others around her, surrounding her with their love. They beckoned, and she went gladly, ready to rid herself of the encumbrances that 102 years had inflicted on her body. She looked back on the wasted body on the bed, laboring to let go of the life that held it prisoner to the aches and pains of old age, marveling that it had served her so long.

She looked at the great-grandchildren, the nieces and nephews, and

199

distant cousins gathered around her body, seeing clearly the family resemblances in them for the first time. Alma, more like her sister Martha than her own mother, Jake's Saralyn. And Cindy, with her dark hair and dark eyes, so like herself when she was young. That young scamp with the curly red hair was a dead ringer for his great-grandfather Sam. And the thin, bearded one in the corner could have been a young Will.

"Nola, come on," the others beckoned her.

"Just one more minute," she said. "I ought to comfort Alma somehow. I shouldn't leave her like this. Somehow I have to let her know it's all right."

"She'll know in time," they said. "In time, she'll know."

Still Nola lingered, longing to help Alma through her pain. She reached down and laid her hand on her shoulder, and Alma trembled under the touch.

"Are you feeling better now, Mother?" Cindy asked her.

"Yes, somehow I know she's happy now," Alma replied quietly. "I just felt a sudden warmth, like I did when I was a child and she would take me on her lap when I'd been hurt and comfort me."

As Nola watched Alma drying her tears, she remembered the day she cried over the stain on Papa's floor and how she scrubbed to get if off. Except, of course, it hadn't been the stain she was crying over but the ache she felt when Papa died, that and the sense of abandonment she was feeling from Sam's desertion.

Oh, Sam, she thought. It took me so many years to forgive you. Why didn't I put the hurt behind me sooner? Deep down, I knew my bitterness influenced the decisions I made that so affected my life. I just never could admit it, though.

As she looked at the tears that had fallen from Alma's eyes, they seemed to multiply until the whole room swam in a river of tears. She felt as if all of the secret tears she had cried during her lonely life were uniting to drown her.

"No more tears, no more tears," a voice said to her. "There will be no more tears."

"I know," she said quietly. "My family will be all right." She sighed. "I'm ready now."

Epilogue

Cindy and Daniel picked their careful way up the hillside, avoiding the brambles as best they could. The trail was almost obscured by the undergrowth that had crept over the ground. Dense stands of mountain laurel and rhododendron made a thicket so high that they dwarfed the two young people.

"How much farther do you think it is, Cindy?" Daniel asked. "I thought you said it was not very far from the house. I think we've come at least two miles already."

"It's not much farther," Cindy panted. "Mama said it was straight up the trail a'ways. I guess it's been awhile since she's been out here. Nobody keeps this trail open anymore except the animals."

"I sure hope we don't meet any bears," Daniel grunted. "I'd be too tired to run. I'd just have to lie down and let him have at me."

Abruptly they burst out into a clearing, leaving bushes and briars behind. The remnants of an old cabin leaned drunkenly against a rock chimney.

"There it is!" Cindy said excitedly. "This is all that's left of the first cabin that my great-great-grandfather Will built."

"Look at the size of those logs," Daniel whistled. "Wonder how he managed them by himself? No wonder it's stood so long."

"Come on," Cindy urged him. "The place where they're buried is just up this trail a bit."

"It looks like somebody has kept this trail clear," Daniel observed. "It's been mowed fairly recently."

"Yes, some of my cousins come up here every so often and clear things out. They put a fence up around the graves a few years ago. One of my cousins lives over this ridge, and he comes and checks on things every once in a while. On Decoration Day, someone always comes and puts

201

flowers on the graves. We come other times too, but we always come on Decoration Day. Look, there it is."

They came to the iron gate in the fence surrounding the four graves and pushed the latch back so they could enter. The little plot was neatly mowed, and the weathered stones stood out starkly against the mountain sky.

Cindy pointed down the hill. "There's a spring under that rock over there, Daniel," she said. "Take these jars and fill them up, please. I'll divide the flowers out so that we can put some on each grave."

Daniel brought the jars of water back to Cindy, and she filled them with the spring flowers she had brought. They carefully placed them on each of the four graves, then stood back and surveyed the scene.

"One of the last things Great-grandmother Nola asked my mother to do was to promise her she would bring flowers to put on her parents' graves on Decoration Day. She never missed a time coming until she got too feeble to walk up here."

"Who will come when you can't come anymore?" Daniel asked her.

"Why, I suppose I'll just have to tell my children the stories about their great-great-grandparents so that they'll want to come, too," Cindy replied. "I've never minded coming, and I don't think they will either. I always feel like there's a part of me here in this place. I hope they'll feel the same way."

They lingered awhile, talking about the lives of the people who lay beneath the earth. Cindy repeated stories to Daniel that her mother and great-grandmother had told her. They became caught up in the events that had shaped her family's lives, not noticing the lengthening shadows until a sudden chill swept across them.

"Oh, Daniel, look how late it is!" Cindy exclaimed. "We'd better get started back, or we won't be able to find our way back to the house."

They gathered up their baskets and, closing the gate before they left, quickly got on their way down the mountain trail. By the time they reached the laurel thickets, the sun was beginning to go down behind the mountain. What little light was left soon disappeared when they entered the thicket.

"I'd better go in front," Cindy said. "I think I can find the trail better than you can."

"Well, if you can't, we're sure in trouble." Daniel laughed shakily. "I sure can understand how you could get lost up here."

Together they stumbled on through the dense growth, feeling their way along. Sometimes they had to get down on their hands and knees to be sure they were still on the trail.

"Stay close to me," Cindy said to Daniel. "Whatever we do, let's not get separated. It's so dark in here. When the moon comes out, maybe we'll be able to see better."

"Don't worry," Daniel nervously replied. "I'm right with you."

Finally Cindy came to a dead end in the thicket. No matter which way she turned, she met with thick bushes. Just as she was about to panic, she felt herself being directed back into the path and a feeling of calm came over her.

She was so exhausted, she could only gasp out a whispery, "Thanks, Daniel. I thought we were lost."

At last Cindy stepped out into the clearing around the old house, and she laughed shakily. "I'm so tired I might fall down."

"What did you say?" Daniel panted from several feet behind her. "I sure am glad you finally found the path, Cindy. I thought we were going to end up spending the night in the laurel bushes."

Cindy turned around and stared at Daniel, trailing behind her. She sat down abruptly.

"Daniel," she whispered, "didn't you lead us out of the thicket? Didn't you lead me back to the trail up there?"

"Who? Me?" he asked. "What are you talking about? I couldn't have led us anywhere. I couldn't see my hand in front of my face. I was following you all the way down."

"Well, if you didn't, then who did?" Cindy whispered.

Daniel looked at her for a moment, then shrugged. "I don't know. It's been a long day, Cindy. It's time to go home." He went into the old house to gather their things.

Cindy stood for a moment, peering out into the darkness. She listened to the gentle whispers of the night mountain air. Despite the chill, she felt calm and comforted.

"We're going to be all right," she said softly. "Thank you." Taking a deep breath, she turned and joined Daniel in the old house, where he was lighting a lantern to chase away some of the shadows.